PRAISE FOR *MR. PSYCHIC: A NOVEL*

Funny and Entertaining!

He goes from being a person who avoids human connection, out of fear of being hurt or abandoned, to being a person willing to let himself love and be loved by a true Soul mate. An entertaining read, cleverly written, and will bring a smile to your face. Five stars from me.

— SADSACK

Mr. Psychic stole my heart.

Mr. Psychic is a wonderful read! Dermot Davis and H Raven Rose transform the main character, George, from a priggish elitist who thinks he has his life perfectly planned into Mr. Psychic, a soulful, open, and loving human being. It's a fun journey, and you'll love the characters.

— LINDA S. AMSTUTZ

Wildly Imaginative Romp w/ Goofball Aliens.

This novel is an absurd, funny, satirical science fiction tale that takes a dim view of humanity's place in the cosmos. Its premise is that a congress of advanced aliens has been monitoring human behavior from afar, concluded continued human existence is undesirable, and decided to exterminate the lot. The question then is: Will humanity survive?

— O. BARNACK

… laugh-out-loud funny …

I don't usually read science fiction, but the description sounded intriguing. This book is definitely fiction, but one hopes the science is not real. It is laugh-out-loud funny and should appeal to anyone with an off-beat sense of humor.

— SADAZIK

Waiting with baited breath for the sequel

I really liked this book. I'm a fan of end-of-the-world books, and particularly enjoy books with strong female leads. Add a spiritual (but Not in your face spiritual) slant, and you had me at page one ... I will definitely wait with baited, acetone breath for the sequel(s).

- RITZ

Continuing in sight?

...An exciting science fiction told with a coherent protagonist. Would have liked to read the sequel right away - that ultimately decides the quality of the story, because there has to be something to come:).

- UMSTEIGER

Harrowing, Thrilling Read

I read *Dark Eros* straight through in one sitting; I couldn't put it down. It's very well written, with a compelling heroine struggling to escape a horrible relationship and get her life on track against terrible odds.

- JAMES D.

Some things strange and sinister

Some authors have an uncanny knack for writing the dark and disturbed. H Raven Rose is one of those authors. At the very opening of Dark Eros you want to clutch a can of mace, or a small 9mm handgun, before you continue going down this dark path.

- CYNTHIA VESPIA

Books by Dermot Davis and H Raven Rose

Mr. Psychic

Encounter

Books by H Raven Rose

Dark Eros: A Novella

Double Happiness: Shadow Selves

The Big "O": A Romantic Comedy

Dread Zone

Bugocalypse: La Cucaracha V 1

Books by Dermot Davis

Brain: The Man Who Wrote the Book That Changed the World

The Older Woman

Stormy Weather: A Novel: Are You Dreaming Now?

Fatal Eclipse

The Younger Man (3 Book Box Set)

CAGED: A Short Reads Novella

ENCOUNTER

Published by eXu Publishing

ISBN: 978-1-957125-08-4 (trade paperback)

eBook Edition: 2014
First Trade Paperback Edition: 2025

0 9 8 7 6 5 4 3 2 1

ENCOUNTER

A COMEDY ABOUT ESCAPING YOUR CUBICLE... WHEREVER YOU ARE IN THE UNIVERSE

DERMOT DAVIS

H RAVEN ROSE

DEDICATION

For our parents... with great love.

CONTENTS

BOOK PREVIEWS

> *Two things are infinite: the universe and human stupidity; and I'm not sure about the universe.*

> — ALBERT EINSTEIN

THE EARLY SUMMER SKY, OUTSIDE OF THE cottonwoods, an hour or so north-west of Santa Fe, New Mexico, was the ethereal tint of robin's egg blue. On Cerrillos Road, south of I-25, a brontosaurus family—a mother, father, and a baby—appeared to graze amidst dusty, green-gray, leathery, and scaly skin, dappled with sunshine, among woody brown and green desert trees and shrubs.

It was late afternoon. The sun beat down, and the light and desert were hot, dusty, and golden. Lizards, snakes, birds, and insects moved amidst cacti, ocotillo, creosote bush, brittlebush, and perennial and annual desert grasses that grew in the semi-arid landscape. The green and dried stems, trunks, branches, leaves, and spines of cacti created a subtle palette of vibrant colors and textures, featuring shades of green, brown, peach, and lavender. Silvery mica glinted in the sand and dirt of the desert dust.

A beat-up 1967 blue Ford pickup, once ultramarine blue but now pathetically faded, roared past the three life-sized dinosaur sculptures. Going about 90 miles an hour, the pickup truck left shimmering dust motes glistening in its wake. The truck barreled down the road. It managed to turn right, at the very last possible minute. Tipping a bit sideways, it just made the turn into the Los Alamos National Laboratory parking lot.

Barely avoiding crashing, the truck skidded and slid sideways into a parking spot. The faded blue and heavily dented driver's side door opened, and Hank Walsh got out. A forty-something, run-down, bloated excuse for a man, he was one of those men who could be handsome... if they weren't severely depressed, apathetic, overfed, frequently intoxicated, unkempt, and entirely lacking in ambition. He drained a beer, crushed the can, and threw it into the truck bed, where it joined several others, and belched. He then walked toward the building.

The hallways of the über clean, high-tech, high-security national laboratory were silent. Periodically, scientists and geek types would traverse the hallways—the hallway floors so clean and shiny they were reflective—as they made their way to meeting rooms, offices, or laboratories, throughout the compound. At the end of a hallway, outside of a nuclear physics lab, Hank apathetically trooped past Dr. Blake and Dr. Delaware, two clean-cut, excitable, professional nuclear physicists. They were holding research papers, covered with marks and diagrams, and quite obviously comparing notes and in some kind of intense discussion.

Deep in conversation with his colleague, Dr. Blake was surprised when an unexpected stench assaulted his nose. He covered his nose and looked around. He saw Hank, who had clocked in, now wearing coveralls over his street clothes, pushing a high-tech floor cleaning device down the hallway.

"What the..." Dr. Blake asked, his tone of voice making it clear that his question was rhetorical. Then, interrupting himself, he first looked at his watch and then at Hank, turning to Dr. Delaware.

"Can you believe it? It's not even 9 AM? What a seriously—"

"—misunderstood genius," whispered Dr. Delaware, interrupting his colleague. Dr. Blake stared at his coworker with incredulity. He raised his eyebrows as if to emphasize his skepticism. Dr. Delaware nodded at Dr. Blake.

"—I was thinking drunken bum," Dr. Blake said, now alert to the propriety of being polite, softly enough that he could be certain that Hank would not hear.

"Ever look into linear perturbations?" Dr. Delaware asked in a conspiratorial tone, as if thrilled to know factual information that others did not know.

Dr. Blake shrugged as if to indicate a) of course he had, but b) what did that have to do with the drunken bum adjacent who was now stinking up the corridor?

"An approximation scheme set to describe a complicated quantum system in terms of a simpler one to convey the underlying structure?" Dr. Delaware continued as if Dr. Blake might not know.

"Of course," Dr. Blake said, somewhat defensively, as if his associate had called into question some core aspect of his basic intellect.

"He wrote the book on it," Dr. Delaware said with great satisfaction.

"He's working on perturbation theory here at the lab?" asked Dr. Blake, with disbelief in his voice. He looked at Hank. True, sometimes scientists were terribly quirky; a scientist might engage in an odd exercise to stimulate his mind and work through a scientific problem.

Dr. Delaware frowned. Hank, now at the far end of the hall, stared upward as if focused upon something compelling that only he could see.

"Sadly, no. He's a janitor now, but he used to be something

truly special; one of those rare minds with a gift for theoretical genius and serious application potential. It's a pity that he's devolved; I could really use his mind... if only there were some way, some way to—" Delaware continued.

"To what?" Dr. Blake said, laughing uproariously, "To rewire his brain? To jumpstart his scientific genius? That's a good one," Dr. Blake said and grinned as if now he had the intellectual upper hand over Dr. Delaware.

Dr. Delaware frowned. He was obviously a little miffed by Dr. Blake's clear implication that he was incorrect in thinking that there was something worth redeeming in Hank, or Hank's capacity for critical thought.

"There's a huge correlation between depression and high intellectual potential," Dr. Delaware finally responded, almost huffily.

"You build a device like that, in your spare time, which we don't have, my good man, and I won't use it on some dude like that guy," Dr. Blake said, jerking his head in Hank's direction. "I would use the thing on someone with real potential."

Dr. Delaware looked at Hank for a long moment and then turned to face Dr. Blake. "The greatest darkness has the potential to reveal the greatest light," Dr. Delaware said sagely.

"Ah, now, don't go getting all Kabbalah on me, Delaware, not unless you wish to jeopardize my opinion of your mind," Dr. Blake said and then looked down at the research papers in his hand. "Now, where were we?"

BILLIONS OF DAZZLING STARS SHIMMERED IN THE VAST black darkness of outer space. With a flash of light, a space vehicle decelerated from lightspeed and penetrated a fraction of space.

A bizarre, otherworldly space station came into view.

The orbital space station complex was constructed from subatomic particles contributed by the alien civilizations from many universes, galaxies, and planets that orbited. The elemental particles were loosely bonded to create a strong, yet flexible, rainbow-iridescent, colored material that shimmered and appeared to materialize and dematerialize alternately. It was, for beings that possessed the ability to breathe, breathtaking.

Inside the mammoth spacecraft, the size of which would be incomprehensible to humans, life forms from all creations and realities rushed about, attending to their duties and lives. Inside of a hallway, which led to an intergalactic meeting room, late arrivers, diverse and curious-looking life forms, from differing planets of origin (and some from realities which contained nothing that could be described as planets even, failing to be solid or have mass at all), opened doors and rushed into a large meeting room.

Strange sounds and shouting could be heard from within the closed doors. Inside the intergalactic meeting room, significantly dissimilar members of the intergalactic space federation council faced off in a heated debate.

"Despite opposition and ongoing debate, we must weigh and carefully vote on the fate of planet Earth," said Xerb, the Intergalactic Space Federation Council President, carefully and slowly.

"Huguw-huguw, huguw-huguw," a Draconian council member laughed. His laughter squeaked and grated like large pieces of broken glass emitting a low, ragged pitch as they were dragged across a chalkboard.

"It's a simple vote for a situation that, however upsetting for various factions, has an obvious solution," the Draconian council member said when it could finally contain its mirth.

The Zeta Reticuli Grey council member stared at the Draconian with cold rage.

"Obvious? The Zeta Reticuli Greys have billions of ZeRe invested in licensing rights and ongoing experiments on planet Earth's life forms. Our contract won't expire for three more secundi," the Zeta Reticuli Grey council member said.

An obviously peaceful, loving being, the Arcturian council member, who exuded good vibes, patiently lifted its appendage, indicating a desire to speak. The Intergalactic Space Federation Council President nodded, indicating it was okay to proceed.

"Some of these so-called life forms are earthlings. Although primitive, some of them possess a rudimentary self-awareness. Surely they should be given due consideration... protection and rights?" the Arcturian council member asked.

Before anyone else could respond, Q, a Zycorp Spokesperson and special consultant to this council meeting, spoke:

"Those 'earthlings' are subjects and have been genetically engineered by us to be exactly as they now exist. As such, we carry the patent for their modified DNA. Our company has been cultivating these life forms for deons, and they have become very valuable resources to the corporation's bottom line. They may have a very inferior consciousness, but their biological, etheric, and physical attributes were carefully genetically modified by us and were so designed to be exploited."

<hr>

DEEP INSIDE THE SPACE STATION, BURIED DEEP WITHIN hundreds of thousands of offices, within a suite of research labs, various types of alien beings—hundreds of thousands of them—worked in identical cubicles.

N and his clone, N2, an alien being and his first genetic

copy, sat alone in their work cubicle, watching a number of human subjects on a bank of monitors.

"Man—" N2 said.

"Don't call me 'man' or dude, N2," N interrupted, his voice filled with irritation.

N2 rolled his many eyes.

"Whatever, N. Anywayz, we've been doing this for a while... we should get to experiment on some of these subjects. Maybe help 'em live an interesting life, for a change. Whaddya say?!" N2 asked with great enthusiasm. N2 twitched with excitement and curiosity while N looked at him in horror.

Then N looked around, terribly nervous over N2's bold statement. Shaking with fear, he checked to see if N2's statement might have been overheard.

None of the other beings in any other cubicle were paying the slightest attention to the two of them. N sighed with relief and turned to face his genetic copy.

"Get off the crazy. We observe and evaluate subjects, and then prepare reports. What are the first three words in our job description manual?" N asked N2 pointedly. N2 looked like he was thinking, but his source copy knew him better and wasn't expecting an answer anytime soon.

"Record. Data. Only," N said flatly, with the slightest hint of menace in his tone.

"Get off the crazy," N2 said in a wicked falsetto tone, mimicking N's words. Then, pointing at the vast array of highly technical equipment before them, he spoke intently in a serious tone: "Don't be such a fraidy cat. What else have we got going on? Seriously, I'm bored out of my skulls."

N stabbed his appendage toward the equipment. Hank was now on screen. "What's this?" N2 asked. "What happened to the Jeffrey specimen?"

"The Jeffrey subject passed in his sleep," N answered. "You

were right. Sleeping for five Earth days was not a normal occurrence. This is our new research subject." N2 looked at Hank, on screen, getting out of his pickup.

"You've got to be kidding me. See, this is what I'm talking about. Another pea-brain earthling chump," N2 said sadly.

"Is there any other kind?" N asked with contempt.

"Don't be that way. Some of them are geniuses... Like Elvis and Tesla," N2 said as he watched Hank with a mix of resignation and sorrow.

"Elvis Ann Tesla? What'd she do?" N asked, his voice dripping with hatred. N2 was horrified by N's hatred of and for humans as well as his ignorance.

"You are freaking unbearable," N2 said. "If you applied yourself and got some promotions, we'd be observing interesting earthlings that... live interesting lives."

"Oh, sure," N scoffed. "First of all, you'd have to define what you find 'interesting.' Secondly, by my definition of 'interesting,' no earthling I've ever seen did one interesting thing in their entire lifespan."

"And you're okay with that? See, that's exactly my point. You criticize primitive life forms for being boring when all you do with your life is watch them be boring. What interesting thing have you ever done?" N2 challenged.

Appearing unfazed, N continued to study the monitor that featured Hank.

"I see," continued N2 when N refused to engage. "Let's watch this new subject until he sleeps and doesn't wake up. That sounds like an exciting way to spend our lives."

"Subject approaching alcohol store," N said into his voice recorder and enlarged the monitor view. The cubicle immediately transformed into the extraterrestrial equivalent of a 360° theater in the round, and, suddenly surrounded by a high definition image, it was as if they were now outside a New Mexico convenience store.

HANK SLAMMED HIS PICKUP TRUCK DOOR. CRICKETS chirped in the night. Bleary-eyed, he ambled toward the store-front and entered the tiny convenience store.

The convenience store was jam-packed with processed food and drinks, alcohol, cigarettes, and cheaply made curio items. Hank knew exactly what he wanted and where to find it. Slamming down a 12-pack of beer, Hank faced the Native American store clerk. He grabbed a pack of Smoky Chipotle beef jerky from a counter shelf, grunted, and pointed toward the cigarettes and lottery tickets.

"Same old, same old?" the clerk asked.

"Uh-yuh," Hand said.

The clerk grabbed two packs of locally made native smokes, removed five Area 51 Alien Abduction scratchers from the lottery card display, and laid them on the counter.

"Five, right?" the clerk asked.

"Uh-yuh," Hank said. The clerk rang Hank's items up on his old-fashioned punch register and bagged Hank's purchases.

"That'll be $10 for the Area 51 Alien Abduction scratchers plus $35.52 for the rest... for a total of $45.52. That it?"

"Uh-yuh," Hank said and slapped down some cash.

OOBLIVIOUS TO THE GLITTERING STARS THAT HAD SLOWLY begun to light up the cobalt blue night sky, Hank drove his pickup home. Steadying the steering wheel with his knee, he popped open a beer and guzzled it down. The pickup barreled down a deserted road, made a hard turn into a side road overgrown with weeds and brambles, and finally pulled up to his beat-up house trailer.

Hank put the pickup truck in park and switched off the ignition. He sat for a few moments in the silence broken only by the sound of crickets and the distant howl of a lonesome coyote. He finished his beer and tossed the can into the back of the cab, through the open truck cab rear window, and belched hugely. He popped a new beer before getting out of his vehicle.

The house trailer was rusty and old. Knocking back his drink and carrying his sack of treats, Hank ambled toward his broken-down, none-too-clean abode. He stepped over metal junk and overgrown plants to finally reach the front steps and front door. He tromped up the stained cement steps and wrenched open the door.

Inside the trailer, the barely furnished and tiny, cramped space was littered with empty beer cans, used Area 51 Alien Abduction scratchers, empty cigarette packages, cigarette stubs, and other trash. Old filthy shag carpet covered the floors.

Hank flopped into his barcalounger and dropped his paper sack on the floor within easy reach. He grabbed the remote control and clicked it. His ancient TV, with a bent hanger functioning as his antenna, came on.

The picture was fuzzy and snow-filled. At times, it was difficult to see any picture at all, but that did not appear to bother Hank one bit. He sank back with a grunt of contentment.

Hank slurped on his open beer. Then, with lethargy, as if it almost took more energy than he could muster, Hank used his teeth to rip open a pack of jerky. He took a bite and chewed slowly. He grunted and then farted. His deliberate chewing emphasized his resemblance to a cow chewing its cud.

After he had eaten all of his jerky and guzzled all of his

beer, Hank smoked and stared at the set. Periodically he grunted and farted some more.

Later, while watching what appeared to be the evening news, and despite his efforts to keep his eyes open, Hank scratched off his lottery scratch cards and seemed to have no reaction when he did not win.

The local news went off, and the almost indiscernible, blurry color images of a modern TV broadcast transformed into the almost indiscernible, blurry black-and-white images of an old movie. Hank's apathy did not change, though he obviously grew more and more sleepy.

Still watching the snowy screen of his old TV, Hank's head began to snap forward periodically, each time he almost fell asleep.

Each time, at the last moment, before his head entirely fell onto his fat-swollen abdomen, Hank would fart and grunt as he jerked back awake.

Finally, unable to keep his eyes open, Hank fell asleep sprawled in his recliner. He snored. The tiny, static-filled TV screen flickered.

INSIDE N AND N2'S TINY CUBICLE IN THE REMOTE SPACE station, N2 adjusted a control. The flickering, static-filled image, a duplicate of the image on Hank's old, broken-down television screen, appeared on their monitor screen as a wide shot of Hank in his trailer. "Look at this... this... lump of..." N2 said.

"Humanity?" N said in a tone that was fake-helpful.

"I can't watch this anymore," N2 said unhappily.

N2 surveyed the other alien beings and various life forms at adjacent cubicles. They were a mishmash of the curious, bizarre, and outlandish. None of them, including Beetle Blatt, a tiny, dark, almost evil-looking Zygon with an oversized membranous egg head, paid them any attention. N2 turned to face N once again.

"Aren't you sick of this?" N2 asked, his voice filled with despair.

N looked around. The extraterrestrials around them fervently watched their assigned human subjects on their monitor banks and used strange, mysterious electronic devices to compute and/or record human behavior data.

Just like desk-jockeys on Earth, they mostly appeared supremely bored.

"It's our job. Our activity," N said calmly, as if he were entirely at peace with their daily endeavor.

"Our job? Oh, yes, siree-bob. It's our task, assignment, bother, burden, business, calling, charge, otherwise known as the daily grind, activity, all right. But, N, there are a million other activities in life. This galaxy is ginormous," N2 declared slowly yet fervently in a sing-song voice.

N was not impressed by N2's line of reasoning. He looked around at the clean, safe, compact, highly technical environment that was their shared workspace.

"What would you know about the galaxies out there, N2? All you've ever seen in your life is the inside of a test tube, the canteen, and this workspace," N replied.

"Besides, I'm just a glott away from retirement and my pension. A single glott. If I can hold on 'til then," he said logically, being careful to sound as positive as possible. N2, knowing that N was equally bored with their gig, narrowed his many eyes.

"Retirement?" N2 sneered. "They put you on a ship and dump you off in that freaky retirement outpost on the periphery of the galaxy where you eat, shit, and sleep... and then you die. And that's something you're looking forward to?"

"You're forgetting something," N replied. "I won't have to do this... anymore."

"Yippee," N2 mocked. "Besides, how can you retire? You don't have any memories to retire with. It's like you never even existed."

"I have memories," N said defensively.

"Memories of what? Watching earthlings drink beer, watch TV, and scratch their rear ends?" N2 continued. "You do know that the fewer memories retirees have, the less they live, once they retire? It's a scientific fact, look it up."

"I have memories," N insisted. "Besides, I still have time."

"That's right! You do have time, so make it count," N2 encouraged. "This is why it makes perfect sense to..." N2 discreetly looked around. Seeing that it was all clear, he then lowered his voice and whispered the rest into his N's ear.

Enraged, N jumped up, his many eyes widening with a combination of rage and fear. Fiercely grabbing N2 by a tentacle, he hustled him from their shared cubicle and out into the space station hallway.

N DRAGGED N2 THROUGH THE SPACE STATION HALLWAY toward a public restroom. N quickly looked around to ensure they were alone. The restroom featured a variety of mechanical and other waste management and disposal devices for different types of beings. N checked to make sure that the room was empty. Seeing that it was, he then slammed N2 against the wall a few times.

The noise of N2's body banging against the wall reverberated fairly loudly.

So N thrust N2 aside long enough to hurriedly flush a couple of waste devices and create a noise cover. He then faced his double, his many eyes flashing with fear and rage. N2 appeared flummoxed.

"What have I repeatedly told you about openly discussing violating Zycorp Regulations? Huh? You son of a Brettnick! Want to get us iced?" N shouted.

"Not to?" N2 said uncertainly. He was wobbly from being repeatedly thrown against the restroom wall.

"Correct. Because why?" N screamed. N2, still dazed, waved a tentacle.

"Uh, because I... because we'd be iced?" N2 said tentatively.

N flushed some more waste disposal devices again, to create more noise, then grabbed N2 and banged him against the wall to emphasis his words.

"That's right!" shouted N, "Iced, axed, booted, bounced, discharged, dismissed, expelled, given the heave-ho, otherwise known as let go, sacked, or terminated!"

Unable to take any more abuse, N2 wrenched himself from N's grasp. "Okay! Okay! I get it," N2 snarled and rubbed himself with various tentacles.

N slammed N2 against the wall once more for good measure.

"One glott," N said again for emphasis. "One single solitary glott and all of this... all of these sad, miserable, achingly boring, repetitive, stupid, imbecilic tasks are over. Done. Finished. No more. Get it?"

Hearing the sounds of someone approaching, out of breath, sweating, and red-faced, N pulled back from N2 and quickly composed himself. Their coworker, Beetle Blatt, the small, sinister Zygon, entered and approached a waste device. Despite their mutual dislike for each other, he nodded at N as he passed, realizing that he was intruding upon some unusual activity that might be in contravention of Zycorp regulations. He eyed them both suspiciously.

N and N2 quickly faced the nearest waste devices as if to use them. However, the waste devices they now faced were not designed for their body types, so they had to do some serious bodily contortions to make them work.

Glurrrrrrrrrrrrrrrrrp. Spilch. Spilch. Spilch. Splwat. Beetle Blatt made terrible sucking and farting-like noises as he used several suction devices and a long sharp implement to release his body waste. N2 shuddered at the noises that Beetle Blatt's body made. N studiously avoided a reaction.

Finally, expelling the last of his unwanted bodily detritus, Blatt flushed his waste device and turned to wash his extremities.

"Wassup, hater?" N2 said to Beetle Blatt in a nasty tone as Blatt walked past him to the series of cleansing devices on the wall near the door.

Beetle Blatt washed his extremities and ignored N2 and turned to N. "You haven't been contaminated by this idiot and gone pro-human on us, have you, N?" Beetle Blatt asked derisively. N shuddered, and he wasn't entirely faking it.

"Ecological balance is not dependent upon the existence of humans or any other unconscious species. We observe their actions/inactions and do not interfere," N said. It was obvious from his tone that he was reciting a regulation. Blatt's tiny little wedged-on face, in the middle of his bulbous egg head, frowned and spoke: "Any moron can quote Zycorp Reg—"

"Agreed. Any brown-nosing moron can quote Zycorp Regulations. Right?!" N said, his tone fraught with meaning, as if he were insinuating that Blatt were the brown-noser in question. Beetle Blatt was oblivious to N's innuendo.

"But do you know what it means?" Blatt asked N, entirely ignoring N's statement and follow-up question. N frowned, and his many eyes squinted with irritation.

"What is that smell?" N2 asked and looked meaningfully at

Blatt and then laughed raucously. Blatt and N ignored N2. Then N2, unwilling to give up so easily, inserted himself between Blatt and N. He crowded Blatt, but Blatt stood his ground.

"You're a smart boy and I know how to deal with smart boys," N2 said, doing his best James Cagney impersonation as Lieutenant Commander Morton in 'Mister Roberts'.

Beetle Blatt was not remotely threatened by N2 and imperiously waved him away. "None of that, you derivative duplicate," Beetle Blatt said and stomped out.

N2 was supremely embarrassed that Blatt had referenced and made fun of his being a replica. Plus, he'd been unable to intimidate the much smaller Blatt. He frowned and tried not to cry. N, seeing that N2 was upset, tried to make him feel better. "Ah, don't listen to him. He probably wishes he had a copy," said N.

N2 grew more upset. "...Sorry, sorry," N added, "I meant clone."

N2 entirely lost his joie de vivre. Dejectedly, he turned to exit the restroom.

"I would do what you suggested earlier, except, you know, except for Zycorp Reg.," N said, trying to cheer up his clone.

With great surprise, N2 faced the being that was an exact duplicate of him. "You would? You'd do that for me?" N2 asked excitedly.

"Well, of course, you know, we have to adhere to Prime Directive... which legally obliges us not to interfere... unless they ask for help," said N, and he watched with sadness as N2's excitement and joy deflated to nothing.

"If daily lottery scratch-offs and a twelve-pack of American boozle every night isn't a desperate plea for help, then I don't know what is, N," N2 said.

"We have an employment duty, not a moral duty, here," N

added. "Plus, those behaviors are not a universally recognized explicit distress signal."

Alarmed that N2's vital energy looked like it was sinking to a level that could seriously jeopardize his function, N added, "But maybe the guy will do or say something borderline. I'll reread the Zycorp Regulations guide, just in case."

Although N2's energy levels did appear to stabilize, they didn't increase. N2's only physical response was to shrug his shoulders.

Dejected, N2 walked out of the space station restroom with N following close behind. N wished that he could do something to make N2 feel better, yet he knew that it wasn't possible. He was nearing retirement and had too much to lose. Failure to follow Zycorp Reg. wasn't like forgetting to communicate with a friend or failing to do a personal task, he considered. A Zycorp regulatory infraction was a serious professional issue that could result in termination, banishment, and possibly even death.

He had heard rumors that, due to an explicit or implied employer-employee agreement somewhere in the tiniest fine print of the Zycorp Reg. manual, the corporation could legally kill a worker for certain infractions.

Rumor or not, he certainly didn't want to test that gossip himself to determine if it was truth. As the Zycorp Corporation had a no-failure policy, he had adopted a similar personal no-risk policy. No, it was simply not possible to do as N2 wanted, and N could not imagine a reality in which it would be possible.

N AND N2 REACHED THEIR CUBICLE. TO N'S SHOCK, THERE was a "Dweeb Meeting—Now!" message blinking red upon his computer screen. "You stay here, N2," N said and grabbed some official-looking technology (not because he needed it but because he felt that holding it made it appear that he had just been hard at work on a Zycorp task of some kind). N2 sat in a chair, quite content to be left behind while N hurried out of their cubicle.

N KNOCKED LIGHTLY ON THE DOOR OF MALLOW DWEEB's office. A grunt-scream was issued in response, the door slid open, and N entered the office. N looked around the cluttered room, which was piled high with technology. The room hummed with computers and other digital components, from which numerous lights flashed. N faced Mallow Dweeb, his obnoxious squid-alien boss.

"Good morning, sir. What did you need to see me about?" N asked, so nervous now that he had difficulty controlling his quivering tentacles.

"Your retirement," Mallow Dweeb said in his grunting-screech of a voice. N's wobbly eye-filled face blanched with fright.

"My pre-retirement paperwork was entirely in order, wasn't it?" N asked hurriedly.

"It was," Mallow Dweeb wail-growled. "However, due to regulation zzz.1822, your date of retirement eligibility has been recalculated."

N sighed with relief. "To when?" N asked casually.

"It used to be one glott but now it's six glotts," Dweeb grunt-screeched with what was obviously great pleasure.

"Six glotts? But why?" N asked, great shock evident in his voice.

"Regulation zzz.1822 stipulates that the work assignment of employees who bring in a clone to complete their hite is increased by one third. So, your 20 glott hite has become a 26.33 glott hite," Mallow Dweeb responded.

"But why? And when was this added?" N asked, more than a little plaintively.

"It became obvious to Zycorp that many of these so-called "identical" clones did work that was... substandard to their originals. Reg was addended in the last update," Mallow Dweeb replied casually. His grunting-screech voice made his every statement sound as if he were under extreme duress.

"So, because I cloned myself, we must observe and record humans for 130 plus more Earth years? But our subjects will all be dead?" N said helplessly.

"As always, you'll be assigned more subjects if any terminate," Mallow Dweeb grunt-screeched with great satisfaction. N stared, speechless with horror.

"Okay, N. Keep up your good work," Mallow Dweeb finished, dismissing N.

N was horrified; although dismissed, he could barely drag himself from the room.

It was late, and the space station hallways were emptying. As the earthlings' circadian rhythms were synchronized with the work-sleep cycles of their alien observers, most of the other aliens in N's department had left their stations to rest in their quarters. Back in their work cubicle, N, despondent, lay with his head on his desk. Incapable of knowing how to comfort him, N2 looked on in sorrow. N2 sat and stared at their monitors. N didn't speak for hours.

"Hey," N2 finally spoke. "Did you know that this section of the rig has secret storage rooms full of high-tech secret stuff that nobody is supposed to know anything about?"

N didn't respond or even look up from his desk.

"Yeah, some whistle-blower in tech support leaked a bunch

of files. It's all over the web… I know how to get us in, if you're ever interested," N2 continued.

N didn't even acknowledge that he was listening, but instead, he mindlessly performed some analysis work. Then, every so often, overcome by sorrow, he laid his head on his desk and wept. Feeling helpless to improve N's state of mind, N2 would also weep.

Finally, after hours of silence, N spoke. "I'll do it," he said ominously.

N2 was slow to process what N was talking about. N2 looked at the monitors and then at the work desk. Was there some task that N was committed to doing? He saw nothing of the sort before them.

"It's totally against rules and regulations… but let's do it," N said.

"Do what?" N2 asked, not believing he had heard correctly. Was it possible that N had changed his mind about interfering with an earthling subject, he wondered?

"That thing and that other thing," N said, trying to communicate without being explicit. He looked around furtively as if someone might be spying upon them.

N looked meaningfully at their monitor. Hank, dead drunk, snored in his barcalounger. N2 looked from N's tilting head, where he seemed to be pointing to the screen that showed Hank, and began to catch N's drift. N2 lifted a tentacle and shifted his many eyes, surveying their cubicle and work space.

"Seriously?" N2 said, finally getting it. Then N2 got up to dance and jump, wild with excitement, and did all he could not to shout or call out with delight. N watched his clone with a mix of bemusement and sadness.

"Seriously," N said, signaling that N2 should tone down his happy dance. Barely containing his excitement, one of N2's primary tentacles shuddered and shivered in apparent ecstasy.

"Why'd you change your mind, dude?" N2 asked happily.

"One, after our fight in the bathroom, I used self-reflection. I realized that I was angry because in all my negative working life I've never had one glicket of humor or satisfaction. You are right: I have no positive memories to retire with. And two..."

N paused for a long moment. "Two, Dweeb pushed our retirement to over 130 human years into the future," N admitted. All of N2's many eyes widened with shock. He stared.

"That's what that red level meeting was about?" N2 asked incredulously.

N nodded. "The son of a Brettnick found a tiny little Zycorp Reg. clause that—" N became so immeasurably upset that he was unable to continue. He knew that in some quarters, there was a certain stigma associated with having been cloned. So, too upset and too mortified to provide N2 with details about the exact regulation in question, N stopped speaking altogether.

Waiting for more, N2 stared expectantly. N tried to think of a better, less potentially hurtful thing to say.

"What?" N2 asked expectantly.

"In short, we... are not going to retire when we thought we were!" N said hurriedly.

"How can that be?" N2 asked.

N decided that he would not, in fact, explain how it could be to N2. He felt unable to choose to hurt his genetic copy in that way unnecessarily. It was in that moment that N realized that, although generally against his nature, he had developed a respectful regard for his clone.

"How can that be?" N2 asked again, his many eyes goggling in inquiry.

"Let's focus on the future. That suggestion that you were making earlier?" N said quickly, hoping to distract the frequently highly distractible N2. "Let's do it!"

N2 whooped and waved multiple tentacles all at once.

"That's what I'm talking about! Let's make some memories, dude," N2 said.

In that moment, N realized just how attractive N2 was to him.

It shouldn't have come as a surprise, being that the life form looked exactly like himself... and he did love himself, after all. So, it was with great love and equally great surprise that he inadvertently found himself sharing his compassion for N2's inferior status.

"Please don't be offended, N2, but I feel very sorry that you're a clone and considered... substandard by some," N blurted out.

N2 stared at N, completely horrified.

"Substandard? Says who?" N2 asked as he tried desperately not to cry.

"Jealous people, that's who," N answered, trying to salvage the situation. "So, moving on... moving on to, uh, positive memories... and the next best thing," N said.

"Yeah, moving on, dude," N2 managed to say, trying desperately to regain his cool, several of his eyes wide and full of tears.

"And stop calling me dude," N said playfully, hoping to cheer up his clone.

N tugged N2 into a standing position, and the two extraterrestrials surreptitiously surveyed the cubicle area.

It was late, and all they could see was a lone iridescent robot cleaning the floors. What they didn't see was their work colleague, Beetle Blatt, who was hiding and appeared to have been eavesdropping on their conversation. Impulsively, N grabbed N2's primary tentacle and tugged him out of their cubicle.

"What?" whispered N2.

"Shush," N replied as he hustled N2 through numerous empty hallways, past offices and random rooms. They passed a couple of in-love Arcturians, but otherwise, the section of the space station was empty. Finally, they traversed a long hallway and emerged outside a strange, blank wall.

N2 looked at N, his eyes goggling with surprise, not sure where they were or what was going on.

"Where's this purported 'secret' storage room?" N asked.

N2 grinned and pulled out a remote control device. He waved it in front of the blank wall. "I found a hack on the interweb," N2 said with unabashed pride.

"While holding down the menu key on the universal remote, you make the figure eight in the air like this..." For a brief moment, a door shimmered out of nowhere and, with a last quick look around, N and N2 leapt through the temporary entrance into the secret storage room.

N and N2 looked around at the strange room. "How cool is this?" N2 whispered excitedly.

Although the storage space appeared deceptively small from the outside, inside, the room was enormous and filled with technology. Gadgets and peculiar devices made of various strange and curious materials were piled high up to the ceiling.

"So much stuff," N2 remarked. "What exactly are we looking for?"

N dug through a panoply of tech and equipment at the back. He grabbed an extraordinarily small box and then held it up with a happy expression, as if it were a trophy. "Here it is! The Quantum Mind Jump," he whispered and grinned.

"We're doing all this for a consciousness testing machine that they mothballed deons ago?" N2 asked. "The thing is in storage because it never worked?"

"Shhh! We'll talk about this later. Now, come on. Let's get out of here," N replied and tugged at his clone with a tentacle.

"Wait a minute," N2 said and stopped moving. "It's against

Zycorp regulations to take anything out of here without permission. What if we get caught?"

Looking askance at his clone, who now, all of a sudden, was concerned about company regulations, gave N some pause for thought. Did his clone have a few loose chips upstairs, or was his quirky and unpredictable behavior an inherent part of the cloning process?

"Okay," said N. "Good question." Looking around, N gave the mind jump device to N2. "Swallow this, real quick," he said as he hurriedly grabbed something else off a shelf and shoved it down the front of his jumpsuit.

"Seriously?" asked N2, looking at the device and wondering what it might taste like.

"Hurry," N implored, helping him shove the device down N2's throat.

"Now get us out of here," N said.

N2 waved the remote control at the same part of the wall by which they entered. Nothing happened.

"What's the delay?" N asked.

"It's not working," N2 answered, checking to see that he was depressing the correct key on the remote. "Maybe it's a different hack to get out?"

"You've got to be..." Exasperated, N was too upset to complete his sentence. "Tell me we're not going to be trapped here in storage?"

"Is there someone we can call?" N2 asked as he pressed every key on the remote.

"Don't talk stupid. You think that if I had any friends on this rig, I would have cloned you? Depress the same key but reverse the movement." N suggested.

N2 did as instructed, and the wall shimmered, and an exit door appeared. They quickly exited into the hallway outside.

"Wow. That was..." N said and stopped short when he saw

Mallow Dweeb, their obnoxious squid-alien boss, and Beetle Blatt waiting in the corridor.

"You certain of this, Blatt?" Mallow Dweeb said to Beetle Blatt as he squinted at N and N2 with suspicious eyes.

"Yes, unequivocally," Beetle Blatt said, and his tiny little wedged-on face sneered at N and N2 from within the middle of his bulbous egg head.

Dweeb looked N and N2 over. There was a noticeable slight bulge in the front of N's jumpsuit. Blatt quivered with excitement. N2's eyes bulged with emotion. He looked at N. N, quite nonchalant, gestured to his clone that he shouldn't worry.

"Whatcha got there, N?" Mallow Dweeb asked.

N patted his jumpsuit, as if he were nervous. "Uh... nothin'," N said and grinned dumbly. Beetle Blatt laughed maniacally.

Mallow Dweeb took a step toward N and prepared to search him physically.

"Dweeb, sir, you know that touching him will be a Zycorp Reg. violation—" N2 declared calmly, though the threat in his tone was unmistakable.

"Only if he's not guilty," Beetle Blatt said snidely.

"Guilty of what..?" N asked innocently.

"You're hiding something," Beetle Blatt insisted.

"Yeah, as a matter of fact, I am," sneered N, and pulled what looked like a telephone directory from his jumpsuit and waved it about. N2 was so nervous that he appeared to be on the verge of fainting.

"My copy of the updated Zycorp Regulations," N said proudly and thrust it toward Dweeb, "Do you have yours yet?"

Dweeb inhaled sharply and took several steps backward immediately. Looking over the proffered copy of the Zycorp Regulations, he frowned and menacingly turned on Blatt.

"Apologies, N," Mallow Dweeb said, his voice filled with

thinly masked rage. Beetle Blatt was dumbfounded and speechless.

"N, N2… I'm sorry, but I got some bad intel," Mallow Dweeb said and glared at Blatt.

"No shitsky, bossola," N2 said and now smiled happily.

"Oh, my, that was close, and very nearly a disaster," said N as he gave Beetle Blatt a nasty look. "You almost got our boss fired because of your stupidity, Blatt." Dweeb turned on Blatt, his face growing red and swollen with rage.

N and N2 exchanged a glance and hurried away.

As they departed, Mallow Dweeb could be heard screaming gutturally in an alien language. N2 glanced back and saw Dweeb waving his arms threateningly at a prostrate and terrified Beetle Blatt.

Inside a project room at the Los Alamos National Lab, Drs. Blake and Delaware faced a complex equation on the blackboard. Stumped, they paced anxiously.

"We're obviously overlooking some crucial concept or data," Dr. Blake said.

"Unless our basic assumptions about gravity are incorrect," Dr. Delaware retorted. "But, obviously, the gravitational theory held by the entire scientific community can't be incorrect."

"Why limit our concerns to gravity alone? Perhaps our entire assumptions about entropy and the universe as a closed system are entirely incorrect," Dr. Blake replied and then rubbed his forehead in an attempt to stimulate better thoughts manually.

Hank entered with a mop and bucket. The pair of doctors stopped to look at him.

"Sorry. Thought it was empty," Hank mumbled. As he shuffled backward, the contents of his mop bucket spilled. "Fuck, shit... damn it all to hell," Hank muttered to himself.

Delaware shared a conspiratorial look with Blake. Blake shrugged. What the heck? Might as well try, his shrug seemed to indicate.

"Leave that, uh, Hank. Perhaps you could help us with something?" Dr. Blake said.

"Oh, yeah?" Hank said, propping his mop handle against the wall. Dr. Blake looked at their equation on the chalkboard.

"Gravity is a weak force. Acting alone, it can't possibly account for the homogenizing nature of the cosmological universe. Right?" Dr. Blake said, phrasing two statements, which he followed up with a question (which he surmised would indicate whether Hank understood the two statements).

As Hank's dumb expression hadn't changed, Dr Blake wasn't sure if he should even continue.

"O-kay," Hank said as he seemed to be reading the equation line by line, which gave Dr. Blake some hope.

"We're stumped. Besides our core assumptions about entropy, there must be some other factor, some other force in the universe that's affecting the increasingly evolving complex structure of the cosmos," Dr. Blake stated.

Dr. Blake shared a brief, doubtful gesture with Dr. Delaware as they then looked expectantly at Hank.

"Have you considered ETs?" Hank asked finally.

"ETs? What is that? I'm not familiar with the ET theory," Dr. Blake replied, looking at Dr. Delaware for corroboration.

Equally perplexed, Dr. Delaware first shrugged his shoulders and then had a sudden realization.

"For God's sake, man. You don't actually mean extra-terrestrials, do you?" Delaware practically shouted.

"Why not? If there is intelligent life out there, don't you think it is affecting the universe? Same way intelligent life is affecting this planet? Intelligent life interacts with—and in most cases reverses—the effects of entropy in a closed system, does it not?" Hank replied calmly.

"Surely you don't believe in—" Dr. Delaware said.

"Don't believe in a lotta things but that don't mean they don't exist," Hank said.

"Thank you so much for your input," Dr. Blake said in a dismissive tone, rolling his eyes and turning his body away from Hank. Catching the scientist's drift, Hank grunted and shuffled out of the room with his janitorial gear.

"Thought you said he was a genius? ETs? The guy's a friggin' idiot," Dr. Blake said to his colleague and they both laughed a little hysterically albeit nervously.

INSIDE THE SPACE STATION HEALTH CLUB, VARIOUS ALIEN beings worked out on anomalous machines and equipment, some of which bore more resemblance to torture devices than to modern exercise equipment. Others mixed and mingled, socializing and chatting, as N and N2 attempted sit-ups on a floor mat.

"Plan?" N asked N2.

"What?" N2 asked, straining with great effort to even do a single sit-up.

N looked around to be sure that they wouldn't be overheard.

"We need to make plans..." N said. N2, still straining to complete a sit-up, stared blankly at N.

"...for how we're going to actually use that Quantum Mind Jump thingie," N added.

"Plans?! Plans?! We don't need no stinking plans," N2 said,

ala the Mexican Bandit, from the movie "Blazing Saddles." N rolled his many eyes.

"Forget earthling culture for eternity, will you? I really think we need some kind of a plan," N declared, obviously having heard the film reference before.

"I toldja, it's all about spicing things up. Right? We point it at the Hank subject and see what happens," N2 said.

"You mean point it at the image of the Hank subject, and that's exactly my point. We don't even know if the device will work non-locally."

"If it doesn't work... then it doesn't work. We'll think of something else," N2 replied calmly.

"Yes, but what if it does work and this test subject, Hank, starts behaving in some crazy, offbeat fashion..?" N asked.

"That's what I'm talking about!" N2 said, getting wildly excited. N stared.

"A crazy, offbeat fashion? The dude is going to think he has superpowers or something. Maybe he'll start climbing tall buildings, trying to walk on water and stuff," N2 added.

"Exactly! Whatever he does will mess with our test results," N said.

"We're scientists. It's what we do," N2 said.

"I think it's safe to say that we're cubicle jockeys, technicians even, but scientists... No. That, we are not," N said sharply.

Then, before N2 could speak again, N spoke:

"Plus, the QMJ was never approved for complex organisms or life forms. It only worked on amoebas in a controlled environment."

N2 is astounded by this statement. He stares at N with a bit of awe.

"Really? I didn't know that," N2 said.

"I was there for some of the early QMJ tests. It wasn't pretty," N said and, tilting his head to reflect, was soon lost in thought.

INSIDE A TEST LABORATORY, A GROUP OF ALIEN SCIENTISTS from various species, wearing protective gear, test the QMJ on a simple organism. A younger version of N, working as a technician in the background, observed and took digital notes.

Alien Scientist #1 slowly turned a dial on the Quantum Mind Jump. All of the scientists watched intently as the simple organism exhibited rapid growth. With the increasing turn of the QMJ dial, the amoeba-like organism seemed to act with a corresponding acceleration of energy and intelligence.

The alien scientist observers smiled and nodded happily to each other as they ended the first experiment.

Alien Scientist #2 then retrieved the test subject chosen to be next, a complex organism which was housed in a cage-like container on the other side of the lab. With palpable excitement, all of those present watched as the Alien Scientist #1 slowly turned the dial on the QMJ.

In an instant, the complex organism morphed into a horrific giant mutant and killed one alien scientist before exploding and making an enormous mess.

The lab was now a disaster scene. ET medics and a clean-up crew worked on slime-covered injured alien scientists. N cowered in terror beneath a desk.

"OKAY, OKAY. SO WE WON'T TURN THE DIAL SO FAR, ALL right? We're professionals," N2 responded, bringing N back to the present.

N stared at N2 as if he were absolutely insane.

N2, oblivious to N's expression, ogled a female alien who was walking by. Then it became clear that, in fact, he was seriously lusting over her Earthling, "Prince and the Revolution" knock-off T-shirt.

"Zarkwad, I wish I had one of those Earthling t-shirts," N2 said mournfully.

"Space station to N2," N said, sarcastically.

"I would give anything for that kind of Earth swag," N2 said, still staring lustfully after the t-shirt.

N smacked N2 with a tentacle. "Pay attention, N2. We need to test the QMJ. We need to figure out how to give it a trial run."

"Not a problem," said N2. "We could try it out on Beetle Blatt and everybody else we don't like in Quadrant A6."

"Don't be ridiculous. They'd be sure to explode, and it would take us too long to clean out the mess and destroy the evidence."

"Then let's just use it on the earthlings. If they explode, we won't have to deal with the mess," N2 answered logically.

"Then there'll be an investigation and they'll want to peer over all our work for the last three glotts and question our data-collection methods... Who needs that? No, we need to test it out first. If a bunch of specialists couldn't make it work... well, let's just say that there's a reason they completely abandoned this technology," he said quietly.

Unseen, Beetle Blatt, sweating heavily, approached them from behind.

"Test, shmest. It'll either work or it won't," N2 said dismissively.

"What'll either work or won't?" Beetle Blatt asked meanly.

N and N2 turned and looked up at Blatt with alarm.

"Uh, my new... uh, my new data collection method," N2

answered, and it sounded more like a question than a statement. N rolled his many eyes. Blatt would probably see right through the blatant lie.

Beetle Blatt looked N2 up and down suspiciously. "You're up to something. I feel it in my gut," Beetle Blatt said and exposed his quite rotund, fleshy gut. It was swollen, bright red, and slightly undulating.

N rolled his eyes as N2 pretended to gag. Beetle Blatt sneered in response. N2 tried to avoid retching. "Put that away. It's disgusting," N said calmly. Beetle Blatt faced N2.

"You stole something from storage, and I'm personally going to do an inventory to determine exactly what it was, you dwork-fobber," Beetle Blatt said to N's clone.

"Oh, come now. Don't be ridiculous, besides, don't you have better things to worry about," N said calmly, "like keeping your job." A change came over Beetle Blatt. Rather than continuing his arrogant blustering, he slumped down and became obviously despondent. He sighed loudly.

N and N2 exchanged a puzzled glance.

"I'm ridiculous," Beetle Blatt said, suddenly sounding and acting terribly sad. "I probably blew my upcoming review because of you two. No way Dweeb'll promote me now," he added, and sighed again, even more deflated.

N2 looked at N and mouthed the words, "Is he crying?"

"Don't be upset with us. We entirely support your promotion," N said to Beetle Blatt.

Blatt stared at N and N2 in disbelief. "You do?" Beetle Blatt finally said.

Then N and N2, realizing that Beetle Blatt wasn't going anywhere, got up off the floor. "Guess I'm giving up on my sit-ups," N2 said happily.

"You really support my promotion?" Beetle Blatt asked again, as if he could not believe it.

"Absolutely. We'd love for you to be promoted... to another star system. Far, far away," N said and nodded eagerly. He really meant every word.

"That's right. Far, far away..." Beetle Blatt said, his egg head wobbling, and punched the air, "...from these filthy, ignorant, stupid, disgusting humans. Arggghhh! I wish I could exterminate them all... before they spread."

N2 glared at him. "Humans are not filthy, ignorant, stupid, and disgusting," he said, and then thought a moment before continuing to speak. "Well, some of them are. Maybe even a lot of them. But they are an evolving species, and they do have some desirable attributes," N2 said defensively. He hated the arrogance and ignorance of certain alien beings. He really did.

"Attractive? Humans?" Beetle Blatt said, his voice filled with shock and scorn.

"They have something called culture, which most civilizations would die for. Music, for instance," N2 replied, barely able to contain his anger.

"That... that noise?" Beetle Blatt said.

"It's only noise to untrained ears," N2 replied snidely.

Beetle Blatt squinted at N2, then grunted and slapped his red, bloated, ginormous belly. "You are saying that I have an untrained ear?" Blatt asked.

N looked back and forth between N2 and Beetle Blatt. "Of course not, Beetle Blatt. N2 isn't saying that at all... Anyway, your species doesn't have ears," N said.

"Right?! Just unattractive thin nasal membranes resembling Martian craters..." N2 shouted.

"Why, you..." Beetle Blatt shouted and lunged for N2.

N2 got the jump on Blatt and held his throat. N stared at his clone, quite impressed. "Do you wanna piece of me, asshole?" N2 asked.

Beetle Blatt was ready to give up, now that, given N2's

obvious fighting abilities, he was the underdog. "What do you mean?" Beetle Blatt asked fearfully and tried to escape N2's grasp.

"Mess with me and I'll kick your..." said N2, faking a kung fu kick, "...sorry ass into the future."

"He doesn't have an 'ass,' or know what that means so, unfortunately, he can't even translate that," N said to N2 in a helpful tone of voice.

"Yes, your threat is meaningless," Beetle Blatt said, glaring at N2.

"Oh, yeah? Why is that, punk?" N2 asked.

"Because I don't have a... an 'ass.' Or haven't you noticed?" Beetle Blatt said and laughed as if N2 were an idiot. N2 looked Blatt up and down with derision.

Two very forbidding alien gym security guards appeared. They towered over the three beings. N rolled his many eyes in irritation.

"Is there a problem here?" one of the gym security guards asked.

"No. No problem at all. This asshole was just leaving," N2 said.

"You filthy dwork-fobber—" Beetle Blatt shouted at N2 and took another swing at him. N2 gracefully dodged as the alien gym security grabbed Blatt.

"Is asshole your name or your species?" the second alien gym security guard asked Beetle Blatt. Beetle Blatt turned in rage and tried to lunge at N2.

N2 leaned around security and spoke. "It's his species. He comes from a very, very long line of assholes," N2 offered helpfully.

Beetle Blatt, even more enraged by N2's comments, was so incensed that it took both alien gym security guards to prevent him from escaping.

"I'll have to ask you to leave, asshole. No fighting outside the gym's Reptilian wrestling rings," one of the alien gym security guards said to Beetle Blatt.

"I'll figure out what you're up to. Then we'll see who's the asshole," Beetle Blatt said to N2 in a menacing tone as he was hustled away.

"That would still be you, Blatt. Bye, bye, asshole. Give my regards to all your asshole friends and family," N2 shouted after him as Beetle Blatt was forced toward the space station gym exit. "I'm going to get you guys, if it's the last thing I ever do," Beetle Blatt shouted as he was forced out of the space station gym.

"What?" N2 wheedled as N gave him a glance of reproach.

Inside the space station, in the intergalactic zoological gardens, extra-terrestrials and their families browsed near enclosures containing various species of beings, both flora and fauna, from all over the galaxy.

Anodyne New Age music (instrumental musical tones) looped rhythmically. Played from subtle, high-tech speakers, hidden among the purple, red, and orange foliage, the music served as a sedative for the creatures. Giant blossoms, in muted pastel tones, opened and closed very slowly, as if breathing in and exhaling in response to the melody which they were broadcasting.

With the QMJ in a backpack, N and N2 walked past the enclosures and scanned the area for a potential test subject. They stopped at an ugly, motionless creature that resembled an earth octopus.

N2 read an exhibit plaque aloud: "Astroctopi, native to Q-Ten Quadrant... level six intelligence."

"A level six? That's pretty dumb," N stated.

"Apparently, it sits around all day in a motionless stupor and only moves once a week when it needs to get food. Then it takes a dump," N2 replied.

"It's perfect then, I guess," N said doubtfully as he reached into the backpack, exposing the QMJ dial. Making sure that they weren't being seen, he turned the dial slowly. They both cautiously watched the animal. It didn't move or change at all.

"Don't you need to lock in its frequency first?" N2 asked. N flushed red with embarrassment.

"Yeah, of course. I know that," N said as he pushed a button, thereby extracting a long coil and light-head from the QMJ. He pointed the coil at the animal and pressed a button on the light head. Laser lights shot out, triangulated on the beast, and projected its form and measurements as a hologram.

"Okay. Locked on," N stated. Then he slowly turned the dial. They waited. As the creature moved ever so slightly, N and N2 exchanged an excited look.

"He moved... well, a tiny bit!" N said and then turned the dial up a few notches. The animal moved even more.

"It's working! It's working! Crank it up, N," N2 said.

N turned the dial even more. The animal stood up on its tentacles and started to move, albeit a bit comically. N and N2 stared, wholly fascinated by the being.

"What's it doing?" N2 asked.

"I don't know. Looking for food?" N replied.

The animal moved its tentacles and wobbled about, as if dancing. N's face lit up with understanding. "It's moving to the music," N said quietly.

"Oh, that. That's called dancing. Humans do it, too. Far out!" N2 said excitedly.

The astroctopi grooved to the music. A bemused yet somewhat enchanted crowd of celestial families gathered. A little alien child pointed, and his tentacles waved in delight.

"Turn it up more. Let's see if this cat can sing!" N2 whispered to N.

N secretly turned up the dial, yet again. The astroctopi wildly gyrated happily, and, to the crowd's delight, danced up a wall... then it exploded.

The alien families screamed and turned to run as the animal burst apart. Various beings were slimed before they could get away. An alarm sounded. Weird and wonderful security beings approached on the run.

In the confusion and pandemonium, N and N2 slipped away and managed to escape unwanted attention. Ersatz night fell. It was an artificially induced evening, a darkening of the sky from cerulean blue to ever-deepening lavender, created by the futuristic manipulation of light, humidity, and temperature.

In another part of the alien zoological gardens, N and N2 searched for another subject. They stopped at an enclosure holding what looked a lot like a Neandertal. The creature was well-endowed and quite obviously male. N and N2 looked it up and down nervously.

"This is a hominid... and a primate," N said tensely. "I guess it's a logical choice."

"Are you kidding? It's perfect," N2 said and then turned to examine the exhibit plaque: "Level seven intelligence. Aside from some grunts, no language abilities or higher cognition."

"I guess," N said, looking around with nervous circumspection. "Plus, there's no one else around."

Triangulating on it, N pointed the laser light-head at the hominid and projected its form and measurements as a hologram. "We need to go slow with this one," N cautioned.

"Yeah, sure. Slow is obviously the key," N2 replied confidently, as if he really knew what was best.

Once more, N looked around and, seeing that the coast was clear, he secretly turned the dial. The hominid turned quickly and stared at both of them.

"What's it doing?" N2 asked.

"I don't know," N replied.

"Do you think that it's thinking?" N2 asked.

"I doubt it. This species can't think. It probably just noticed us, maybe sees us as food or something," N answered.

"Okay, turn it up," N2 said.

N turned the dial up. The hominid grunted in a way that seemed quite meaningful. N and N2 exchanged a look. N appeared shocked. N2 shrugged.

"Is it trying to communicate? It really looks like it's trying to tell us something," N said, quite obviously stunned by the hominid's reaction.

"That's pretty advanced, right?" N2 asked.

The hominid grunted more frequently now, as if trying to converse with N and N2.

"It's talking to us! Talk back," N said excitedly.

"I don't know grunt. Do you? Turn it up some more. Maybe it'll actually start speaking or drawing pictures," N2 replied.

N turned the dial up. Desperately trying to communicate, the hominid gestured with his hands and grunted in a series that sounded like sentences. N2 faced the hominid and analyzed its gestures.

"Wow," N2 exclaimed. "If we all knew sign language, we could totally be having a conversation right now."

"This device is definitely working," N added.

"Your name is Hand Face?" N2 asked the creature, trying to decode its gestures.

The hominid shook his head and said, "No," then continued signaling. N and N2 stared intently at it.

"It's totally understanding us!" N2 said.

"You don't like the food?" N asked the creature.

The hominid nodded, "Yes!" N and N2 got terribly excited and paced in front of the creature's enclosure. N2 grabbed N, but N quickly shrugged him off for acting too excited.

"This is amazing! Turn it up," N2 said.

N turned up the dial. The hominid abruptly stopped signaling. N and N2 stared at it. "Oh, shit," said N2, his worry as he shielded his face, anticipating being slimed.

"Brain..." uttered the hominid. His word was garbled, yet intelligible. N2 was stunned and stared at the creature. N fidgeted with the QMJ controls.

"Did he just talk?" N asked N2. Turning to the creature, N touched the edge of its enclosure and motioned, as if to encourage it to come closer.

"Brian?" N asked.

"Maybe that's his name," N2 said to N.

"What is y-o-u-r n-a-m-e?" N2 asked the creature, enunciating very slowly.

"Brain..." replied the hominid and rubbed its head.

"His name is Brain! This is far out!" N2 said.

"Brain... h-u-r-t..." the hominid said, enunciating slowly like N2 did.

"What did he say?" N asked, distracted by the QMJ controls.

"His name's Brain Hurt," N2 said excitedly.

"Brain h-o-t..." the creature said.

"Holy cannoli, he's really talking. Turn it up!" N2 said.

N turned it up. The hominid reacted with apparent rage. It grunted and screamed garbled words. It pounded against its hi-tech enclosure. Then it stepped back and spoke again to N and N2.

"Brain f-r-y..." the hominid said, its words were a bit clearer. N and N2 strained to understand. Then the hominid's head and body exploded. N and N2 got slimed. An alarm sounded.

"Oh. His brain was getting fried," N2 said.

"You know what it means, don't you?" N said..

"Uh, we fried his brain?" N2 asked.

"Obviously," N said and thumped N2. "But first he spoke... which means that he developed self-awareness! What normally takes ages... the evolution of consciousness... the machine made happen in seconds!" N exclaimed.

"The Quantum Mind Jump totally works!" N2 replied.

"Yeah, and this stuff really stinks," N said with disgust as they both wiped greasy cellular slime off of themselves. N and N2 turned to leave. They barely made it to the front of the next animal enclosure before alien security beings ran past them. Acting innocently, they hurriedly made their way to one of the side exits.

***

Back inside their work cubicle, N and N2 observed Hank. They both look bored out of their minds. "Come on, dude. This is worse than mist-gazing at midnight on Tarskle," N2 said and sighed heavily.

"Yeah, like you've ever been to the moons of Tarskle," N replied.

"On the holo deck, I have! Many times!" N2 retorted. "You do know that the brain can't distinguish between real and fantasy, right?"

"It's too dangerous," N said, changing the topic. "The Hank subject's brain looks like it could explode very soon all by itself."

"You're concerned about the subject?" N2 said.

"Of course not. I'm concerned about my retirement," N replied.

"But you promised. What about those positive memories for retirement?" N2 said. "You won't live long without memories."

"I'll get engram implants," N said.

"You can't get implants, dude. They don't last, or you'll end up totally confused like what's his name?" N2 said, his voice filled with concern.

N laughed. "Like you?" he asked.

"I had implants?" N2 asked.

A fellow worker, D2, popped his head over the cubicle wall. "Hey, you two, check out X^2 News. You won't believe what's happening out there," D2 said.

N changed one of his screens to X^2 News. An extraterrestrial X^2 reporter stood before a mob scene. Behind the being, angry alien demonstrators carried placards with signs that read: "Humans Are Beings Too," "Even Primitive Life Forms Have Rights," "Society for the Prevention of Cruelty to Humans," "Just Say No to Humans as Experimental Subjects," and so on.

N and N2 watched the screen as alien beings from around the galaxy ranted, screamed, and protested. The extraterrestrial X^2 reporter gestured to the increasingly violent scene behind them. "Ugly scenes here again, at the HQ of the Intergalactic Space Federation, as the interested parties meet again to debate the future of elementary life forms living on an inconsequential world, in the boondocks of the Galaxy, known as planet Earth," the X^2 reporter stated.

The computer screen showed interviews with various interested alien parties.

"We retain ownership of these... creatures. Ongoing food and drug testing programs, mind control and behavior modification programs... means there isn't a product or service in our catalogue that was not first tested on planet Earth," said Q, speaking for Zycorp.

A dark neosaurian-reptilian type of being, and a member of

the Intergalactic Space Federation Council, responded angrily to Q.

"Though they seem an insignificant species... on the periphery of the galaxy, it may be important to allow their existence. As we all know, when a flybble flaps its wings on Tauryon, a hurricane is created on Vartex," stated the Draconian Council Member, the dark neosaurian-reptilian life form.

"The conceit that genetically engineered human DNA may somehow spread and infect the rest of the universe is entirely preposterous," said the Zeta Reticuli Grey Council member, a small neosauroid grayish-white being, genetically engineered for high intelligence.

The very petite and slender horse-like Arcturian Council member stood and waved its arms.

"We motion that all races agree to withdraw from planet Earth entirely and allow natural human development to proceed unimpeded," stated the Arcturian Council member with great love.

The Draconian Council member stood back up to add another few cents to the debate.

"As a selfish, warlike species, killing each other and their planet, their days are numbered. Why wait for the inevitable when an obvious catastrophe and an uninhabitable planet are in their future? An evolved species with no planet of their own should be given the opportunity to live on a planet such as this, to respect it, treat it with care, and live in peaceful accord with the intergalactic federation," the Draconian said.

"Hear, hear," agreed many members of the Draconian delegation.

The image then switched back to the reporter.

"As talks continue for two more Tauryon cycles, stay tuned to—"

N switched off the report. He looked upset. "Your tear ducts are enlarged," said N2. "Are you upset about something?"

"If they wipe out the earthlings," responded N, "then we're out of a job. If they leave the earthlings alone... then we're also out of a job. Either way—"

"—Koo-koo-ka-choo, we're screwed," interrupted N2.

Resolutely not amused and unimpressed with N2's lack of reverence, N looked briefly at N2 and then reached beneath the counter to take out the QMJ.

"What are you doing?" asked N2, suddenly alarmed. "Someone will see it!" he added, furtively looking around for who might have eyes on them. Every living entity in the immediate vicinity was focused on their work, most of them looking almost hypnotized from staring at their boring screens for such long periods.

Without responding to N2's concern, N pointed the light head of the QMJ at the screen, which showed Hank snoring loudly in his barcalounger.

"OMG, what are you doing?" asked N2, his alarm growing.

"Ever peruse the Zycorp Regulation manual fine print at length?" asked a calm and collected N.

"No," answered N2, still looking out for eyes looking in their direction.

"Well, in a minuscule 1.1 font, Zycorp Regulation zzz.919 stipulates that employees who fail to do any portion of their assignment fail to get a pension," continued N, still focusing his attention on Hank. "Not... one... ZeRe," he added.

"Gad-farqing-zooks!" responded N2, genuinely amazed, yet still not understanding N's intentions.

"Well, if the last 19 glotts of my hard sweat and toil with this company have been meaningless..." continued N, "the least we can do is acquire some positive memories."

N2 now seemed to finally understand N's uncharacteristic

display of reckless abandon of Zycorp Regulations and instantly became excited. "That's what I'm talking 'bout," N2 said, a little too loudly. "But we still don't know if the QMJ will work non-locally," he said, in a more hushed tone.

"We'll soon find out," answered N, the light head of the device now positioned to his satisfaction.

"Let's do this," said N2, now all fired up.

N engaged the QMJ and triangulated Hank with ease. "It's locked in," he said with resolute assurance.

"Far out!" N2 almost shouted. "Crank that baby, dude!"

N slowly turned the dial. Beetle Blatt, paper in hand, appeared out of nowhere. N2 quickly moved to block Beetle Blatt's visual discovery of the QMJ while N bent down and casually hid the machine out of sight, beneath the counter.

Intensely focused on his intention for the cubicle visit, Beetle Blatt waved a document in the air with what could only be described as malicious glee. "Guess what I have here, N?" he asked.

"Your transfer papers?" answered N, who was pretending to enter data into the side console.

"An inventory report," said Beetle Blatt. "I could tell you what's missing... but then you two already know that, yeah, huh?"

Beetle Blatt looked at their expressions closely, his eyes darting from one to the other, hoping to catch them in some guilty or tell-tale look of collusion. N and N2 were acting sufficiently calm and composed, however. They focused their eyes on their respective tasks and barely looked at their inquisitor, Blatt, at all.

"Even if something were missing," N2 said as he extracted data from the video feed, "there's no way you can prove we took it... which we didn't."

"Oh, yeah?" exclaimed Beetle Blatt, excited that, based

upon N2's obvious nerves, his relentless grilling might be smoking them out. He focused his vision even narrower upon N2, his face getting closer and closer to N2's.

"What's missing, Blatt?" asked N, hoping to deflect his attention away from N2.

N2 quickly swiveled in his chair in order to input data into the data energizer and to avoid Beetle Blatt's obnoxious stare.

"No way that this son of a Brettnick generated a report of inventory so quickly, he can't even get his work done on time," N2 said to N, as if Beetle Blatt wasn't even present. "He's totally bluffing."

"We'll soon see about that," exclaimed Beetle Blatt, outraged at the accusation. "I have a meeting with Mallow Dweeb first thing in the morning. You have till then to come clean and stop me."

Blatt gave them each one more threatening glance before he walked off, hoping that his dignity and integrity were still intact. N and N2 quickly stopped what they were doing and both watched Beetle Blatt return to his cubicle.

"Do you really think that he's bluffing?" N asked N2.

"Totally bluffing," answered N2, as if there was no doubt in his little mind. "I don't know about you but that stare of his felt so invasive, I feel like he just raped me with that dark horrible egg headed gaze of his."

"I know. Me too. I understand they mate with those nasty things," N agreed.

"I didn't know that. A Zygon mates with its egghead?" N2 asked incredulously.

"So I hear," N said and shuddered, "Though I can't imagine who or what would want to mate with one of those creatures.

N2 stood up and shook himself, similar to how a dog would shake off its wet fur. "I think we need to tie one on," N2 said, as if that would solve everything.

"I don't know what that means," said N. "I obviously care less for human colloquialisms than you do, but okay, I'm basically following you, with blind trust, at this point. Let's go tie it on!"

N2 led N to the space station sports bar, which always seemed to be full of hardcore partiers, no matter what time of day or night.

Actually, it was probably because there was no day or night in space that it always seemed like a good time to party. Or perhaps, the monotonous occupations of the alien workforce were so unbearably dull that any chance they could get, they would choose to spend their hard-earned ZeRes on the best inebriating beverages that the vast universe provided.

N and N2 found the quietest spot that they could find, way at the back, which, compared to the space station canteen at the same time of day, for instance, wasn't really quiet, at all. Empty drink cups and other strange containers littered their seating area, which gave them an indication of how bad the service was; no surprise there. Wait staff in space were notoriously bad.

When the Octogonian Reptilian Waitress eventually arrived, they made sure to order extra rounds of the sports bar special, which was a highly intoxicating, verging-on-toxic brew made from the famed lotus-berry bush, which was abundant on nearby planet Xterra Bundish Loca.

They needn't have ordered so many drinks, of course. After a few sips of the potent drink, they were soon both so inebriated as to be incapable of operating any kind of machinery or device. In short, they got totally wasted.

"I'm so relaxed," exclaimed N, slurring his words. His body melted into the shape, contours, and crevices of the vinyl-like booth.

"Are you relaxed, my clone, old buddy?" N asked N2.

"I'm so relaxed, it's unreal," N2 happily agreed.

"Progeny of my genes, my DNA twin," exhorted N, his tear glands enlarged, his underused, tiny emotional center in his brain stimulated by the drink. "Your genetically modified DNA may be just a teensy bit off, perhaps, but... I love you," N said mushily.

N2's emotional center was equally stimulated, and his tear ducts had no problem releasing their water-based contents. He sobbed with joy and gratitude.

"Maybe I should get a few more of us." N continued. "I have a few ZeRe saved... be worthless in prison."

"Hey, N., be careful," said N2 as N tried to stand up straight but failed to do so.

"You can call me man... or dude, even," said N, warmly.

"I'm really getting used to your humanisms. It's probably what defines us, as separate beings, I'd say," N added.

"Holy crap!" exclaimed N2. "I've never heard you talking like this before. You must be so wasted."

"Yeah, I'm wasthed," N slurred, "but when are we going to tie one on?" He swayed back and forth.

"When are we going to tie one on, dude?" he asked again, and struggled not to fall over. N2 laughed so much at his identical original that he fell to the floor and rolled over several times beneath the table as N continued to sway and speak.

"Sheriously, dude. When are we going to tie it?"

Bending down to help N2 rise from the floor, N lost his balance, with tentacles flying, and subsequently joined his first-generation copy on the floor.

"We should tie it on more often, you and me," N said with utmost seriousness as they lay on their backs, looking up at the sparkling stars visible through the glass-domed enclosure.

"You got that right!" said N2 in between bursts of uncontrollable giggles.

N and N2 were woken by the sound of their wake-up-and-stay-up alarm, which went off at the same time every workday, which was every day.

N painfully rolled his body in the direction of the alarm clock and switched it off, silencing the deafening noise. N2 sat up in his bed and took some time to adjust to his surroundings. They were in their space station allotted quarters, alright, but he had no idea how they had suddenly ended up there.

"How did we get here?" he asked.

"We have no time to question," responded N in a grave tone. "Look what time it is."

N2 turned to look at the digital time scale-o-meter: Stardate Intergalactic Time: -310586.4070089556.

"Wow, it's really early. Or late," he said as he sat up and grabbed his sore head with several shaking tentacles.

"How did it get to be so early?" N2 asked.

"The tie one on beverages must have caused some time confusion in the brains," reasoned N.

"Or we've been abducted again," N2 conjectured.

"That was just that one time," N corrected, "And they promised not to do it again."

"Yeah, like we can trust those Reticuli Zygots, sons of breaches," N2 said, inspecting his body for signs of any unauthorized midnight incursions.

Realizing that N hadn't moved in quite some time, N2 looked to his buddy for clues. N's eyes were enlarged with alarm as he read the morning feed from the promotometer. "What is it, good buddy?" N2 enquired with forced calmness.

When N didn't respond or move from his position, N2 moved closer to get a look at what he was reading. "What is it?" N2 asked, now alarmed.

"Looks like we've been side-swiped," answered N with immeasurable gravitas.

"Violations of Code 6 and Code 7 of the Zycorp Regulations. We're going to be iced."

"Iced?" N2 almost shouted with horror.

"Beetle Blatt must have reported on us," N said, after considering the situation for a moment. "Theft of Zycorp inventory and leaving our stations without permission and without due concern for data encoded within the time-allotted workload. We are pre-iced, a temporary measure, until an investigation can be instigated and completed," he added.

"An investigation? We'll be found guilty! We'll be iced for good!" N2 babbled, his body spinning, tentacles waving, with uncontrollable panic.

"I don't want to be permanently iced," N said, as if thinking out loud.

"Of course you don't want to be permanently iced! Who would want to be permanently iced?" screeched N2, still spinning.

Then he stopped suddenly and accidentally whacked N with an out-of-control tentacle. "There is no way we can face an investigation and avoid freezing. We need to hide," N said calmly.

"Hide?" asked N2. "Hide for how long?"

"Hide permanently," answered N, almost retching at his ridiculous solution.

"How can we hide permanently? They can trace our DNA footprint within nano-digitals on this rig. We'd need a DNA scrambler to begin with. But where would we hide? How would we eat?" N2 cried.

N2 was so distraught, he was nearing a meltdown. "We need to get off the rig," N concluded, "make a break to a secure planet that doesn't have an extradition treaty with the Zeta Reticuli or the Zygons."

"That's a great idea," responded N2 sarcastically, "except

we're way out in the galactic boondocks and have no way of getting back to the tri-solar serio-seismal planetary system. We're so going to be iced!"

Looking very pensive, N walked closer to the space domicile see-through barrier and looked out at the vast universe beyond.

"The only transport vehicles on this hunk of material have a maximum transportation limit of 260,000 zonk-giles. There's only one habitable planet within a 260,000 zonk-gile radius," N commented.

"Earth?" N2 questioned.

"They'd never find us on earth because they would never be allowed to send anyone to look for us there."

"That's right!" said N2, warming to the idea.

"They'd be breaking every Intergalactic Space Federation Council treaty and protocol if anyone even set down one tentacle on planet Earth. That's brilliant!" N2 added.

"Zycorp doesn't care about treaties, N2. They only care about profits. They won't send anyone after us because to do so would contaminate their research on humans. Alien interference on Earth would completely distort the data, rendering it meaningless. As soon as word got out that Zygons and Zeta Reticuli were visiting Earth, even if it were to extract another alien species, every contract would be pulled from here to the Circle X-TC quadrant. Zycorp business would implode in just two mini-moes of a nano-glott!" N said in response.

"Hot doggonit. We're going to Earth!" N2 dreamily exclaimed.

"Just think. Remember when you thought you would retire without any memories to cherish? Now, you're going to make so many memories, your brain won't have enough space to put them all!" N2 said happily.

"Yeah. Let's hope we get to live to enjoy those memories," N responded gravely.

N AND N2, MOVING FURTIVELY, SNUCK THROUGH THE corridors of the space station, attempting to avoid attracting notice. Making their way to their workspace, they quickly stopped and hid when they saw Beetle Blatt and Mallow Dweeb talking conspiratorially just outside their work cubicle.

"Nutzoid," N cursed. He grabbed N2 and hustled him back the way they came. "We'll have to leave every possession we own and just make a run for it," N evaluated the forced N2 in the opposite direction. N2 frowned and hurried along. He'd thought they could maybe sneak in and out without being noticed.

TIME SEEMED TO MOVE SLOWLY AS N AND N2 nonchalantly made their way past strange and different alien beings, all on their way to work. Periodically, the two would look around to ensure that they weren't being followed. Sneaking into a large storage bay, N and N2 made sure they weren't seen entering.

"What are we doing here?" asked N2. "The Starcars and docking bay are way over the other side," he said, then gasped, "Are you stealing stuff?"

N quickly filled a backpack with numerous technical gizmos, which were amazing and curious in their appearance, that he had selected from among hundreds. They were stored on huge shelves, which rose to the ceiling.

"Earth has an atmosphere and anomalous gravitational fluctuations that will make it hard for us to assimilate easily. We need to bring things with us or, among other deleterious side effects, we'd begin to age at 3.57 times the rate we are now," N finally said.

"Yikes," exclaimed N2. "Stock up, dude."

N opened up a read-only screen on one of the storage computers and, typing in some quick commands, began scrolling through a long list of names. "Now what are you doing?" asked an inpatient N2.

"We need to know if we made the do-not-travel list. If that's the case, then the Starcars will be programmed not to take us," N stated calmly.

N2 flailed, tentacles askew. "Are we listed?" N2 asked, panic revealed in his voice.

"No, not yet. But if they're staking out our work cubicle, it can't be long before they upgrade the search to level six," N said. He was calm, as if the situation was bringing out a sense of control. They exited the storage room and took a look around.

"Let's move, N. I'm not equipped to deal with stress beyond the workplace, which is like, zero stress," N2 whined.

N almost smiled. "You'll be fine, N2. We're going to stroll over to the docking bay, just as if we were walking to the staff canteen. We do that every day, right, N2?"

"Yeah. Speaking of which, I am getting a little hungry," N2 said, brightening.

"We'll stop for a bite on the way. Let's move it," N said, and almost laughed aloud at N2's foolishness. Taking a deep breath, the two beings started.

N and N2 walked quickly, toward the docking bay, as calmly as if they were walking to the staff canteen. "Where are you two going?" a Vulcan sentry asked them as they approached one of the Starcars.

"It's our staff commander's birthday and we all chipped in to get him some take-out," N said.

N2 looked at his buddy N with astonishment. He had

no idea that the being was so resourceful and such a convincing fibber. "Is this Starcar all loaded up?" continued N.

"I don't see you two listed," the sentry said, checking his check-out list.

"Yeah, it's a last-minute thing. We won't be on the list. You could call our commander... but he doesn't know anything about it. It's a surprise, so that it would ruin his birthday, but you could call him," N said sadly.

"What kind of take-out?" the sentry asked suddenly.

"Hugo's on the cusp," replied N quickly, without batting any of his multiple eyelids.

"You're going to Hugo's?" the sentry asked with lip-smacking interest.

"Wild-caught space eel and terra-yaki spam for all," N2 said helpfully. N smiled happily and nodded.

"Seriously?" asked the sentry, his eyes aflame with sudden desire.

"Hey, can we bring you back some?" N2 asked quickly, as if the thought had just occurred to him. "It's so great... but looks like you know that."

"I can't afford that kind of—"

"No problem," interjected N, "We collected way too much Ze-Re to feed our small department. There's going to be major overages."

"Can't remember the last time I had wild-caught eel," the sentry added, salivating just a bit, as his tongue involuntarily licked his many lips. "But I can't," the sentry then concluded, stepping more firmly to block their path.

"My commander would ice me, then replace me with one of my younger clones," the sentry added kindly.

"Oh, too bad," replied N, his voice filled with faux sadness, thinking hard about what to do next.

"Yeah," agreed the sentry, in an even sadder tone of voice, "It really is too bad. I love space eel."

Unable to come up with any further scheme, which would get them safely past the guard, N and N2 turned to make their retreat.

"Now, what?" N2 asked N in a whisper.

"Let's find somewhere to hide and come up with a better plan," N responded. They walked away as the sentry returned to his post, and once out of sight, hid behind some transport cars. A large unauthorized double-decker starbus touring craft made a very loud and clumsy landing at the docking bay. Some warning lights flashed, alerting all security personnel in the area to investigate.

As they did so, the doors of the craft slid open and out poured a colossal mass of mixed and quite colorful alien races, who very soon revealed themselves to be demonstrators and activists. Shouting chants and waving placards, their sheer numbers and exuberance overwhelmed the small number of security personnel.

"Stop human experiments now!" they chanted loudly and angrily.

"End the cruelty now!" they raged. It appeared that the group was associated with the Aliens for Ethical Treatment for Humans group, as the placards they waved sported slogans like:

Let Them Be!, Free The Unevolved Human Scum, Shame on Your Higher Self!

Seeing their chance for escape, N and N2 wasted no time in running to the first available Starcar. They quickly dived in and closed the door swiftly. Before N2 had time to secure himself in the passenger seat, N had started, backed out, and accelerated the craft right off of the docking bay and into open space.

"Wow," N2 declared as he watched the off-planet space

station fade off into the distance, "I've never been off-rig before. This is wild."

"Strap yourself in," advised N, "we're about to hit warp speed." He carefully avoided mentioning to N2 that he actually had been off the space station before. No point in upsetting his only clone.

"Wow," repeated N2, securing himself in his seat. "I've only seen warp speed in the—"

Flash! Before N2 could finish his thought, the craft accelerated, and a sea of white stars elongating in a blue shift was all that they could see and experience, as the Starcar peaked at its utmost outer limit of acceleration. Both N and N2 distorted visually. "Ye-ow!" N2 attempted an ecstatic yell, "Yippee ki-yaye!"

His words, though, were garbled until they made the jump to warp speed, and both of them wobbled and vibrated wildly, saliva dripping from N2's mouth. The vibrations were so intense, it sounded as if the Starcar might shake completely apart. Finally, when they had made the jump and everything seemed normal again, N checked the navigational aids and set course for Earth.

N2 watched each passing cluster of shimmering stars and galaxies with ever-increasing excitement.

"We're going to Earth," he mused out loud. "We're actually going to Earth. No simulation, no engram memory implants... we're actually going to Earth!"

"I would try to conserve your energy, if I were you," cautioned N. "This is a Starcar. It's going to take some time to get there," he added.

"Can we make the first stop Disneyland? Or Disney World? Disney World or Disneyland; it doesn't really matter. Maybe Disney World. I could go either way. You choose," N2 said magnanimously.

"Where?!" he asked, then added, "No! We can't change our destination now. We're going to Earth," N said with irritation.

Disney World is on Earth. So is Disneyland. They're both on planet Earth. They just call it a world. Human humor," N2 said and laughed with actual joy.

"Why do you want to go there?" N asked curiously.

"According to the guidebook, they are both the happiest places on earth," N2 said in all seriousness. He was over-stimulated and quite obviously ecstatic.

"We'll see," said N, unconvinced. "Let's turn on the news." N punched a button. A tiny, high-resolution monitor seemed to appear. It was actually a projection.

" X^2 newscast, local news" N instructed.

The screen instantly showed an X^2 reporter standing before the angry group of alien demonstrators as they were being pushed back onto their starbus.

"As you can see, behind me, more negativity than this sector has seen in a glott. Could it be that the debate about humanity and planet Earth is decreasing consciousness throughout the universe? And, in related news, two Zycorp employees are on the run," said the X^2 reporter, in a sinister tone of voice.

N and N2 exchanged anxious glances as poor images of both of them, overworked, stressed, and much less attractive than normal (N2 had one eye bulging in a particularly nasty way), appeared on screen. The reporter reappeared on screen with Beetle Blatt.

"Yes, I worked with them. It's safe to say they're capable of just about anything. Typical human sympathizers, they absolutely exhibited criminal tendencies and—" Blatt said, but was cut off.

The camera quickly shifted back to the Alien X^2 Reporter.

"Suspected of stealing valuable technology, anyone who sees them is asked to contact the network at this tele-coordinate immediately," the X^2 Reporter said. As contact information flashed on screen, N killed the broadcast.

Seeing themselves on the X^2 news report, depicted as criminals, seemed to shock them both. They remained quiet and stared blankly ahead as they hurtled through space toward an unknown world and an equally uncertain future.

"We're believed to be criminals," N said glumly after a very long silence. "It's so... so unfair! We... we never did anything... and they're calling us criminals?"

"Steal equipment from storage, tie one on during work hours, take a Starcar out into the universe... and suddenly we're criminals? Unbelievable," agreed N2.

"On the run? Seriously?" expounded N.

"Seriously," N2 said in response.

"This is a vacation. We're entitled to a vacation. Do you know how many vacation glotts I have saved up, which are legally owed to me? I've lost count. Every time I ask to use one up, guess what they say? Administration replies, 'Now is not a good time.' It was never a good time. Well, guess what? This is a good time! This is my time... this is our time!" N barked.

"Yeah," chimed in N2, "you got that right! They don't give us vacation, we take vacation. 'Cause that's how we roll! Give me five up top," N2 said as he raised a tentacle. With his tentacle still poised and waiting, N2 noticed an immediate shift in N's mood. He dropped his tentacle.

"What?" N2 asked as N put the Starcar on autopilot and hurriedly grabbed his backpack, as if he had just remembered something terribly important.

"We can't go to Earth with tentacles. We can't just show up on planet Earth looking like this. We look like their..." N struggled to remember the word, "...their 'monsters,' the scariest things... things that terrify them, right? They'd kill us on sight."

"Not if we go to Disney World. They have creatures there.

Crazy-looking aliens with huge heads and small bodies. Weird creatures. Furry. Scaly. Strange. Humans love them. Just like they'll love us. Everyone at Disneyworld will want to hug us and take still pictures of us and feed us hotdogs and candy..." N2 salivated at the delicious thought of such happy-making things.

Finally, N found what he was looking for, a compact, hand-held device with a multi-directional wand.

"What's that?" N2 enquired with mild interest.

N smiled pompously, his savacous glands elevating in size. N2 paid even more attention: if N was getting all puffed up, the device must be pretty important.

"It's a multi-phase shape-shifting device. It used to be top secret Zeta Reticuli military tech before they perfected the applied distortion science and put this baby out to seed."

"What does it do?" N2 asked.

"The army used it to change a soldier's appearance..." N said and paused for effect, and then made eye contact with one of his clone's many eyes, "...into that of the enemy... so that they could then infiltrate and spy without being discovered."

"You're going to change our appearance to human?" N2 asked, his excitement barely contained.

"If they've got human on this thing," N answered, turning a dial through a vast selection of alien life forms, hominid and otherwise.

"Ah, here we go... human." N paused, looking a bit puzzled. N2 smiled happily and waved a tentacle.

"That device has a human as one of the settings? Far out! We're going to look like humans! That's wild!" N2 said and bounced up and down in his seat.

"Yeah, except I didn't realize that there were so many different types of humans," responded N glumly.

"Different types?" N2 asked curiously.

"Yeah. There's homo habillis, homo erectus, homo sapiens, Australopithecus, Neandertal, Cro-Magnon..." N said, obviously quite overwhelmed.

"Maybe it doesn't make any difference... if they're all human," suggested N2, "Let's just pick one."

"Okay, I guess," agreed N, "Lean back."

"Why am I going first? We don't even know if this thing works?" N2 asked suspiciously.

"Alright," said N agreeably, as he thrust the device into N2's hands. "I'll go first."

"How do you work it?" N2 asked as he scrolled through the on-screen list. "Oh, look, there's even more choices. Negroid, Caucasoid, Mongoloid, Pygmy... Pygmy has a nice ring to it. Do you think Pygmy sounds good?"

"Sure. Okay, so you want Pygmy?" asked N as he grabbed the device back.

"Sure," replied N2, now not entirely certain, "just as long as I look like Elvis."

"I don't see that species listed on here," said N as he input critical data, such as N2's original species, height, weight, and so on, into the device.

"Just stand still, for a nanosecond," N said as he waved the wand in the direction of N2's body. "One human Pygmy, coming right up."

As the device shot out a steady stream of bio-discrete-photons, N2's body began changing from head to toe into a tiny human. Seeing the distressed reaction that appeared upon N's face, and inspecting his "new" tiny arms and legs, N2 freaked out. "What is this? This doesn't look like a full-size human being. Is this human?" he squealed in a tiny voice.

"I'd say that you're humanoid, all right, but I don't think that you should be so... small," N answered, looking at the device with a puzzled expression.

"Increase my size!" N2 demanded. "I refuse to be this small! This will be a disaster in Disneyland!"

"Humans come in all shapes and sizes. Don't be such a judgmental being." N suggested.

"You don't understand," shouted N2. "I'm not being judgmental, I'm being practical! I'm so small that they won't let me on the rides!"

"Yeah, probably get beaten up by the child humans, too. I've seen news videos; some of them can be quite vicious. Let me try it again," N agreed.

"Okay, but I should tell you that I'm feeling really groggy and my head feels like it's being squeezed into a..." N2 swayed, as if he was about to faint, "...squeezed into a... Let's just say that I really don't feel too good right now," he managed to finish.

"Alright," N said with more than a bit of urgency. "Try to remain conscious, and I'll change you into something else. How does Neandertal sound?"

Unable to answer, N2 was losing consciousness fast. N made the adjustments and quickly converted N2 from a tiny Pygmy to a huge Neandertal.

N2 expanded in size as he morphed into a huge Neandertal body. His bulk was so massive, his new form was squished into the passenger seat of the Starcar. He became so large that his head and face, really almost every part of him, nearly filled the quite roomy passenger seat adjacent to N and the driver's seat.

"Wow," N exclaimed, shocked by the transformation. "How do you feel?" asked N as he looked down at the device with concern and confusion.

"Okay, tha gud," N2 grunted, sounding more primitive by the second, barely able to speak, squished against the ceiling and his seat. "Feel brain breathe, know I mean?" N2 grunted as he seemed to be fully relaxing into his new form.

"Try to relax," N advised. "We need to change you into a

modern human. Why don't they give a listing for just a modern human?" N asked as he scrolled on the device screen for a more appropriate form. As he chose "Mongoloid," a message flashed on the tiny screen of the high-tech device. "Craps!" N blurted out.

"What's up?" N2 asked in a deep and ancient voice.

"It says that we can only change you one more time, or it could be critical," N said.

"Crit cal for 'chine or, uh... me?" N2 grunted and thumped himself for emphasis.

N stared at N2, quickly trying to calculate whether to leave him as he was or risk changing him into yet another form, which could even end up being worse. Obviously, his clone's ability to communicate had degraded with his current change, and he was also enormous. N hated to judge, especially since N2 was always quick to point out when he was being judgmental. Still, at the same time, N2 no longer seemed intelligent enough to be able to successfully hide out on Earth for any appreciable length of time.

"I don't know, it's probably not a big deal, but for safety's sake, let's give it one more try... and whatever you get, you're stuck with. So, you choose," N said, being unable to select from the remaining choices and hoping to abdicate all responsibility.

"Gee, tanks... N," N2 replied gutturally. "What options again?" He was so large, he really couldn't turn his head or move, but his diminished capacity for thought made it so that he didn't even complain.

No, N thought, looking at his clone, Neandertal was definitely not the way to go. "Look," N said, having a burst of inspiration, "...they probably have some significance in order. Why don't we choose the last one?"

"What last un?" N2 grunted.

"Homo sapiens sapiens," N replied.

"Sapiens sapiens?" grunted N2, as if the words were very disagreeable to him. "That doesn't sound right. Why are they using the same word twice?" he tried to ask, but it sounded like: "Th do so ri. Why us sa wo two?"

In order to respond appropriately, N leaned closer and struggled to understand N2. He in no way wanted to alert N2 to the horrifying consequences that the transformation could result in for him.

"Mabe so gud, na it two," grunted N2 cheerfully.

"Okay," N said casually, taking N2's response as being in the affirmative.

"Homo sapiens sapiens, it is, then." N held his breath as he turned the dial to the very last option on the list. As he did so, N2 inexplicably began singing what sounded like an odd rendition of New York, New York. His singing actually sounded like what a very primitive and unevolved primate would sound like as he grunted out the song. Not waiting for N2 to finish, N engaged the device.

N2's rendition grew intelligible as he slowly shrank and twisted, finally morphing into a burly, six-foot-two human—a relatively handsome Caucasian male with a modern look, sporting a full head of blondish-brown hair.

"New Yuck, New Yuck—" N2 finished with a flourish. "It's the song Frankie Sinatra sings," he clarified, in case N didn't get the reference. Relieved beyond his wildest imaginings, N nodded happily: N2 finally seemed normal enough.

"Far out!" N2 declared when he checked out his new body, moving it around as if he were trying on a costume. N let out a huge breath and began breathing again.

"You look great," exclaimed N with considerable relief. N2 finally fit properly into his passenger seat, and his words were intelligible. "How do you feel?"

"I feel great!" replied N2, "No, I feel gooood," he corrected himself, breaking into his rendition of the song "I Feel Good," made famous by James Brown.

"Okay, here, do me," N insisted, passing the device into N2's hands. "Whatever you do, don't change the settings!"

Without breaking rhythm, N2 continued his song, pointed the device, and transformed N into a wiry, thin, yet strong Caucasian male with brunette hair, approximately five feet five inches in height.

"Hey, we're different!" N2 almost shouted. "We look totally different! I mean, really different! Look at us! Look at you. We're so different! How can we look so different? We're clones?"

"When we get arrested, it'll be the first question we ask the military, okay?" N answered as he reviewed his new form. Despite his unfamiliarity and secret distaste for how he looked, he was nevertheless delighted that he didn't become something worse.

"This feels... terrible," N deduced. "No wonder humans are so unhappy all of the time. These bodies feel like prisons. Phew, it even stinks," he added, lifting his right arm and smelling his armpit.

"I like it," said N2. "I like the way I look. Do you think I got the handsome body because of luck or some other intangible feature like instinctual and emotional intelligence or something?" N2 asked and then laughed as N frowned, his new face and expression looking hilarious to N2.

"Don't be ignorant. You're not handsome. We both look ridiculous," chided N.

"Say something else," N2 said as he watched N's lips move and couldn't stop laughing.

"Let's get a move on. If they think that we're criminals on the run, they'll have posted every space rig and outpost of the entire known universe with our descriptions," N stated.

"Who'd recognize us? We don't look anything at all like our normal physical descriptions!" N2 remarked happily, trying to contain his mirth.

"We don't, but our Starcar does," N said.

Just as N spoke, a set of colorful, flashing lights was seen in the distance behind them.

"What's that?" N2 asked.

"Space cop," N answered. "We need to change the shape of the craft before he gets close enough to triangulate us." Swiveling in the pilot seat to fully face the complex controls before him, N consulted the range of dials, screen, and flashing lights on the control panel.

"Better hurry," said N2, watching the approaching lights with interest, "it's gaining on us."

N quickly found the shape-shifter program he was looking for and rapidly scrolled through the thousands of possible shapes.

"What kind of craft would a human drive?" N wondered out loud. "Do they even have any craft capable of star flight?"

"Cadillac!" shouted N2, "humans love to drive a Cadillac. I know that for a fact."

"Cadillac," N quickly keyed into the console. "It's asking me to select from a bunch of numbers," N responded with increasing agitation.

"What numbers?" N2 asked.

"One nine five-o, one nine five-two... there's a whole bunch," N said. N2 had no clue what to suggest. Not waiting for a reply, N selected a number at random, "With fins or without fins?" N then shouted.

"Fins?" N2 responded, looking anxiously behind them. Their pursuer was gaining fast.

"With fins," N selected. "Color? Oh, never mind," said N, as again he selected at random.

"Hurry," said N2, getting more alarmed. "They're gaining fast!" he screamed just as N slammed a button on the panel. The craft shook and vibrated, making horrible noises. They covered their ears as, with a screeching groan, the craft contracted in size. In doing so, it threw N2 forward. He crashed against the front control panel. As the craft contracted further, N2 was thrown back into the passenger seat.

"What have you done?" shouted N2. "The Starcraft is imploding! We need to eject!"

"There is no eject!" shouted N.

"I don't want to die in space!" N2 screamed.

"I can't hear you!" N replied against the din.

There then followed an abrupt silence. In an instant, the Starcar ceased its hyper-exertions. "I don't want to die..." N2 stopped shouting mid-sentence. They both looked around at their new, cramped surroundings. The Starcar looked totally unfamiliar and less than a sixth of its original size.

The inside looked exactly like a 1950s Cadillac. A vibrational "knock" on their window caused them both to jump in shock. A space cop, lizard-like in appearance, with a great spiny ridge on his head, floated outside their window.

In a spacesuit, on a starbike, the lizard had pulled alongside them. He gestured for them to turn on their two-way communication device. "What seems to be the problem, space officer?" N asked, once communication was established.

"License and registration," the space cop stated, looking around the inside of the peculiar craft with suspicion and extreme curiosity. Despite his lizard-like face, his facial expressions looked like he was asking himself what the heck these guys were flying in.

"Yes, of course," N replied, wondering to himself exactly where he might find such things.

"What does he want?" N2 whispered.

"Identification," whispered N, turning back to the space cop. N smiled. "We don't have the things you ask, sorry," N responded as N2 rummaged around his seat and the side panels of the door, hoping to find something that might suffice as identification.

"You must have a license and registration. It's a galactic requirement. If you can't produce it, you'll have to turn around and come with me," the reptilian said.

"Oh, here they are," N2 exclaimed with great surprise and relief. He'd opened the glove compartment and found what appeared to be official ID discs.

"Hold them up to be scanned, uh, being," the space cop demanded, looking N2 over. N2 smiled.

"Department of Motor Vehicles?" the space cop asked, reading from the registration. "What kind of species are you and what star system are you from?" he asked with intense suspicion. He especially checked out N2, who had been grinning broadly and goofily in order to appear friendly.

"We're homo sapiens sapiens," answered N proudly, pausing for effect, "from the planet Earth."

"You don't say," said the space cop with derision. "Didn't know earthlings were capable of intergalactic space flight?"

"Yes, most beings are not aware, sadly. It's recent history, the last few glotts, actually. We'd appreciate it if you could get the word out, seeing as how so many think we're all backwards and... whatnot," N said.

"I'll see what I can do," replied the space cop, not meaning a word.

"Yeah. We're tired of being treated like... uh, idiots, and... the poor relatives of the universe," N2 chimed in, still smiling like an idiot.

The lizard space cop looked past N, who was now entirely mortified, and gave N2 a more thorough once-over.

"End the discrimination, man. We shall overcome," N2 added and gave a peace sign. The space cop stared silently at N2, unable to determine whether the being was doing something illegal, and scratched his scaly head in an effort to think of something.

"Is there anything else, officer?" N asked politely.

"No, I guess things here are in order. Have you seen any other traffic on your journey?" the reptile asked.

"No, sir. We were just remarking how quiet our travel has been," N replied nervously as he wondered frantically to himself why this being wouldn't depart already? The encounter was making him so terribly anxious, he couldn't stop his new human body from shaking.

"What's in your trunk?" the space cop asked, sensing that something was just not quite right with these two weird "homo sapiens sapiens." Unfamiliar with the concept, N looked all around for a 'trunk.'

"Trunk? I don't think that we have a—" N stated, then N2 hurriedly interrupted him.

"Control. Open trunk!" N2 commanded the control panel. A tiny trunk on the back of the Cadillac popped open. N and N2 watched the cop on their video screen as he went back to investigate.

"What's in the trunk?" N asked N2 with concern.

"I don't know. It's a storage area for whatever humans like to take on their travels," N2 replied, looking around anxiously.

"Control," commanded N, "list contents of trunk?"

"Typical human road travel objects," the computer replied, "toolbox, beer, beef jerky, travel souvenirs, sexy magazines, and assorted sex toys."

N kept his attention focused on the video screen. At the trunk, the Space Cop was rifling through the stored items. Then he paused and again scratched his head. He picked up and was obviously taken by the human sex toys. With great interest, he held up a full-size blow-up doll of a human female, clad only in a négligée.

"What's this thingie?" the reptile asked.

"Oh, that's a travel souvenir..." answered N, not quite sure.

"...from Earth," added N2, with much innuendo.

"What's it used for?" the Space Cop asked, holding it this way and that.

"Humans use it for all kinds of things," N2 replied, winging it. "When they are away from home and their loved ones, they like to take them to their beds. It helps them sleep."

"You don't say," the Space Cop commented, totally smitten. Obviously excited by this idea, the spiny ridge on his scaly head and neck stood straight up. He squeezed the blow-up doll gently, entirely intrigued by the "souvenir" thingie.

"You can keep it," N suggested. "We don't need it, we, uh, have each other... so, uh, we didn't use it. It's still new."

N2 gave N an annoyed look. Like the reptilian cared about them "having each other" and whether or not they had 'used' the thing. Mesmerized by his new plaything, the cop slammed the trunk shut and then rapped it twice.

"Alright. Move along," he ordered. Gently squeezing and examining his blow-up doll with a scaly appendage, the Alien Cop returned to his vehicle. N and N2 watched nervously as the Alien Cop happily strapped the doll behind him, hopped on his starbike, and then sped away.

"That was close," N said, allowing himself to breathe deeply again.

"You told him he could keep our toy?" N2 griped. "We've got each other," he mimicked sarcastically, "We never even got to play with it once!"

"Don't worry, N2. There will be lots of other toys to play

with when we get to Earth," N said sarcastically. N2 smiled and settled back in his seat.

"You're right. When we arrive, we can choose any Earth toy we want. Let's shift this baby, see what she can do!" N2 replied.

N increased the speed, and the transformed Starcar jerked forward, soon approaching the intergalactic maximum efficient cruise speed. Space flew by, and stars shimmered like sparkling diamonds.

From the outside, their ride looked just like a 1950s Pink sporty Cadillac, complete with tailfins, cruising through the vastness of outer space.

As a punishment, along with his ordinary workload, Beetle Blatt was instructed to man the cubicle vacated by N and N2. Preoccupied with his other tasks, however, he paid little attention to the screen, which displayed Hank, who was currently snoozing in his barcalounger. Though asleep, Hank looked quite different from the last time he was observed. He seemed more peaceful within himself, and, having lost weight, the man appeared more attractive.

Beetle Blatt's attention was drawn to the screen as Hank sat up and rubbed his eyes. Not fully awake, he looked around at his cramped trailer, which, as usual, was littered with beer cans, lottery scratcher tickets, empty cigarette packages, and empty food take-out boxes. Looking briefly at his tiny, static-filled TV screen, which flickered between images and snowy static, as if switching channels, he fell back asleep.

Beetle Blatt stood and returned to focus on a screen on his mobile control panel. On that screen, he could see the results of some secretive sleuthing. Having searched through various databases for the serial number of the Starcar that had recently gone missing, he hoped to use that information—and his Intergalactic Positioning Device—to locate its whereabouts.

If successful, he could try to deduce precisely what N and N2 were up to. He was convinced that whatever they were scheming, and wherever they were, it had everything to do with him, either directly or indirectly.

If he could solve and prove their conspiracy and catch them breaking Zycorp Reg., it would stand him in great stead for his upcoming promotion re-evaluation meeting with Mallow Dweeb. Successfully locating the missing Starcar's ID number, he performed a quadrant search to track it down.

When he got the "live audio feed" option, Blatt inserted an earpiece into his nasal cavity and tilted his head sideways to enhance his focus.

"How are you feeling, man?" Blatt felt a human voice say.

"Hungry. Did you bring any Zycorp ready meals?" N2's voice answered. Blatt now recognized that he was successfully tapping N and N2.

"Check the meals-to-go port-sack," N replied.

Garble, garble, garble... Losing audio, Beetle Blatt snorted in irritation and then adjusted the earpiece to try and improve the audio connection.

"I know that we're not really criminals. You know that we're not really criminals. Garbled... get the heck outta dodge, take a little road trip, make some memories, let things cool down a bit," one of the two said. Blatt wasn't quite sure which being was speaking.

"Holy Mother of Reptilia..." followed by garbled words.

Beetle Blatt slammed his desk in irritation and tried adjusting the earpiece again.

Garbled, garbled... "...wonder what the food is like on the blue and green globe?" N asked.

"Planet Earth?" Beetle Blatt said out loud. A coworker in an adjoining cubicle, Mantid, an insect-like creature that resembled, yet was much larger than, an earth praying mantis, stopped working. It stared at Beetle Blatt suspiciously.

"Queltip device?" he asked, his voice an almost indecipherable little squeak.

"What device?" Beetle Blatt responded, feigning both innocence and ignorance.

"Device in Zibbie's xylmohop," Mantid said, as he stretched quite a distance and suspiciously tapped Beetle Blatt's gadget with one of his spindly legs.

Beetle Blatt mimed to indicate he had forgotten that he was wearing the thing. "Oh, this. This is... It's my..." Blatt mumbled. Unable to think quickly, he stood and faked intense embarrassment. Mantid observed him, unmoved and unconvinced. "Queltip device?" Mantid asked again.

"A hearing aid, because I don't have ears," Beetle Blatt answered and, faking a sense of deep shame, he hung his tiny egg head, grossly over-acting.

The mantid tilted his head, as if wondering what Blatt was trying to convey with his gesture, and then, gurgling with laughter, he patted Blatt on his back, as if he were a lower life-form.

"Whatever, Blatt," it said. "Don't give up the day job," he added, as he minced off on his pincer-like long legs.

Making sure he was alone again, Blatt looked furtively around, pushed the gadget tightly into his nasal membrane, and listened again with intense concentration.

"Now who needs to 'Get off the crazy?'" was all he could intelligibly make out, as most of their conversation was corrupted beyond recognition.

As Blatt tried various adjustments on screen and on the device itself, he failed to notice that on the earth-screen before him, Hank was engaged in a characteristically odd set of behaviors. In what appeared to be an altered state of consciousness,

Hank organized and meticulously cleaned his house trailer for the first time.

It appeared that he was so entranced and at glorious peace with the world that he was practically levitating. Once cleaned to his satisfaction, he sleepwalked back to his barcalounger and soon returned to a deep sleep.

N LOOKED OUT AT THE PANORAMA OF STARS ALL AROUND them as they sailed through space.

"We could lay low in Cygnus X... watch the birth of some baby stars," N said, speaking his thoughts aloud, as the Caddy flitted through glittering celestial bodies. N2 giggled for a long moment.

"You like a little mutation with your stellar dust and gas?" N2 finally responded.

"What?" N said defensively.

"That place produces a peak X-ray flux density of $2.3 \times 10\text{-}23$ $Wm\text{-}2Hz\text{-}1$, which is 2.3×103 Jansky," N2 read off the wikistellar entry on the onboard computer. "It would poison us. Plus, baby stars die out there."

"Helluva way to go, though," reflected N, sounding unusually pensive, "birth and death, intertwined."

"We're going to planet Earth," N2 stated. "You promised, plus, we'll be safe enough there. It will be fabulous."

"Guess we're taking our chances with warring and savage earthlings, then," said N.

"That's what Zycorp wants us to believe. Makes it easier for them to sell their services. You should know better, man," N2 said, defending Earth, yet again.

"Whatever... man," replied N, feeling overly weary.

"It's okay," N2 said, realizing that N was almost at his limit.

With the push of a lever, N2 pulled out a little spray bottle. The Zycorp label read "While Away the Hours" and featured a picture of a sleeping moon wearing a nightcap. N2 held it up to N. N stared blearily at it.

"Ready for cryosleep?" N2 asked and then, puff, he sprayed N without waiting for a reply.

Thud! N took a single breath, and his head fell against the side window. He fell right into a dead sleep.

"That's what I'm talking about," N2 said. He then fiddled with the dash, searching the screen console for Earth music. Finding what he was looking for, N2 twitched, shook, and squeakily sang along with the first Earth song that came up, "I Know What Boys Like". Excited out of his mind, he fervently sang along to the lyrics.

<hr>

THE DOCKING BAY OF THE SPACE STATION DREW AN increasing number of protesters, as the first anti-human experiment factions had arrived and gained notoriety.

Predatory protestors, consisting mainly of Draconian and Zeta Reticuli species, carried signs with pro-experimentation slogans. They chanted and shouted as they marched against the hippie-like, peace-loving protestor-beings.

"Humans are animals! Humans and animals are one!" they shouted, "95% animal DNA - research for ZeRe. 95% animal DNA - research for ZeRe."

Another protesting faction, the peace-loving, very gentle, horse-like Arcturian beings, displayed their support for letting humans be. Harmoniously, they chanted with vocal tones that resembled humming:

"Humans are beings, too. Humans are beings, too."

The Arcturians accompanied their quiet song-chants with their famed "Dances of Universal Peace-Love-Joy."

Lookers on were mesmerized by the beautiful, exotic, choreographed Arcturian routines. The dance they were performing was so beautiful that the Minx-Alien X^2 Reporter motioned for the X^2 cameraman to get a wide shot of the chorus. She then jumped in front of them to make her report.

"Behind me, Arcturians demonstrate for humans and in the process, they reveal their customary and quite lovely, indigenously unique, high frequency love for all beings... yes, love for all beings... including humans," she began.

Enraged that the gentle and loving Arcturians were getting serious camera time, Draconians and Zeta Reticuli ran angrily towards the Minx-Alien X^2 reporter. The Minx-Alien X^2 reporter immediately activated her self-protective defense shield as the demonstration took a more aggressive and possibly dangerous turn.

"Yet the demonstration grows ugly... as Draconians and Zeta Reticuli protest their right to harvest humans for ongoing research..." she gasped out.

The Minx-Alien X^2 Reporter ran from the Draconians and Zeta Reticuli, yet still managed to continue her report, "... because, as they state, a 5% difference between humans and earth chimpanzees makes people the ideal research laboratory animal. This is Amunica Ray from X^2 News reporting," she shouted.

ON THE EARTH-SCREEN MONITOR, HANK WOKE UP AND looked around his tidy trailer, his expression one of obvious extreme puzzlement. Beetle Blatt, holding a Zycorp Regulation manual, checked his time piece, took a huge deep breath, then left the cubicle to walk to the office of his boss, Mallow Dweeb.

"Unfortunately, we've had to go with another applicant," Mallow Dweeb announced, not even waiting for Beetle Blatt to get himself seated.

"Because I did that media interview?" Blatt asked.

"You did a media interview?" Dweeb asked.

"No, of course not. Zycorp is renowned for rewarding a being who diligently follows regulations." Blatt rescinded smoothly. Dweeb looked him up and down.

"You do follow regulations," Dweeb finally admitted.

"Yes, I do," Beetle Blatt stated proudly.

"Top of the class," Dweeb acknowledge diffidently.

"So what's the problem?" Blatt finally asked when it became apparent that Dweeb wasn't going to add anything further to the conversation.

"The 'problem' is that you only follow regulations. You're what we refer to as a perfect worker. But Zycorp likes management to be someone... someone who—"

"Someone who doesn't follow regulations?"

"Someone who thinks outside the rectangular."

"That's the first I've heard of this. Since when does Zycorp encourage employees to think independently?" asked Blatt, seriously confused and decidedly angry.

"And where does it actually say, 'Think outside the rectangular?'" Blatt enquired further, flipping through the virtual pages of the Zycorp rulebook on his handheld computer.

"It doesn't," Mallow Dweeb admitted, "but we do expect our brainier workers to... show initiative. Sadly, you've shown zero of that." Mallow Dweeb then proceeded to rubber-stamp "Failure" in bright red ink on Beetle Blatt's application. Blatt stared down at the document in complete and utter shock.

"So sorry. Now, go away," Dweeb said, returning to his

work. Beetle Blatt didn't move for a moment. "Now!" Mallow Dweeb added, speaking sternly.

Beetle Blatt stumbled to his feet and managed to get himself out the door without fainting or falling into a big, helpless heap on the office or hallway floors.

THE 1950S INTERSTELLAR PINK CADILLAC STARCAR SHOT past a moon, then slowed down. N2 consulted a holographic map as N slowly woke up.

"Where are we?" N asked groggily, checking out his unfamiliar surroundings.

"We're approaching one of the Earth's moons," responded N2, trying to concentrate on the map.

"Earth has more than one moon?" asked N.

"What? No. I guess I was looking at Jupiter. Which one is Earth?" N2 asked. "Oh, never mind, I found it. Wow, it looks so blue!"

Still trying to come to full waking consciousness, N rubbed his head. He didn't notice that he had drooled all over his chin. "What's the plan?"

"Well, I don't know about you, but I'm starving. Ideally, we could find a nice little diner on the moon and eat some human food," N2 responded, almost licking his lips at the thought.

"I mean, what's the flight plan?" N squinted his eyes to focus on the holographic map.

"Huh?" N2 said absentmindedly. "Dash! There are no restaurants on the Earth moon, yet. Now, there's a business opportunity we could consider—"

"You've been flying this thing... you're taking us into Earth's atmosphere, and you don't have a flight plan? We could end up in the ocean, N2! What are the landing coordinates?" N asked as he checked out the on-screen flight trajectory.

"Just a seci-dot," N2 answered, as he frantically searched for something on the holographic map. "I can't find Anaheim."

"Roswell, as everybeing knows, is located at 33.3942° N, 104.5225° W. Our current flight plan is going to miss it by ten point five degrees. I'm putting us back on auto land," N said, keying in some commands.

"Why Roswell?" N2 asked derisively.

"All landing craft capable of earth landings are automatically programmed to land at Roswell. It's mathematically the optimum landing point for our craft in consideration of Earth's electro-magnetic biofield. Not to mention that it's barely populated with earthlings and we can land without being discovered," N said emphatically.

"Screw Roswell," discounted N2, "This is a normal earth space vehicle, we won't be detected. We fly into the local airport, which is LAX, and then head to Anaheim. They'll just think that we're a normal human spacecraft. It's perfect."

"What's in Anaheim?" N inquired.

"Happiness is in Anaheim!" N2 replied. With a crazed expression, N2 let out a manic laugh and shifted the Starcar's gear into atmo-approach, level-seven.

N shook his head, disapproving. "What are you doing?"

"Who put you in charge?" N2 asked as he took control of the craft. "You're not the boss of me."

"Yes, I am! You're my clone! Just because we're off-rig doesn't—"

"You promised! You said we could go to Disneyland!" N2 pleaded.

"I did no such thing!"

"Yes, you did!"

As they continued to argue, the Starcar whizzed right

through the glowing stratosphere on a direct descending course toward Los Angeles International Airport.

Too upset to work, Beetle Blatt was unable to focus on anything. Sitting in the cubicle, he stared blankly into space. Mantid, noticing his co-worker's lack of work progress, slowly inched his way over to his work station.

"Zibbie crying?" Mantid finally asked.

"No, of course not. Zygons don't cry," Blatt replied.

"Zygons are too proud to cry?" Mantid inquired.

"No, it's impossible for us to cry. We don't have tear glands," Beetle Blatt said defensively.

"Too bad Zibbie no promoted," Mantid said, in an attempt to commiserate.

"Too bad I didn't catch N and N2. Would have been promoted for sure. They stole a QMJ from inventory," Beetle Blatt said, not bothering to hide his bitterness.

"Zarkwad. Thought was bluff," Mantid noted.

"Zygons don't bluff," Beetle Blatt said numbly.

"What did they want with a QMJ? QMJ not work on clone being," Mantid stated calmly and logically.

Blatt nodded in agreement and sighed heavily.

"Their choice of device stumps me. They have some devious plan, but I..." Beetle Blatt thought about it some more. Mantid had inadvertently said something significant. His words gave Beetle Blatt a powerful idea. He quickly left the cubicle. Curious, Mantid followed.

Beetle Blatt hurried to one of the security kiosks in that sector, and in his mind, he was already preparing an excuse to give to the security personnel. Luckily, however, the security kiosk was unmanned. Quickly, Blatt keyed in commands on a touch-screen interface. Mantid joined him.

"What Zibbie does here?" he whispered with caution. "Such action contravene Zycorp reg."

Beetle Blatt tapped the visual command screen, which soon displayed holographic surveillance footage of N and N2. "Thinking outside the rectangular," he said enigmatically.

Speeding up the image, Blatt then stopped it and played it at normal speed when he saw something of interest. The holographic cubicle surveillance footage clearly revealed N and N2 using the QMJ on their human subject, Hank.

Blatt gasped and pointed, almost unable to believe it. "They used the QMJ... on a human subject!" he exclaimed.

Almost in horror, Mantid stared at the hologram.

"Why do that?" asked Mantid, totally shocked. "That corrupt and destroy all human data from that moment!"

Returning from their lunch, the two security personnel turned the corner, shocking them both with their sudden appearance.

"You are not authorized to be here," one of the guards said. His tone of voice was quite ominous: "What is your purpose?"

"We wondered about our missing co-workers, N and N2. Have they been found yet?" Blatt lied as he quickly disengaged the security footage.

"Those beings are considered criminals and enemies of the corporation. If they are ever found, they will be iced, no questions asked. We apologize for any inconvenience to your work department," one of the guards, a robotic Zylock, answered.

"Yes, it is an inconvenience, but good to know that you are doing your jobs. Come, Mantid, let us leave these good sentries be. We thank you for your time," said Beetle Blatt as he shuffled Mantid away.

As the guards checked for anything remiss at their kiosk, Blatt quickly pushed Mantid along and into another corridor, out of sight. Rushing back to his cubicle, Beetle Blatt enlarged the earth-screen to get a better look at what Hank was up to at that moment.

On screen, Hank parked outside his local convenience store, got out of his vehicle, and then slammed his pickup truck door closed. Crickets chirped in the still night. Clear-eyed, Hank walked with purpose towards the storefront.

Beetle Blatt and Mantid watched with interest; Beetle Blatt took digital notes from time to time. "Earth being has been doing this every Earth day cycle. It is the same, always. At first, I mistook him for a robot," Blatt clued in his partner. "Watch with attention. Store clerk will ask, "Same old, same old,"" Blatt said, conferring with his notes. They both watched the screen with intense focus.

Having selected his items for purchase, Hank put a large bottle of upscale spring water in front of the Native American Clerk. Not noticing Hank's purchase, the Native American clerk greeted Hank as he always did. "Same old, same old?" he asked.

"Not tonight," answered Hank, softly and kindly. The clerk automatically turned to grab two packs of locally made native smokes and some Area 51 Alien Abduction scratchers before processing what Hank had said.

He then halted his robotic movements and looked at Hank, a serious expression of confusion on his face. "Not tonight, did you say?" the clerk inquired with surprise, double-checking.

"Correct. Not tonight," responded Hank, looking clear-eyed and happier than ever and more put together than normal. He was a man at peace.

The clerk looked at Hank, as if for the first time, and then glanced at the glass container of pure drinking water sitting on the counter. This was very different, he thought to himself.

"Spring water? That it?" The clerk, looking stunned, hadn't yet rung up or bagged Hank's water. Was Hank playing a practical joke? He wondered. He stood perplexed, looking at Hank as if expecting some kind of explanation for what he perceived to be an unusual turn of events.

Hank gently placed some money on the counter and smiled. "Yes, please," he answered.

Dumbstruck, the clerk slowly and carefully bagged Hank's purchase. Hank noticed a collection jar for a needy indigenous family who had lost their father in a car accident, on the counter. Pulling a few bills from his worn leather wallet, he stuffed them into the jar.

"Holy cow," the clerk couldn't help saying, "That's the first actual wampum donated round here since the Clint man was Potus."

Hank bestowed an almost beatific smile on the clerk. In an instant, the clerk recognized that type of smile; he had seen it on some of the village elders and the tribal shaman. He was, in this moment, on the receiving end of the smile of an enlightened man. The fellow before him was a man at peace, someone who acts and feels a sense of oneness with every other living being.

Beetle Blatt and Mantid stared raptly at the earth-screen. Blatt checked his console to consult previously recorded data, while Mantid looked on.

"The subject," Blatt said as he looked at his console, "This Hank earthling... his intelligence quotient has shifted significantly."

"Will distort all subject results?" Mantid asked.

"Zarkward! The entire program is compromised!" Blatt announced with shock. When a different thought occurred to him, he then smiled.

"We should report," said Mantid, as he stood to go.

Beetle Blatt grabbed him, however.

"Wait," he said as he keyed in some commands. "Pay attention," Blatt suggested. "I think I know what those two criminals are up to."

Blatt and Mantid sat back down to watch as Blatt queued up some video footage of the Federation Council President, who came on screen.

"On their current life trajectory, Earthlings do pose a threat to all other life forms in the universe. Immediate extermination, however, is not advised at this time," reported the Council President as he addressed the Federation assembly.

Beetle Blatt fast-forwarded through the footage. "You look for something?" Mantid asked.

"Wait," replied Blatt, not yet finding what he was looking for, "I think this will solve the puzzle." Blatt selected the segment he was looking for and then ran the recorded footage.

"The defining question," the Federation President continued, "and what the council requires proof of, is whether the Earthling life form has a natural capacity for evolution toward advanced awareness. If one member of the species possesses that attribute, revealing the potential lying latent in the entire breed, then they are, therefore, worth saving. Until then, the future of Earth, and Earthlings, is indeterminate."

Beetle Blatt stopped the recorded footage, quickly rewound it, and replayed a segment.

"If one member of the species possesses that attribute, revealing the potential lying latent in the entire breed, then they are, therefore, worth saving."

Looking as if he had just had a major epiphany, Blatt stopped the recording. Mantid waited for clarification.

"One person can save the entire human race?" he asked Blatt.

"Correct. One person who can show advanced awareness," Blatt answered, still working it out in his mind. "They used the

QMJ on the Hank subject to rescue the human race," Blatt finally declared.

"Why they do this?" Mantid then asked. "Why them two want to save human race?"

"To get my job," responded Blatt, as if coming to the punch line of the whole seedy conspiracy.

"But that is against Zycorp Regulations?!" Mantid squealed.

"Exactly," answered Blatt, his mind still working through the intricacies of the unfolding plot. "They are thinking 'outside the rectangular,' that's what they're doing. Exhibiting managerial lackey potential. I had never suspected them of such devious behavior. You?"

"No," answered Mantid. "They seemed to have very low intelligence."

"Which makes their plot all the more ingenious. But where are those 'assholes' now I wonder?" Blatt asked as he keyed in the identification number of the Starcar for the Intergalactic Global Positioning program to locate. The screen revealed the location of N and N2's Starcar: they were near Earth's moon, about to make a descent towards Earth.

"Look, they are going to Earth," Blatt exclaimed.

"Who go to planet Earth? It is armpit of galaxy." Mantid said and laughed.

"Don't you understand? They wish to save humanity," Beetle Blatt said.

"I do not understand," admitted Mantid. "Why they care about lower form mammals?" he asked.

"That's just it. They don't care about humans. They want to get promoted. They want my job!" Blatt snarled. Mantid stared at him, still quite confused.

THE CLOSER THEY GOT TO EARTH, THE MORE N AND N2 argued.

Uncharacteristically, N was acting with increasing anxiety.

"I don't give a zarkwad about humans. Truly. They stink... they're addicted to sex, food, drugs, and killing. They disgust me," N stated angrily.

"You'll probably get to like them, once you get to know them," N2 encouraged. "Why are you so angry, all of a sudden? Are you scared?"

"Of course I'm scared!" admitted N. "We're about to land on Earth, the scariest farqing planet in the known galaxy! We're about to get up close and personal with earthlings, for Hokum's jest! They eat beings like us down there. Any life form with a diota of intelligence would be terrified of them! That's why you're not scared," N practically screamed.

"Your negativity is killing my joyous excitement buzz," N2 chided quite gently.

He then quickly turned his head as something outside shot past them really fast. "Did you see that?" asked N2, excitedly. "That must have been a Rüppell's Griffon... earth's highest-flying bird. I've only seen them in stories my parents used to read to me at night."

"What parents?" asked N incredulously. "You came out of a test tube. You don't have parents."

"I do on the holo deck," N2 answered lightly.

"Whatever," derided N, who had his eyes fixed with dread on the beautiful blue planet ahead. "I'm thirsty," N then announced.

Rolling his eyes upwards, N2 ignored him still.

"Seriously, I'm just so thirsty. I don't see why you couldn't stop on a small asteroid or somewhere else. Let's change course for the Lyra constellation. Take a leak, get a drink," insisted N.

Trying to blot out N's negative anxiety, N2 sang, "I Know What Boys Like" under his breath.

"Aren't you thirsty?" N persisted, "Wouldn't you like a drink? I know I'm terribly thirsty."

"Disneyland, here we come!" N2 said excitedly.

"What? Oh, yeah, right. The happiest place on earth. Is that like a hippy-peace-freak earthling kinda mantra? To suck you in before they eat you?" N asked.

N2 snorted in derision and again rolled his eyes. "I guess I'll just have to show you. We'll hit LAX, then go to Anaheim," N2 said.

N stared at N2 and mentally tried to change his mind, but N2 didn't budge or react, nor did he say another word.

"Okay, then," agreed N, begrudgingly. "Fine. Super duper. But only if you'll do as I say, no argument, once we leave Anaheim. Once we leave the happiest place on earth, then I'm in charge."

"Yes, yes. Yes, of course," agreed N2, as he crossed his human fingers behind his back.

"You want to go on holiday? Now?" Mallow Dweeb shouted as Beetle Blatt sat before him.

"I'm entitled..." Beetle Blatt nervously answered. "According to Zycorp Regulation zzz.367, each employee is entitled to one intergalactic month off for every two glotts of perfectly completed assignment."

"I'm abreast of Zycorp Reg, Blatt," Dweeb barked.

"Here's my paperwork," Blatt said and handed Dweeb a digital file. Dweeb looked at it briefly, then tossed it on the desk where it bounced and fell to the floor.

"File a copy with Zycorp Regulation Department SP2,"

Dweeb relented. "Have a memorable vacation. Make lots of memories, and return restored to fulfill your term," he added.

"Thank you. Yes, sir," responded Blatt as he squatted down to pick up his digital paperwork.

He turned away quickly to hide his grin, as Beetle Blatt knew that the only reason Dweeb had permitted him to go on holiday was that very curious and as-yet unreported incident Blatt had observed between Dweeb and the Gabaien Worm twins.

"Zibbie going on holiday?" Mantid asked as he watched Blatt pack a bag.

"I can't believe I just got approval," Blatt said, the furry hairs on his legs all puffed up as a consequence of his dark joy.

"Uh-huh, Zibbie going on holiday?" Mantid repeated as he fidgeted and appeared abnormally concerned with Beetle Blatt's actions.

"No one gets approval. He must really like me, after all," Beetle Blatt said, not sounding as if he believed his own words. "I do still have a shot at promotion," he continued, mostly oblivious to Mantid. As Beetle Blatt turned, he accidentally knocked something off of N's desk. He reached under N's cubicle counter to retrieve whatever had fallen.

His eyes widened when he saw what appeared to be an actual Quantum Mind Jump. He touched it to find out. It was an actual QMJ. He leapt back, horrified.

"What you doing?" Mantid asked suspiciously, about to bend down to investigate. Nervously, Blatt quickly stood back up and tried to act nonchalant.

"Found it!" he said as he waved the errant fallen item, a tiny data device, which he had knocked off the desk. "You've never been on holiday, Mantid?" Blatt asked, hiding his nervousness and confusion.

Mantid pretended to reflect, which was utterly unnecessary as his type of being had instant total recall of all experiences and other information taken in. His pause was purely for the comfort of other beings.

"Nary a vaca? Life without a space trip?" Blatt continued, trying to sound cool, hip, and interested. Meanwhile, he carefully copied all of Hank's data into a portable data device.

"No. Never," Mantid replied, emulating sadness. "Where will Zibbie go?"

"On a journey... to entrap the traitorous usurpers intent upon destroying my career dreams and quality of life!" Blatt declared, as if he couldn't keep his secret to himself any longer.

"Oh," said Mantid, "I see," although his difficult-to-read insect-like expression made it seem that he did not understand Beetle Blatt's meaning at all.

Later that night, Beetle Blatt slipped out of his shared quarters. Looking furtively around the darkened, nearly empty, space station corridor, he made his way to the now deserted work area.

Fumbling along and dodging the curious night security celestial beings who looked a bit like intergalactic owls, space station cleaning staff beings, and other employees working the night shift, he finally made it to the work cubicle.

Double-checking that no one was actually around, he squatted down and grabbed the QMJ. Thrusting it quickly under his shirt, he hurried from the work station. Making his way to the docking bay, he arrived at a booth that said "Space Vehicle Rentals." A strange-looking alien greeted him at the booth. "What can I help you with?" it asked.

Beetle Blatt produced a plastic card, which the rental clerk swiped through his digital reader.

"I made a reservation," Beetle Blatt answered.

"Yes, Beetle Blatt," the clerk replied, reading off the details. "A vacation rental for two glickets?"

"Yes, please," answered Blatt.

"Will you be staying in this solar system?"

"No. I'll need hyper jump."

"That's four K ze-re extra, and we will charge by the click," said the clerk.

"Fine," answered Blatt. "And I will need a multi-phase shape-shifting device... to blend in with the local populous."

"Of course," replied the clerk. "They come standard in all our hyper-jumps."

"Oh," responded Blatt, surprised that he didn't need to explain himself.

"Take any of the jumpers lined up on the right," the clerk said with a smile. "Have a great vacation and make some terrific memories."

"Thank you. I will," answered Blatt as he left the booth.

Selecting a newer model, Starrv, Blatt put the weekend bag, with the QMJ inside, onto the passenger seat of the rental. He settled into the driver's seat and looked over the unfamiliar console. He didn't notice a light thump from outside the vehicle.

Blatt started the vehicle and slowly pulled out of the docking bay. Other space vehicles of various makes and sizes came and went, but, as it was curfew for most workers, traffic was light. Putt! Putt! As the Starrv slowly putt-putted out and away into space, Beetle Blatt heaved a sigh of relief. The space station slowly grew smaller and smaller in the rear windows of the Starrv.

Approaching the safe jump-space zone, Beetle Blatt lifted the Starrv joystick in excitement.

"Light speed, here we come," he said out loud. Punching in the coordinates into the console, shifting the joystick into jump mode, he reached over and pushed the warp-leap button. Nothing happened.

"What the zarkwad?!" he cursed and slammed an appendage against the joystick. Unfamiliar with the new-fangled controls, Blatt was confused by the array and complexity of the Starrv control panel.

Perhaps he pushed the wrong button, he considered. Blatt began pressing and pushing buttons and levers, hoping to get it right. Unable to figure it out, he looked out the window to see if he could locate the space rig. Alarmed that he was now adrift and out of range, all he could see around him was a vast and empty void.

"Computer!" he yelled. "Lightspeed!" Waiting for what seemed like an inordinate amount of time to receive some response, he panicked when nothing happened.

"Lightspeed, Zarkdamnit!" he shouted, hoping that, some-how, the Starrv's computer system would come to his aid and instruct the craft to find some get up and go. To his incredible frustration, it did not. Instead of traveling warp speed to its destination, the Starrv putt-putted slowly through space.

N AND N2 WATCHED WITH AWE AS PLANET EARTH CAME closer into their view. Whereas N2 had an expression of rapture on his face, N, looking quite nervous, was unaware that he was biting the lip of his human costume.

"How can a beautiful planet be home to such a warlike species?" N asked.

"Humans are passionate beings," N2 remarked.

"Yeah, passionate good, if you get on the right side of them and passionate bad if they don't like what you say or what you look like," N said, his thoughts beginning to race into a panic.

"What if they don't like us? We won't last a day! Where will we land? How will we survive? They'll cut us open and eat us like animals—" N added.

As N began to scream with fear, N2 grabbed hold of him and, looking straight into his eyes, shook him. "Pull yourself together. Humans don't eat humans anymore... pretty much," N2 shouted as N now whimpered.

"We're not humans! To them we're probably... exotic meat," N replied, truly terrified.

"Look... listen to me. I've studied the species in great detail. We land in America; we'll be safe there. Americans are not cannibals. They're civilized. All we have to do is act cool. We tell everyone we meet, 'Have a nice day,' and we'll totally blend," N2 said, increasingly uncomfortable with N's concerns.

"Americans are good people," N continued, perhaps thinking that if he said it enough times, he too would start to feel safer and more secure. "They only kill humans who are not American. We will blend in with the Americans, and then we'll be safe," N2 said.

"How will we blend?" N asked, feeling considerably calmer.

"It's all about wearing the right clothes," N2 said firmly.

"What are the right clothes?" N inquired.

"Blue denim jeans," N2 answered. "Everybody wears blue denim pants."

"That's it?" asked N, looking down. He was wearing blue denim jeans, as was N2; both of their human costumes were fully clothed in casual wear.

"See, I told you it was going to be easy!"

"Where is America, exactly?" N asked.

They both looked closely at the approaching Earth.

"Huh. Honestly, when I watched all their movies and entertainment, I thought it was all America. I had no idea there were so many land masses. Did you?" N2 said, skirting the issue and sounding uncertain again.

N glared at him. What was he doing, letting this nitwit sound off like an expert and act like he was in control, driving the Starcar towards certain doom?

"Thank the stars for autopilot, huh?" N2 said, and then, tapping the console, he said:

"Computer: destination Los Angeles."

***

MOONLIGHT SHONE SILVER UPON THE DESERTED ROAD adjoining Hank's beat-up trailer. Hank, in pajamas and house slippers, stepped outside into the crisp air and put an armload of beer cans into a recycling bin.

Standing for a moment to appreciate the beauty of his surroundings, he breathed in the fresh evening air, then returned to his trailer.

The inside of his mobile home was now pristine. Perhaps for the very first time in its long life, the inside of the trailer was squeaky clean, and there was a place for everything, and everything was in its place.

Hank entered his tidy bedroom. He turned on a lamp that sat on the bedside table. The lamp lit the tiny orderly room with a soft glow. Hank got into bed and chose a book from the pile of books arranged upon the bedside table.

After perusing the book stack, which included copies of the Talmud, the Bible, the Tao Te Ching, the Bhagavad Gita, the Zohar, and a few others, he chose the copy of Prince Siddhartha and began to read.

Hank fell asleep reading, the sacred text open upon his heart. The letters of the sacred text rose off the book and illuminated as if they were on fire, turning gold, and entered his heart chakra.

Hank dreamt curious dreams, filled with light and shadow, and which included extraordinary visitations of sacred beings from myth and ancient religious texts. Krishna, his eyes wide and wild above his rich, beautiful blue skin, beckoned Hank toward him, where he floated above the clouds, backlit by rays of brilliant golden light. As Hank approached with due reverence, Krishna whispered some sacred words into his ear.

Such dreams were now becoming increasingly common, and Hank appeared to grow in wisdom with each of these nightly encounters with remarkable individuals.

At dawn, Hank awoke and carefully closed the book, which was still lying across his chest. Easing himself out of bed, he fell to his knees and thanked the Creator for his life, the day, the sacred text, his job, his truck, and everything else for which he felt grateful in that moment.

He felt and expressed his gratitude so profoundly and for so long that tears welled up in his eyes.

Feeling thirsty, Hank stood looking into his refrigerator, hoping to find a suitable beverage. From the fresh produce and vegetables in his fridge, Hank selected a handful of beets, carrots, broccoli, and an apple. Giving them a quick wash beneath the kitchen sink, he proceeded to chop them into pieces small enough to fit into his sparkling new juicer.

Then, chanting sacred, ancient prayers, Hank made raw fresh vegetable juice.

Noticing the golden sunlight streaming through the screen door, Hank took his raw juice drink out to the steps of his trailer. Still looking a bit shaggy, due to his erratic shaving routine, he was nevertheless fitter and leaner than ever before, and, soaking up the sun's brilliant rays, he glowed with renewed health.

Noticing the run-down state of his yard, Hank used a scythe

to mow long grass, weeds, green brambles, bushes, and trailing vines and clear a large knoll outside of his trailer. Happy with his landscaping, Hank put away his tools and washed up inside the trailer. He then grabbed his keys and got into his truck.

Hank drove into town and parked on a little side street. He got out of his vehicle and purposefully strode toward a series of little shops and stores. Entering an old-style barber shop with a red and white striped barber pole by the door, Hank sat in a chair to wait for his turn.

With only one other customer, Hank didn't have to wait long before the elderly barber gave him a short back-and-sides and a close shave with a straight razor. Hank got out of the red leather barber chair and looked at himself in the mirror. Freshly shaven with a smart new haircut, Hank liked what he saw and gave the older man a generous tip.

Returning to his trailer, Hank made a simple salad and cooked some brown rice, then sat and slowly ate his light meal as he listened to classical music. He then wrote in his journal for about an hour, and after inserting a new DVD into his player, he attempted some yoga poses, trying to follow along with the instructor on his TV.

Sweaty from his workout, Hank took a long, hot shower, chanting unintelligible words and humming all the while. When Hank stepped from the shower, he was more radiant than ever. Looking into the mirror, he noticed that his eyes seemed brighter and more alert than the last time he checked, which was pretty much never.

He then dressed entirely in white: a white cotton t-shirt and white denim pants. Then Hank followed through on his urge to go outside and meditate on the newly trimmed grassy knoll under a large oak tree near his trailer.

Sitting beneath the great white oak, Hank seemed mesmerized by the vivid green leaves of the tree as sunlight sparkled through them, the golden-green hue striking against the azure blue sky.

His senses on full alert, Hank watched as a butterfly, with delicate iridescent yellow-green wings, sailed past. A few seeds, of unknown origin, floated down to the ground. Hank felt fully immersed in his surroundings and wholly engaged with the moment—a moment that seemed transcendental, magical, and yet paradoxically, frozen in time. Breathing slowly and deeply, his mind alert, yet in total relaxation, Hank felt as if the world he now inhabited was excitedly on the verge of and awaiting some event of earth-shattering import.

REPORTING FOR WORK AS USUAL, HANK ENTERED AN EMPTY room in the Los Alamos National Lab Project Room, pushing his customary mop and a bucket. Although dressed in the same worn, faded janitorial clothes which he always wore, he now radiated an entirely different demeanor. Still mainly invisible to other staff, he nevertheless exuded purity, manly strength, and true peace.

As he prepared his mop, Hank looked up at the half-finished theorem on the chalkboard. He stared at it for a long moment and then returned to his work as he pushed his mop back and forth. Although he diligently kept mopping the checkered vinyl floor, there was a part of him that was thinking very deeply about the theoretical problem.

When the room floor shone bright with cleanliness, he put the mop aside. He grabbed a piece of chalk and, in a focused mind of total concentration, he rapidly finished the theorem. Standing back to check his accuracy, he smiled, obviously quite happy with his work.

INSIDE THE LOS ANGELES INTERNATIONAL AIRPORT traffic control tower, multiple air traffic controllers were hard at work. Squeaks, static, and the dialog of various pilots and controllers created an atmosphere of no-nonsense professionalism among the overworked staff.

Harry Watkins, an air traffic controller just one week away from retirement, stared at something strange on the radar screen before him.

"What the heck?" he said quietly, uncharacteristically spooked by what he was seeing. "Unidentified aircraft, Los Angeles International tower, radar contact 12 miles southeast of Los Angeles Vortac, please identify," he spoke mechanically into the mouthpiece of his headset.

Although just a blip on his radar screen, had Harry Watkins actually seen that the craft he was trying to communicate with was actually a 1950s Pink Cadillac (with fins) making its descent into his airspace and controlled by two extra-terrestrial visitors from a star system not even known yet to science, he might have instead chose not to come into work that day.

Inside the Starcar, N and N2 were still looking around wildly, wondering where the human voice they had just heard was coming from.

"Unidentified aircraft, LAX tower, radar contact. Say altitude. Do you read? Identify yourself, please," the authoritative voice stated with greater irritation.

"I thought humans were idiots! How can they know we're here?!" N asked N2, beginning to panic.

"Chillax. We're on their Earth radar... he just wants to communicate. We speak human lingo and we'll be just fine," N2 said, a bit uncertainly, as he pressed some buttons so that he could transmit.

Inside the LAX tower, Harry Watkins waited for a response, giving his full attention to the movements on his radar screen. "Radar contact, unidentified craft. Please identify," he repeated, sounding sterner.

"Hey, dude... whassssuuuup? So, we're two homo sapiens sapiens coming back home with some takeout. It's all totally chill," said a voice that seemed weird to Harry. It was N2, obviously doing his best to be nonchalant and sound human.

Harry Watkins stared at his radar screen with surprise. It took him a moment to react. "Say again? Identify yourself," he said.

"Okay... so I'm totes obvi a normal, typical human: average height, build, beautiful lime green eyes. I enjoy music, movies, and the works of James Dean, Marilyn Monroe, and Elvis. I'm just a regular human guy," the peculiar voice, N2, said again.

Harry Watkins thought to himself that, yes, now he had heard it all.

"Dude, identify your craft and request flight following or state your intentions. Roger?" Harry said, his words rich with meaning.

"What is with this guy?" N2 turned to N. "I just told him everything about myself."

N slapped N2 on the upside of his head.

"He wants you to identify the craft, not you personally! He wants to know what we're flying, you idiot!" N said ferociously.

Inside the LAX traffic control tower, Harry watched their steady descent as he waited for a response. The strange voice cut the silence once again:

"My bad, duderooski, I was just joshing with you. The craft is a Mark Infinity, plutomium powered anti-gravity twin seater —" Harry looked puzzled as a loud smack sound then cut the voice off.

The Starcar lurched as N took control and stopped their

descent. He shoved his clone away and cut him off by depressing a button. N2 glared at him. "What are you doing?" he asked.

"Zarkwad! What are you doing?" N answered. "You can't tell him about our plutonium-powered anti-gravity craft! These idiots still fly combustible jet engines that are powered by decomposed once-living organisms that died millions of years ago, which they now burn as liquid fuel! He's probably calling the military aircraft of all the earth nations right now!" N screamed.

"Unidentified aircraft, please repeat, you got cut off," Harry's voice was heard.

N depressed a button to transmit.

"We're just making a joke with you, human being. We left our wallet with all our identification back at the space restaurant, so we need to go back..." N said. Then he added, "But thank you for your cool vibes. Have a good moon time," he said, then shut off all communication, keyed in new commands, and engaged stealth.

"Engaging stealth," N said to N2 pointedly.

Harry watched with disbelief as the craft disappeared from his radar screen. "What the—?" he gasped. "Space restaurant?" he then said out loud.

Inside the Starcar, N punched buttons and established a new trajectory for their craft. N2 reacted with shock and disappointment.

"We're not going to Anaheim?" he asked like a disappointed child.

"If they don't know who we are, they'll assume we're hostile. Better to keep away from cities... and humans, in general, totes obvi," N responded irately.

COFFEE IN HAND, DEBATING QUIETLY, DRS. BLAKE AND Delaware entered the Los Alamos National Laboratories project room. As they turned to the chalkboard, they both froze, staring in shock.

"What's this?" Dr. Blake asked. "Someone messed with our theorem."

"Someone... finished our theorem," Dr. Delaware corrected. As they studied the now-proven theorem, line by line, their initial shock gave way to expressions of disbelief.

"This is... extraordinary," Dr. Blake said.

"This can't be correct," Dr. Delaware said, though it was obvious from his voice that the answer to the theorem was, to his great shock, definitely correct.

"Who would do this?" Dr. Blake inquired.

"Do you see what I see?" Dr. Delaware asked.

"Uh-yeah. Somebody just proved the existence of Extra Terrestrials," Dr. Blake said.

"There must be some mistake," Dr. Delaware said again, in a different tone, and it continued to be evident that he meant the exact opposite.

"It's flawless," Dr. Blake said, moving around to view the completed theorem from different angles, with the reverence and appreciation of a man examining an extremely valuable, rare, perfect, and precious jewel.

"Yes, but the implications," Dr. Delaware said reluctantly. He shook his head dazedly.

"Mathematics doesn't lie," Dr. Blake replied. "Are we artists who dream about possibilities, or are we scientists who stand by what the facts reveal?"

"Yes, but this is... earth-shattering," Dr. Delaware said. Dr. Blake said nothing for a long moment. Then he spoke.

"Forget earth-shattering, this is consciousness-shattering," Dr. Blake said.

"Perhaps Drake's equation was correct, after all. There is intelligent life in the universe," Dr. Delaware replied as Dr. Blake laughed nervously.

"I would never have believed it. I mean, I always thought what a load of baloney, you know?" Dr. Blake said, truly experiencing a sense of shock and wonder. He began to weep quietly.

"No wonder we couldn't prove the theorem. Talk about thinking outside the box..." Dr. Delaware said.

"I have to sit down for a moment," Dr. Blake replied. They both took a seat and, for the longest time, stared at the incontrovertible truth revealed by the solved mathematical theorem, which proved beyond any doubt that yes, there is intelligent life on other planets, and extraterrestrials do indeed exist.

A DARK, NEAR-BLACK NIGHT SKY FILLED WITH GLITTERING, silver-white stars floated over a majestic desert landscape. Dramatic and striking, a sky and landscape in dark purple, blues, and sand tones, the scene could have been a picture postcard released by the New Mexico tourist board.

Whoosh! A shimmer distorted the blue-black night sky, as something impossible to see flew past the silhouette of a mesa as if to land on the desert floor.

The Starcar, still in the form of a Cadillac, flew close to Earth. It then stuttered and sputtered, coming to a complete stop and falling to the earth with a thud.

A door swung open, and N2 nervously poked his head out in order to breathe in the night air.

"Is it safe?" said N, still securely hidden in the car, his voice quite obviously querulous with fear.

"It's safe and it's beautiful," N2 said. He deeply breathed in the safe air, apparently his earthling costume had a breathing apparatus, and admired his beautiful surroundings: the desert, the flora, and the star-filled desert night sky.

"No humans?" N asked, somewhat more calmly, yet still hiding out inside the vehicle.

"No humans," N2 admitted, sounding disappointed. N2 looked at the desert floor and slowly began to step down out of the craft.

"This may be one small step for an extraterrestrial wearing a man suit, but it is one giant leap for intergalactic beings," N2 said dramatically and, trying to jump and land, fell face first to the ground. N stuck his head out and looked down at N2.

"What happened? Are you okay?" N questioned.

If N2 was hurt, he didn't show it. Clearly awestruck, he slowly got to his feet.

"Gravity, man. It's the bomb," he said. "Come on out here, N! Earth's gravity is like nothing you've ever felt before. It's probably sexy, I mean, uh, sensual... except I have no idea what that actually feels like," N2 said breathlessly, wobbling to correct his balance.

"Dude, this is wild," N2 added as N stared at him.

N2 reached down and picked up some earth. He smelled it and moaned with pleasure, and his eyes rolled back in his head a bit.

"N, man, smell this. It's so... earthy," N2 said and thrust the dirt in N's direction. N looked down at the dusty, reddish desert earth and sand that hit his upper body.

"As soon as you're ready, we should head back," N said, brushing off the dirt from his chest. "Earthlings may be primitive, but we know now that they do have basic radar," his voice trailed off.

N2 stared at N, who was still cowering inside their vehicle.

"Head back? Are you fobbing me? We just farqing got here," N2 said and laughed.

"Take some earth, pick up some souvenir stones, gather whatever memories you can... we're not staying," N said firmly.

"We're not going anywhere," N2 answered, even more firmly. "The atomic power stabilizers are shot."

"The... what?" asked N, panicked.

"You, in case you hadn't noticed, flubbed the landing. That wasn't abnormal. Maybe you were too busy to notice the dashboard's 'check rod stabilizers' light was flashing. Probably still is."

N quickly turned to check the dashboard. Sure enough, the dashboard's 'check rod stabilizers' light was flashing red.

"What are we going to do?" asked N, not really expecting a satisfactory answer. "We can't get stuck here. We can't!" When he got no response, he stepped out of the vehicle and looked around wildly.

He groaned loudly when he saw N2 rolling on the ground, moaning with pleasure, enjoying his first experience of gravity and the earthiness of planet Earth.

As Beetle Blatt's Starrv putt-putted laboriously through space, Blatt alternately consulted a holographic manual and pressed various controls in the desperate hope that he could finally get the jumper to work.

"Engage the FOB booster? While positioning the TFX override to compress the rear axial modem navigational module," Beetle Blatt read the manual slowly aloud, hoping to make sense of it. He then pressed a different set of levers and controls. Nothing happened. Blatt's egghead wobbled a bit in frustration.

"What the zarkwad?!" he exclaimed with rage.

"Press the red button while holding down the yellow switch," said a soft, distant voice.

Blatt shrieked and looked around the Starrv wildly: was he now hearing voices? Quickly locating his weapon, Blatt turned to check out the rear of the vehicle.

"Is someone there?" he asked, hoping not to sound as fearful as he was feeling. Mantid uncurled himself from his position on the ceiling and dropped down beside Beetle Blatt, scaring the zarkward out of him.

"What the... Where did you—" Beetle Blatt stuttered, trying and failing to formulate a coherent question.

"I sneak onboard," Mantid said calmly.

"Obviously! But why would you—" Blatt screeched, nearly out of his mind with shock.

"I love you, Beetle Blatt," Mantid said, to further clarify the situation.

Beetle Blatt stared at the insect-like being, his expression one of astonishment.

"You what?" Beetle Blatt finally managed to squeak out.

"Not in a feeling way," Mantid clarified and then sighed dreamily.

"As you know, my kind doesn't experience emotions, per se. It's a mental love. Purely mental. I'm in love with your mind," he continued, perfectly mimicking a love-struck being.

"That is... freakishly disturbing," Blatt finally managed to squeak out. Realizing that he was still holding his weapon, he hurriedly put it away.

"There is a human phrase that you may benefit from meditating upon, my Zibbie," Mantid said softly.

"Is that so?" Beetle Blatt huffed. "Well, what is it?"

"It is... what it is," Mantid quoted calmly.

Beetle Blatt snorted and, swinging one of his minor appendages, threw the data/holographic instruction manual through the air toward Mantid. Just get us out of here," Blatt demanded.

Mantid casually caught the data device with his two spindly upper legs and gave what looked like a grimace (but what was actually its attempt at a smile) to Beetle Blatt. Sliding past Beetle Blatt, Mantid settled himself into the command chair and glanced at the data/holographic instruction manual.

Chattering aloud, it made strange chirping and clicking noises as it expertly pressed buttons and dials on the vehicle console. Beetle Blatt's mood greatly improved as the Starrv vibrated rapidly and roared in response.

"Prepare for hyperspace, my Zibbie one," Mantid then said.

Beetle Blatt sighed and grumbled, as if to show his displeasure with Mantid; yet, secretly, his oversized membranous egg head trembled with relief, and he did an internal happy dance. Mother of Reptilia, it was about farqing time. He sighed.

As soon as Blatt strapped himself into the passenger seat, Mantid pressed a rising glowing button and, with a surge, the craft accelerated into hyperspace.

N AND N2 EXPLORED THE DESERTED DESERT LANDSCAPE BY car. Faintly lit by the full moon, in the brightening night sky, the landscape and the movements of the two extraterrestrials upon it were reminiscent of the Earth astronauts' moonwalk. The two creatures, in their human disguises, lifted and dropped heavy rocks, threw pebbles and stones into the air to watch them fall, and hopped about with intense curiosity and glee.

"Earth gravity is wild, dude," N2 said, really relaxing into their adventure. He held up his palms, which were quite dirty, "Look, the earth gets on the hands."

"I know. It doesn't stay on Earth. This stuff gets everywhere!"

N agreed and, as he turned his head, he suddenly froze in horror and stared.

N2 followed his gaze: a pair of approaching headlights, bright white against the increasing darkness of night, lit up the desert terrain.

"Let's get out of here," N hissed.

"Don't be such a scaredy cat. It's just an Earth vehicle," N2 said and laughed.

"Oh, zarkwad, they know we're here," N gasped out, beginning to panic.

"Nah. There would be more than one. Probably a line of them. Plus air vehicles. Correct?" N2 said and scratched his head.

N knew that his clone was correct. Yet his panic didn't lift. They both stared fixedly as a four-wheel-drive SUV approached, its headlights sending two beams of bright light upon the otherwise darkened dirt road.

N looked around with urgency and became even more fearful when he realized that there was nothing in the stark terrain behind which to hide.

"Just relax and act human," N2 ordered N. As the vehicle pulled up beside them, the sudden stop of the car's tires threw dust particles into the air.

"Zarkwad, we didn't even bring any weapons with us, what was I thinking?" N chided himself as he shifted his body so that he was shielded behind N2.

As the car door swung open, N instinctively clung to his clone.

"You boys having car trouble?" a husky female voice asked, as a pair of cowboy boots swung out and landed on the dirt beneath the open car door.

Too scared to respond, the two aliens stood motionless.

They watched as a pair of cowboy-boot-clad feet walked closer and soon became illuminated by the car's headlights.

Marcy Beuchamps, a beautiful brunette in her thirties, placed her hands on her hips and smiled.

"That's a really nice ride you boys got there," she said, obviously impressed and immediately smitten by the beautiful pink caddy, which appeared to be in perfect condition.

"Is this from the sixties?" she asked, admiring the fins.

N released his tight grip from his clone, and the two aliens looked goofily to each other, each wondering exactly where the sixties might be located.

"Uh, yeah, uhm... no. We're not from here," N2 blurted out.

"You and me, both, partner," Marcy acknowledged.

"That's not from around these parts, either. What a classic beauty. What's wrong with her?" she asked, nodding at their vehicle when N and N2 looked confused.

"I think the atomic power rod stabilizers are depleted... due to Earth's gravity and unexpectedly high atmospheric barometric pressure," N2 said and sighed heavily.

Marcy had zoned out during N2's car talk. She shrugged.

"Huh. I don't know anything about cars. You two need a ride into town?" she asked, her tone friendly.

"No," N said hurriedly.

"Yes, we do need a ride into town," N2 said and elbowed N in the gut.

Marcy looked from one to the other. N2 grinned hugely. N pinched N2 and rubbed his belly.

"Yes? No? Do you two need a ride or not?" Marcy asked, seeking clarification.

"Yes. We would like that very much, thank you. He's just a..." N2 said, his voice trailing off, unable to find the right human words.

"I know, I know," Marcy said and laughed loudly.

"Typical male, doesn't want any help. But it's all good. It's not far, and I'm happy to build up some good karma by giving you a lift. Let's go," she said as she got back into her car and cranked it up.

Jumping onto the bench front seat right next to Marcy, N2 didn't give N a chance to argue or resist. Reluctantly, N opened the front passenger door and shoved N2 over, trying to force his way in beside him. It was a tight squeeze, all three of them in front.

"Yeah," Marcy said, grinning broadly at N, "You might be more comfy in back."

Embarrassed, N flushed bright red. N2 grinned as N got out of the front seat, slammed the door shut, and opened the back door. He then got into the back of the car. As soon as he closed the door, Marcy pulled the SUV back onto the road in a cloud of dust.

"Will your car be... okay there?" Marcy asked N2.

"Oh, yes—positively it will. It has a..." he paused for a moment to think, then spoke again, "It has a special security device inside."

"Good," said Marcy, "Better safe than sorry."

With Marcy's attention focused on the road ahead of them, N took a small device from his pocket, dialed in some commands, and pointed it over his shoulder at the parked Starcar.

The vehicle shimmered under a force field and disappeared from view.

"My name is Marcy, by the way," Marcy stated.

"Thank you very much, Marcy. By The Way," N2 said, distracted by and checking out, with fascination, the dashboard and interior of the car. N was gazing out at the landscape, entirely mesmerized by the desert terrain of this part of planet Earth.

Marcy laughed for a moment as the guys exchanged a look, not getting the joke. "What are you guys called?" Marcy asked.

"Uh, you guys used to call us Martians, but not anymore..." N2 said distractedly.

"Oh, really?" Marcy replied, gave N2 an odd look, and then glanced at N in the rearview mirror. N was looking out the back window.

Turning his vision away from the surrounding countryside, N suddenly realized what his clone had said and punched the back of the front passenger seat.

"You wish to know our names, yes? Because N2 likes to make the funny, much of the time," N said and forced a laugh. Har. Har. Har.

"Yes," N2 admitted, embarrassed, finally realizing what he had just said to Marcy.

"That I do... like to make the funny. But our names, yeah, my name, my first name is Elvis, and the dude in the back is named Marilyn."

"Marilyn? Really? More like Marilyn Manson than Marilyn Monroe, right?" Marcy said, trying to find N in her rearview mirror.

"No. Marilyn Monroe is a totally cool name, maybe the coolest," N2 said sternly and frowned at Marcy as if, due to her response, her loyalty to her country were now in question.

"You guys are weird," Marcy said, laughing happily. "I love it."

In the back seat, N's eyes were opened wide with rising fear, the more they drove away from the Starcar. N2, however, was increasingly intrigued by Marcy's personality. He turned to N in the back.

"Do you think Marcy's a sex addict?" he whispered, fully thinking that Marcy couldn't hear him.

N groaned and punched the back of the passenger seat again. Marcy giggled until she snorted.

"You think I can't hear you, Elvis?" she asked a blushing N2, "And the answer is no, I'm not." N2 sank into his seat, embarrassed.

"I do like it, though," Marcy said for effect. N2 grinned.

"Sorry, I didn't realize you had such great hearing, Marcy. I mean no insult... but from my studies, reduced ability to hear seems to be quite common among certain older humans... not that you are old. You appear to be in excellent condition, but you know what I mean," N said.

As he spoke, Marcy laughed harder, as if these guys were really and truly hilarious.

"I know what you mean, buddy," she said and laughed even harder, then added, "You guys really crack me up."

"For instance, certain older humans can't hear some tones at certain Hertz levels. But thank you for your answer to my question. Knowing that you do like "it" is totally groovy, Marcy baby," N2 said.

"You are a riot. You know that?" Marcy said, then laughed and punched N2 on the shoulder, lightly. In the rear, N groaned and sank low into the back seat. Marcy thought they were a pair of idiots. She couldn't stop laughing at them. These were definitely not the kind of memories he had intended to be making.

INSIDE THE STARRV—WHICH, THANKS TO MANTID'S piloting, was now making some serious progress hurtling through space—Beetle Blatt inspected the QMJ.

"How may I assist you once we reach planet Earth, Beetle Blatt?" Mantid inquired, looking fondly over at his beloved.

"Do you know how this machine works?" Beetle Blatt asked, ignoring the insect-like being's query and his amorous glance.

"This generation not for human. It is, in effect, dangerous for them," Mantid stated firmly as he scanned the GMJ with his personal computing device.

"There's a prototype for humans?" Beetle Blatt said, and turned to stare at Mantid.

"Oh, yes. Very covert research," Mantid replied casually. He gave Beetle Blatt a sly little look.

"Why is it secret?" Beetle Blatt asked.

"Your innocence is one thing Mantid very much likes about you, Zibbie. You think powerful beings have good intentions, money-making intentions, work, use and enslave others, not kill, a place for all," the statement stated.

"That's not true. Is it?" Beetle Blatt inquired querulously.

"I love you, Beetle Blatt," Mantid cooed softly.

THE SUV BARRELED DOWN A NEW MEXICO ROAD. DAWN was breaking in the desert sky.

The blues, purples, and dark tones of the desert morphed into lavender, mauve, peachy, and beige hues. Marcy had Country music playing. N2 grooved to the song while happily gazing out his window at this strange, new, beautiful world. N, however, felt that the strange human music was assaulting his ears.

"You like this music?" Marcy asked N2 as she noticed his body swaying.

"I like all human music," N2 said, swooning.

"Human music?" Marcy asked. "What's—"

"He means all music which describes the human condition," N corrected, interrupting her.

"Well, that sure sums up country music," Marcy replied. "Country music is music of the human condition, that's for darn sure," she added.

"Why are you driving alone in the deserted badlands of this landmass?" N asked her.

"You guys sure have a way with words. Are you European?" she responded with a question, casting a sideways glance at N2. Then she and N locked eyes via the rearview mirror.

"English is not our first language," N admitted. Marcy nodded.

"I got that," Marcy nodded. "I'm a journalist, to answer your question. I'm following a story."

"I love human stories," N2 said wistfully.

"Meaning... stories that define the human condition," N clarified and glared at N2. Marcy laughed and nodded.

"Yeah, me too," agreed Marcy.

"Who doesn't?" N2 said, barely able to mask his complete disinterest in human stories. Marcy didn't seem to notice his falseness.

"Yeah, but this isn't that kind of story. I know I might not look it, but I'm a math geek. I write for a magazine called *Abacus*. Don't reckon you've ever heard of it," said Marcy.

"An abacus. Primitive calculating tool used by early humans before the advent of digital calculators," N said, automatically providing the standard definition.

"An abacus may be ancient, but I bet you couldn't use one, hot shot," Marcy shot back, as if he had somehow insulted the inanimate object use for simple calculations.

"Only because our mathematical methods are eons more advanced than counting with sticks and beads," N retorted sharply.

"High-fangled methods up in Finland or wherever you oddballs are from?" Marcy said just the teensiest bit snarkily.

Then she giggled, not really all that riled by N's reactive response.

"Aw, shaddup, Marilyn... Tell us about the story, Marcy," N2 interjected.

"I don't know how true it is, which is why I'm going to check it out, but if it is accurate, it's the biggest bombshell to drop since... oh, since Roswell, I guess. Which is just up the road, incidentally," Marcy said and laughed again.

"The story is about Roswell?" N2 asked, delighted.

"Kind of," she said, distracted by driving, then added. "Uh, no. Not really. It's about this guy—a janitor—with a background in applied physics, to be precise, and a PhD, I should add. Out of the blue, this guy has purportedly scientifically proved the existence of advanced extraterrestrial life."

"What?" N screeched and began to hyperventilate slightly.

"I know, right? Mind-blowing. He has purportedly mathematically proven the existence of aliens," Marcy replied.

"And they say math is boring," N2 said, and he and Marcy laughed uproariously.

Beetle Blatt was now in the Starrv driver's seat with his pedal to the metal. Mantid sat in the copilot seat and stargazed.

"So Zycorp has the technology to help increase the consciousness of earthlings and other beings... but they don't?" Beetle Blatt asked.

"They make most of their wealth from experimenting on earthlings," Mantid replied.

"Yes, drug trials, behavior manipulation studies, DNA and organ harvesting, mind control experiments, viral weaponry..."

Beetle Blatt acknowledged and ran through the list. His over-sized membranous egg head trembled.

"The civilized galaxies benefit from the research, so it's in everybody's interest to consider humans as... inferior, really property, my Zibbie, given that so many of them were genetically engineered experiments to begin with," Mantid added.

Beetle Blatt nodded speculatively, trying to wrap his mind around it.

"So, if they became more intelligent... all that business goes away. No more Zycorp..." Beetle Blatt thought aloud, "So, quite simply, Zycorp doesn't want earthlings to grow in consciousness?"

"It is not well known, Zibbie, but in fact, Zycorp has many technologies, devices, and implants designed to force the devolution of humans," Mantid said carefully, in a very, very quiet voice. Beetle Blatt stared at his insect-like coworker.

"So whoever could prevent subjects, like this Hank earthling, from evolving would very likely be greatly rewarded by the Zycorp corporation," Beetle Blatt said, after he had mulled it over, and then stretched with satisfaction.

"Zycorp would be much in debt... to whomever—" Mantid stated.

"We have to find the original subject, " Beetle Blatt said in an evil tone and gave Mantid a malevolent grin, and his membranous mouth and nose area quivered. The sensuousness of Blatt's pose and tone, which was very attractive and almost gratifying to his traveling companion, caused Mantid to shudder with pleasure.

UNDER A NIGHT SKY FULL OF SPARKLING WHITE-HOT STARS, in the Los Alamos National Lab parking lot, Hank parked in his usual parking space. Three junior lab techs passed by as he got out of his truck. Recognizing Hank, they stopped.

Joking around, they made crazy signs behind his back as all three of them laughed. Hank looked up at them with total acceptance and equanimity.

"Hey, Mr. Janitor, what planet are you from exactly?" one of the techs jeered. They all snorted with laugher as Hank, undeterred, selected what he needed from the bed of his pickup. Irritated that they hadn't provoked a reaction, they tried again.

"E.T., call home," mocked another technician. "Don't forget, Mars needs your mom," he added, still hoping to get a rise from Hank, who seemed totally at peace and unaffected by their mocking.

"Why is this asshole still smiling?" one of the techs asked another, finally getting seriously irate.

"Hey, my favorite Martian, do you still think Earth Girls are easy?" he shouted after Hank. The newly blissed-out janitor, beatific in his enlightened state, smiled and breezed into the building. The lab techs exchanged looks of bewilderment and confusion and, with embarrassment, dispersed to their vehicles.

THE SUV NAVIGATED A SERIES OF WINDING BACK ROADS, some of which were dirt and some paved.

Finally getting on the highway, Marcy looked relieved when she spotted the exit ramp for Main Street. N and N2 exchanged a look as the SUV zoomed past a "Welcome to Roswell, NM" sign, which featured the tagline, "Dairy capital of the Southwest." N look at N2. N2 shrugged.

Marcy took the exit. A few minutes later, staying on Main Street, Marcy slowed the vehicle and parked at a gas station in downtown Roswell.

"Hope you guys can get your car fixed okay," she said, turning to them to indicate the end of the line.

"I'm sure the mechanics here can still fix a 1950's caddy," she added.

"They have sub-atomic isotopes at this facility?" N2 asked, checking out the primitive state of the gas station.

"You'd be surprised," Marcy replied. "Just because we're out of the city doesn't mean they don't know their stuff. Everything's gone all high-tech nowadays."

N2 smiled and shrugged. It would be amazing if they could fix their ride.

N and N2 reluctantly got out of the cozy and safe comfort of Marcy's SUV.

"Bye, Marilyn. Take it easy, Elvis. Enjoy the rest of your vacation," Marcy said and waved. Unsure of a correct and appropriate response, N and N2 merely looked at her forlornly. They waved, and Marcy waved again in response.

"Take it easy, boys," she waved and, rolling up her window, drove off.

N and N2 stood on the deserted main street in Roswell, looking hopelessly lost, not quite knowing what to do next. The night was headed toward dawn, and the sky was a light blue-gray and brightening by the moment. It would be daylight soon. The firmament became solferino, a purplish-red color, as the sun rose over the distant mountains.

Still looking up, N turned his head and reacted with shock. The street lamp beside them had a giant alien head at its apex. The light emanating from it was not very strong; it merely cast an eerie, faint green glow on Main Street. They stared at it with a mix of curiosity and horror.

"Why would they...?" N2 began to ask a question he didn't quite know how to finish.

"Don't ask," N responded.

"You think that's a real head or a..?" N2 asked.

"I don't think it's real," answered N slowly, then added, "But... he sure does resemble someone I used to go to Junior Starlight Academy with."

"Let's find somewhere to hide," N2 suggested.

"What's wrong? I thought that you loved these earth beings?" N asked.

"I do but that alien head is totally freaking me out."

"We do need to find accommodations," N said as he led N2 towards downtown.

The more they walked and took in their surroundings, the more precise a picture of the Roswell community began to emerge. It seemed like all of their questions were answered as soon as they thought of them. Passing a sign that said, "Your Favorite Alien Zone," they stopped outside a building with a sign that said, "Holy American International UFO Museum and Research Center."

Across the street was a UFO-themed Micky D's complete with models of alien beings and flying saucers. N2 laughed out loud. N poked him angrily.

"Okay, now I get it," N2 said with relief.

"What?" asked N, irritated that N2 wasn't letting him in on the joke.

"This town is totally alien-friendly," N2 answered.

"You think?" N asked doubtfully.

"Yeah, look around. All the aliens look friendly, none of them are killing earthlings, and they don't even have weapons," N2 said, looking more and more relaxed. N looked around. It was true. The ETs on the signs and pictures, or in displays, however bizarre, almost looked ridiculously friendly.

"You're right," N agreed, loosening up, "If I were an alien from a foreign planet, I would say that whoever these people are, they definitely love aliens here!"

N2 pointed at a store window display. A busty human female mannequin wore a T-shirt that read:

"I love my alien boyfriend."

The T-shirt featured a giant red heart, and each of the dark, slanted ET eyes of the male "alien" graphic was positioned directly over the female mannequin's breasts.

"Did you hear me?" N asked, "If I were an alien—"

"We are aliens from another planet," N2 interrupted and corrected.

"Yeah, of course, but you know what I mean," N said with exasperation.

"At least we won't stick out here," N2 said happily, "If they knew who we really are, they could totally treat us like gods." He sighed and closed his eyes, lost in a fantasy. N punched him lightly.

"Don't get carried away, Elvis. We should stick to your original plan and find a place to hide." N said. "We can think things over and—"

"There," N2 said, pointing to a sign with an image of an alien that somewhat resembled an angelic cowboy extraterrestrial, wearing boots and spurs, with a crashed spaceship behind it. The sign read, "Alien Motel 11:11."

The words "Aliens welcome!" flashed in neon lights.

"Aliens welcome!" N2 practically roared, "They welcome aliens, can you believe it?"

"Yeah, yeah," N chided, hoping to tone down N2's hyper enthusiasm.

"Let's not get carried away. They are humans, after all. If I've learned one thing watching them for so long, it's that their behavior is totally unpredictable. One minute you're a god and the next thing you know... you're someone's dinner. First thing we need is local currency," N said, making a plan in his head.

"They have machines that dispense local currency," N2 said

and pointed to a bank. As they approached, N and N2 checked out the modern ATM.

"Is this too primitive to hack?" N2 asked. N laughed then said nothing, and for the first time since they had arrived on Earth, the being seemed more relaxed and in control.

N put a slithering mechanorganic prong in the ATM. When it stuck, he wriggled it and forced it more deeply into the ATM. A bit resistant, the prong squeaked, then it went in all the way.

"Nothing's happening," N2 said after a few seconds.

Before N could say, "Wait," the ATM spat out money like a winning Vegas slot machine. N smiled happily and pulled a tiny mesh wallet-like bag from his backpack.

"Earth currency! Well done," N2 loudly exclaimed as N filled the tiny mesh wallet-like bag with cash as quickly as he could. The mesh bag remained flat and appeared empty, no matter how much cash he put into it.

"Now, we can get lodging," N said, looking very pleased with himself.

"I know just the place," N2 said as he stared at the alien motel across the street.

"Well, it does say, 'Aliens welcome, '" N said as he followed N2's gaze. N and N2 crossed the street to the Alien Motel at 11:11. They stared at the large sign outside, which featured a green, pearly, iridescent, slender extraterrestrial with big, dark eyes, resembling a combination of an alien and an angel. The alien angel's crashed spaceship was behind him.

"Let me do the talking," N2 said as they entered the rental office, "I know how to speak cowboy."

Dave Kukowski, the young clerk on duty, sat behind the desk looking bored, leafing through an alien-themed comic book. He had greasy, stringy brown hair and was chewing and popping his gum. Looking up from his reading, he watched the two newcomers who, very nervously, approached the desk.

"Howdy, my cowboy friend, dude. Is it true you welcome aliens here?" N2 inquired.

Switching immediately into his "please the customer" persona, Dave gave both guys the Mork salute from the old TV show "Mork & Mindy."

"Nanu, Nanu," Dave said and grinned.

"Way cool. You speak Ork!?" N asked, impressed.

"I only know the greeting," Dave replied, "I haven't seen that show in ages."

"Feeling mighty neighborly and very much at home here, in this excellent Alien-friendly earth establishment," N2 said with forced friendliness as he looked around the ET-themed office, "We will rent one of your fine offerings."

"I'm so sorry, but I'm not sure that I have a place available. This is our busy season," Dave said, not looking at all apologetic.

"I don't understand why you would not be sure?" N chimed in, his voice revealing his increasing irritation, "The number of places you have to offer is finite, yes? They are either occupied or vacant, correct?"

Both Dave and N2 gave N a surly look.

"Yeah, but human nature being what it is... people make reservations and, well, they may or may not show up. Others don't leave on time, even when you tell them a million times exactly when check-out is, which is at 11 AM, and check-in is at noon. I'll know how I stand a half hour after that," Dave said with irritation, then he indicated the wall clock, which read 8:30.

"What should we do?" N2 asked, more than a little plaintively.

"Well, ya'll will have to come back later. Plenty of places in town where you can kill a few hours," Dave added, and forced a smile. He sat down again and picked up his comic book, making it clear that the two of them had been dismissed.

"We have much currency," N said and spilled wads of American cash onto the counter. Dave smirked and, without even looking at the cash, pulled out a couple of Alien drink vouchers, some Your Favorite Alien Fun Zone passes, and a bunch of coupons for other local establishments.

"Nifty. I'm really happy for you... Yet, you must still wait, like all the rest of us. You guys hang out at the fun zone, then get a couple of drinks at the watering hole next door, because I've got nothing for you. Now, how's that sound?" He said with irritation as he threw the passes, coupons, and vouchers on top of their cash.

"You have a watering hole?" N2 asked, suddenly chipper.

"Right next door," Dave answered, pointing to his left and not looking up from his comic.

"Thank you, pardner. We'll mosey along and be back at the designated hour," N said, then snatched up all the cash and the coupons and hustled his clone out of the rental office. Once outside, the guys looked around. Not much was going on. It was way too early.

The guys trudged around historic downtown Roswell, avoiding eye contact with people, and gave each of the few humans they passed a very wide berth.

Unaccustomed to the scorching desert heat, they soon began to wilt seriously. Looking thinner than when they landed, sweat was pouring off of them.

"Where is all this liquid coming from?" N2 asked as he wiped his brow and examined his secretions, first smelling, then licking his flesh.

"I think it's some kind of natural lubricant," N surmised, inspecting his perspiration.

"Lubricant for what?" N2 asked.

"I think you know what," N responded and rolled his eyes.

"For having sex?" N2 asked incredulously, sounding terribly excited by the idea.

"No, not for having sex, although that would make sense, I guess. I was thinking contact sports," N said and mimed making a pass with a pretend football.

"Oh," N2 said, not entirely convinced, "Perhaps sports humans will see our condition and invite us to play."

"Yes," N agreed, "I'm sure that's how it works."

"Then again, dude," N2 added after a moment's thought, "Maybe some females of the species will wish to make the sex with us." N shuddered as he contemplated that horrifying thought.

"That sounds disgusting," N replied and almost threw up. The two aliens, disguised as humans, trudged along, sweating profusely.

"My body feels like it has a hole in it around the center. I didn't notice that sensation earlier," N2 remarked as they trudged up Main Street toward the Fun Zone. N nodded thoughtfully. After a long moment, he had a realization.

"I think that's an indication that the body requires fuel," N surmised, "We should eat and refuel."

"You mean eat human food?" N2 asked innocently.

"What other kind of food is there on this planet, you dwork-fobber? You see any real aliens eating real alien food in any real alien restaurants?" N asked grumpily. N2 ignored N and looked around desperately.

"Oh, look, there's a human restaurant that says they serve alien food!" N2 pointed.

N turned and then whacked N2.

"Get your eyes fixed, dummy. The sign says 'Hunan'... not 'human,' and it doesn't say 'alien food,' it says 'Asian food.' Apparently, they eat Asian humans in this cowboy desert alien-friendly town. I told you that we need to be careful. We'll eat later," N said, walking on.

Head dropping, N2 appeared truly disappointed. His trip to Earth, in general, and Roswell in particular, was turning out to be very disappointing.

"Not much going on in Roswell, is there?" N2 complained as N gave him a little shove to quicken his pace.

"Come on. Maybe the Your Favorite Alien Fun Zone will be... fun," N said.

"Maybe they'll have a holo deck or sub-optimal, laser-based 5D simulated war games," N2 said, perking up, "I would love to try and beat my current score."

As the two extraterrestrials reached their destination and stood beneath the "Intergalactic Fun Zone" sign, their jaws dropped with disappointment. They discovered that instead of a Fun Zone, as advertised, what stood in its place was a tacky gift shop called "Alien Landing Zone."

Wandering in, N2 looked terribly disappointed to see an extensive collection of plastic extraterrestrial and monster knick-knacks, cheap off-brand candy, and other junk. Sensing his clone's disappointment and feeling somewhat responsible, N got excited when he noticed a door against the side way with a sign over it that read, "Your Personal Area 51."

Grabbing his buddy, he raced toward the doorway and pulled out some cash. He tossed the money to the clerk as they both ran past. The store clerk rang up two adult admissions and apparently didn't object to the exceeding large tip that N had inadvertently given him, as he quickly pocketed the dough.

Full of alien crash-site paraphernalia, Your Personal Area 51 was a conspiracy theorist's nirvana. Like a kid in a candy store, N2 read every exhibit sign, perused each genuine and questionable copy of newspaper reports, and pored over photocopied copies of documents stamped "classified," purportedly government files and inter-department memos.

A grizzled-looking older man, presumably acting as a security guard, sat on a stool and appeared somewhat spooky in the subdued lighting.

"Is all of this real?" N asked the man.

"Yup," the old-timer replied.

"So, what really happened, do you think?" N asked in a tone that indicated he truly wanted to find out what humans actually knew about what was happening in the skies above them.

"Well," said the old-timer, "the Roswell incident, guess you know, was an extraterrestrial UFO crash and a top-secret military cover-up."

"But what do you think really happened?" N inquired.

"Dunno. My daddy always claimed it happened, but guess it don't matter much since no more of 'em have ever dropped in. Kinda wish they would, would sure boost business," the white-haired gent said and looked around sadly.

"Yes, I could see that," said N, "Because real extraterrestrials, coming back to Roswell, would…" he paused. After a moment's thought, he asked, "How would the appearance of real ETs help business, exactly?"

"I guess loads of people would bus in, hoping to see one of them there alien creatures for themselves," the shopkeeper said, "And they'd buy stuff… souvenirs and such."

"The Earth government would not get involved?" N asked, fishing.

"Oh, you bet the feds would be down here all over their sorry alien asses," the old geezer wheezed, "They'd be dissecting those folks quicker than you can say alien autopsy! None of this ET phone home bull hooey, we'd butcher those invaders lickity split."

"Eek," N exclaimed.

"Nah, but don't worry," said the guy. "Not going to happen. What crazy-ass aliens would wanna come to earth?"

"I know, right?" agreed N, as he resisted the temptation to grab his clone and run screaming out of there, "They'd have to be quite stupid to do something like that." N2 nodded agreeably, yet his calm and collected reaction was a pretense.

"Mantid, how much longer before we get to Earth?" Beetle Blatt demanded, "Because I really, really want to be there already."

Sleeping with his body frozen and his eyes fully open, Mantid didn't reply. Blatt waved an appendage in front of his companion's eyes, but Mantid made no response.

"Mantid, how much longer before we get to Earth?" Beetle Blatt asked again.

After receiving no response, Beetle Blatt decided to verify the provided rental jumper data and travel companion and consulted a holographic interstellar travel map. Startled from his task by a weird clicking noise, he quickly turned to see Mantid awake and staring fixedly at him.

Click. Click. Click.

"What's that noise?" Beetle Blatt asked.

"It's just that Zibbie, Zibbie's assertive tone of voice is so..." Mantid said.

"What?!" Blatt demanded.

"Attractive," Mantid said as Blatt realized that the sound was coming from Mantid, who was rubbing his rear mandibles together.

"Stop that, right now!" Beetle Blatt ordered as he stared in horror and shuddered with disgust at Mantid's obvious gratification.

"But why'd you have to pose with all of those play toys? It was really quite embarrassing, and it took forever," N asked, his voice dripping irritation, as the two of them left the building and shop and walked up the road.

"They were not toys. The displays were real," N2 insisted.

"Yeah, like they really have recovered crashed alien spacecraft, complete with dead alien bodies. And they couldn't think of anything better to do with it than put it all in a Intergalactic Fun Zone... for the pleasure of human tourists waiting for their accommodations to be ready," N said.

"It was fun," N2 said, trying hard not to have his buzz dampened by N's negativity.

"How could you get your photo taken with toy aliens? Now they have you on record," N chastised.

"They just thought I was another human tourist. Don't exaggerate."

"They were obvious fakes—made of cheap rubber—and anyway, you can have all the photo ops you want with real celestial beings, once we get off this rock," N said with true exasperation.

"You just don't get it, man, kitchy is cool..." said N2 sadly, "It's a human thing. You wouldn't understand. Having fun in a place like the Intergalactic Fun Zone. It's obviously too far outside your repressed, anal alien ken," N2 said, looking like he might cry.

"Oh, sure, kitchy is cool, for sure, I mean totally," N parroted using a put-on nasal voice, laden with sarcasm, entirely mocking N2.

"You always do this—you're controlling... You try to tell me what to do and how to feel. I don't get to be me. I hate it—sometimes I think that I hate you, Marilyn," N2 said, and, his emotions out of control, turned and slapped N hard.

N stared at his clone, his mouth open with astonishment.

N2 turned and walked toward the cabin rental office.

"The watering hole is now open, and that's where I want to go. I'll check us in and we can get our bodies something to eat," N2 said over his shoulder.

"I'll come with you," N said and hurried after N2, still in shock over the violent episode that they had just shared.

"No, I need a moment," N2 said and refused even to look at N. Unaccustomed to such odd and unruly behavior, N paced, wondering what exactly was up with N2. Perhaps it was the oxygen levels in the air. Or, maybe, planet Earth's gravity was causing horrific stress on N2's central nervous system. It made him quiver to think about what was affecting his clone, yet N could not stop pondering.

N looked himself over: if something environmental was affecting N2, then it was most likely impacting him as well, he considered.

Did his fingers, hands, and arms look a little bloated? He tried to get a good look at himself, but the truth was that he really didn't entirely recall exactly what his human disguise had originally looked like. That meant he really couldn't make a scientific comparison. Perhaps he was a little bloated, he reasoned.

Then again, he considered, maybe wearing a human suit was causing a corollary excess of intense negative and sadistic emotion. Humans were terribly violent creatures. Everybeing knew that. N2 finally came back out of the motel office.

"Here's what's going to happen," N2 said, as he faced his original, "We're going into the watering hole and we're going to have the best time. I want to hear no more negativity about the

Earth, humans, or anything else from you, understood? From now on, we will make only happy memories. Deal?"

"No more negativity. You are correct. What's the point of being on a vacation if we're not making any positive memories?" N agreed quietly.

The two of them trudged to the tavern adjacent to the motel. The establishment bore a resemblance to something out of an old American Western movie.

N and N2 sat at a table in a corner booth in the local bar, which appeared to be decorated to resemble the alien bar in the original Star Wars movie. The staff were dressed as alien creatures and characters, some recognizable and some not.

"Here ya go, fellas," the lanky, buxom barmaid said as she served them tall, bubbling, neon colored, alien-theme mixed drinks, which she had earlier recommended as the world-famous, house special. The core of her body was clad in a tight-fitting leotard-like garment, and the rest of her was dressed like a cross between a faux-fur-suited Wookie and a giraffe walking on its hind legs.

"What else can I get ya?" she asked.

"More of these," N2 quickly said, his eyes wide with anticipation.

"You got a thirst going on, boys. Enjoy," the barmaid said as she left.

Taking the large, yummy-looking drink in two hands, N2 finally began to get excited. "Now, this is what I'm talking about," he said happily, and knocked back his bubbling, bright, neon-colored alcoholic beverage.

N looked at his drink with circumspection but refrained from making any negative or cynical comments.

His head turned quickly when shrieking feedback from the sound equipment on stage sent a piercing screech through the laid-back bar. A sign above the stage read, "Karaoke Night," as a local guy began to sing on the raised platform.

"What's happening?" N asked N2 who, unperturbed, was downing the last of his drink with intense satisfaction.

"Chillax," he said, after emitting a soft burp, "It is earthling entertainment. Sit back and be entertained."

"Yes, of course," N said agreeably as he sipped his drink slowly. "Earthling entertainment is excellent, or so I hear, from a reputable source," he added, and winked at N2, obviously trying to butter up his genetic copy.

N2 finished his drink just as the barmaid returned with two more.

"Here you go, cow pokes," she said. "Drink as much as you want, I've got a tab going for you folks."

By the time N2 knocked back his second drink, he was feeling all warm and fuzzy. Happily looking around the bar, he felt affection for the locals, for the tourists... for everyone. He looked at N and felt a wave of love for his original. Reaching over, he touched N's arm.

"Dude, isn't this the best vaca, evah? Like totes obvi," he asked with a broad smile. Not understanding the question, N glared at N2.

"Vaca, vacation," N2 clarified, then added, "Totally obviously."

"We aren't actually on a," N said as he made quote signs in the air, 'vaca,' dude."

"Dude, you called me dude," N2 said, really excited, "I feel more human by the earth minute." He sighed blissfully.

"You are a strange dude, dude," N said, finishing his first drink. Then, increasingly buzzed himself, he smiled happily at N2.

"Yes, you are the strangest dude, ever," N said with a giggle.

"No, dude. You are the strangest ever dude... ever," N2 corrected, smiling.

"I was being ironic, though, you know that... right?" N asked as he began his second drink.

"Sure thing, dude," N2 replied, still not tiring of the word.

N genuinely laughed, even if he didn't quite know what he was laughing at. He stared at the beads of water on his drink cup. Taking a few more sips of his brightly colored, bubbling drink, he surveyed the other patrons with greater warmth in his heart.

"I'm sorry for what I said before," N2 admitted, "I just need some downtime. It's a bitch being a worthless clone of a being, practically worthless... probably soulless... definitely lonely."

N stared at N2 in horror; he hated having the sordid facts of life laid before him so bluntly.

"Jeez, dude. So we're here, but let's continue to enjoy the human entertainment, okay? Some earthling music, one or two more drinks, your bit of 'down-time,' and then we go get lodging and hide out," N said.

"Yup, yupper, yuppers," N2 said, suddenly perking up, "Music, drinks, good memories. One of everything... and then we're outtie, man!" N2 shrieked ecstatically. N groaned to himself and slapped the side of his head, not quite sure what he was getting into with his very emotionally erratic and unpredictable clone.

When N2 leered at a chick walking by, his tongue practically hanging out with lust, N bopped him on the upside of his head.

"Don't you go native on me, N2," N warned, "There's enough humanity to deal with here already."

"It was her shirt, dude. Didn't you see that? It was a vintage Grateful Dead Woodstock tee," N2 declared, being entirely honest and totally bowled over.

Looking incomprehensively at his clone, N uncharacteristically grinned.

"When are you going to get on up there and make some earth music yourself, dude?" N asked and nodded toward the stage, "You obviously totally love the noise these humans make."

"Do you think I should?" N2 asked. N thought about it for a minute.

"Maybe not," he said, "I guess we keep it all low key, stick with enjoying the entertainment from afar, have a few more drinks, make a few more memories."

That's what I'm talking about," N2 exclaimed, wildly excited, "More drinks, more music, more memories. Keep them coming, dudes," he said and stood to wave to the waitress to order more drinks.

Some time later, N2 was still laughing hysterically and pounding shots. N held his nose and managed to drink a shot.

"Well, that's last call," the barmaid said, somewhat tetchily. "We're closing in fifteen." N and N2 exchanged confused looks.

"Why is she so angry?" N asked, waving his arms about tipsily and accidentally sweeping his wallet-like bag off the table.

"I dunno," N2 replied. "Maybe because we keep drinking and we don't get drunk or run out of cash or I dunno. Hey, your thingy," N2 said, pointing to the dropped bag on the floor. As N leaned down to get his special bag, N2 took advantage of N's inattention and left their table.

N, bag retrieved, sat up, and, looking around for his clone, he was shocked to see N2 on stage.

The karaoke machine was playing "How Soon Is Now?" by The Smiths as N2 posed suggestively with the microphone, looking particularly ridiculous.

N2 sang soulfully along with the lyrics. Some badass locals

at the bar stared at N2 as he seemed to be crooning suggestively to them.

Practically screaming, putting everything that he had into it, N2 sang. The barmaid offered N another drink, but N shook his head, no. He knew he was drunk and well past his limit. He looked at his arm. It appeared to be swelling.

N2 sang, now hitting his stride. Getting better, the more he sang, the locals were now emotionally reacting to his version of the song, as if he were pretty talented.

Still focused on the bad-asses at the bar, N2's extreme emotion and hyper-soulful rendition of the song caused some of them to lose it.

Some of them tried to hide the tears in their eyes; one or two unsuccessful locals sobbed quietly, snot dripping down one redneck's face.

N watched his clone with pride, and even though he didn't know the words or the song, he found himself attempting to sing along. His eyes had difficulty focusing, however. Every so often, he noticed that for a very brief second, a tentacle would show or N2 would morph into a Neandertal, and grunt instead of singing. A moment later, again very briefly, N2 morphed into a Pygmy human and quickly reverted to his normal human disguise once more.

Suspecting that N2's human camouflage may have some kind of bug or glitch, N realized that he was drunk, and so he couldn't rule out the possibility that he was hallucinating this. What he was seeing could be the result of his own first experience of intoxication. He looked around to see if anyone else in the crowd was reacting with shock to what was happening with N2 on stage. They weren't.

When N2 quickly morphed into a Neandertal, yet again, and then back into a Homo sapiens sapiens, N jumped to his feet and tried to decide whether he should walk towards the stage.

N2 was singing about his being human and needing to be loved, entirely oblivious to his erratic and rapidly morphing physical appearance. N saw that his clone's real tentacles were burgeoning intermittently; his extra-terrestrial body threatened to bust right out of his human disguise and ruin everything for both of them. N shuddered in fear, imagining being brutally murdered by an angry human mob disgusted by the sight of real aliens.

N2 sang, in a strange, squeaky little voice, as a tiny little Pygmy human.

Only the sober barmaid seemed to notice N2 losing his human form. She quickly did a double-take. N2 looked solidly human again, so she stared at him for a long moment. Seeing nothing out of the ordinary, she then shook her head. It was obvious that she thought that she must have been seeing things.

"Is that it for last call?" the bartender asked her.

"That's it for me," she said, meaningfully.

"Long shift?" the bartender asked.

"Long shift and too many Roswell freakazoid weirdoes... who don't even tip," she complained, "Seriously. I've got to get out of this place," she said and turned to finish closing out the tables in her station.

As N2 gyrated and rapidly morphed between the three earthling disguises that he'd tried, periodically, a bit more of his actual form showed through. Oddly, many of the locals were too inebriated, think drunk out of their minds, to notice.

N decided that immediate action was required to avert a major catastrophe. N2's tentacles were now all over the place as N2's original form threatened to dominate. Launching his body at N2, who was still standing on the karaoke stage, N seemed to fly six feet through the air. Then he crashed into and knocked

N2 to the floor. The people watching stopped what they were doing; some stood up, and a woman screamed.

"And all my hope is gone…" N2 continued to sing. When he tried to wave off N's attentions, he quickly saw that instead of a human arm, he was pushing him off with his very own tentacle. Instantly sober, N2 realized the enormity of the screw up and they both scrambled to their feet. Taking advantage of a shocked and hushed bar crowd, N2 took a grand bow and rushed his original out of the bar.

It was now dark and cold outside as N and N2 looked around wildly. Expecting the crowd to come running out of the bar in pursuit, they prepared to run for their lives. After a quick trot down the street, they looked back and, to their great relief, the two realized that they were not being followed.

N2 looked down at himself and gave a little scream: he was rapidly shifting between four forms. The molecules of his being seemed to speed up. It appeared that, at any moment, he might explode into a gloppy mess of molecular soup.

"What's happening?" he practically squealed.

"Must be the alcohol affecting the—" N said, but didn't get to finish.

"Help me, N," N2 begged as N pulled the Zeta Reticuli military tech multi-phase shape-shifting device from his flat carry bag. He had to squint to focus, his inebriated state causing his body to sway and his hands to shake.

"What are you going to do?" N2 asked with alarm.

"We need to… uh, we need to reset," he said, having to think hard.

"Oh," N2 said as he watched with trepidation as N fumbled with the device.

"Homo… something, wasn't it?" N asked as he dialed through the settings.

"Sapiens, I think it was," N2 answered quickly, his human

form now seriously losing its hold. "Hurry," N2 said as his tentacles waved in the air.

"Homo sapiens sapiens!" N declared happily when he found what he was looking for on the device.

"Is this even going to work?" N2 asked as he reverted more solidly back to his original, alien form.

"If you have a better suggestion..." N said as he pointed the device towards his clone.

"Do it!" N2 said, now completely alien.

As N engaged the device, N2's form morphed more and more rapidly through his three alternate forms until, finally, to their shared relief, it reverted to his original form and held.

Exhausted, inebriated, and looking unusually red and bloated (presumably as a result of their excessive consumption of human alcoholic beverages), the two faux-humans took a moment to get their bearings. Then, grabbing hold of each other for mutual support, they trudged toward the "Alien Motel 11:11."

Having secured a room, N slept fitfully in the Mid-century modern rental, which, just like all the rooms, had a "Roswell Alien" theme. N2 sat in an armchair watching TV. Like a precocious child who was too excited to go to bed and sleep, yet too tired to keep his eyes open, N2 tried to stay awake long enough to watch John Wayne in "Rio Bravo."

"Sorry, don't get it done, Dude," John Wayne told Dean Martin.

Bleary-eyed and disturbed by the sound of the TV, N opened his eyes and freaked when he saw a bizarre giant menacing ET, with enormous fangs and an ugly mug, crouched over him. Screaming, he fell out of bed.

Both of the aliens' facial and body skin was unusually wrinkly and stretchy; it almost hung off of them. They had huge bags under their eyes and appeared severely aged, very thin, and quite greenish. They were obviously dehydrated.

"Keep it down, dude," N2 told him. "I'm trying to watch the entertainment."

More awake now, N looked up and saw that the frightening ET was actually a statue and obviously part of the Roswell Alien-themed décor. Holding his head in pain and feeling too weak to stand, N crawled back onto the bed.

"What is this feeling? My brain feels like it was taken out and left soaking in the salt baths at Iosphere Flats for ten cosmic cycles," N said.

"Yes, I feel the same," N2 groaned as he switched off the TV, "I've concluded that it's an alcoholic hangover. How many times have we seen the Hank subject get them after heavy consumption?"

N got up out of bed and wobbled toward the bathroom.

N2 then stared around the room, as if looking at it for the first time. The sun was coming up outside, and they'd both been too drunk to get a good look at it the previous night. The room was over-the-top, ET-inspired Americana kitsch, and N smiled as if he truly and genuinely liked the décor.

"I do so feel very at home here, N," N2 said.

"Of course... Hank! I forgot all about Hank!" N said from the bathroom as if his brain was slow to compute, "Isn't it weird that he solved that mathematical equation?" N2 didn't answer.

N2 wobbled and groaning again, managed to make his way toward the bathroom. He entered as N was leaving. Needing water, he ran the tap and slurped from the stream. N returned with the Zeta Reticuli military tech multi-phase shape-shifting device and refreshed both of their human disguises.

"Hey," N2 said, "I was stable. I don't need that anymore."

"You may be stable for now, but we both need to remain that way, especially when we are in public," N said, "Luckily, the human brains were intoxicated and couldn't trust their vision and make any kind of reasoned thought. Being seen by humans, I mean, their seeing how we really look, could turn out very badly for us."

"You don't know what that thing is doing to us at the molecular level," protested N2, "You can't just go around zapping living tissue and biological organic particles all the time, dude," he said loudly and then dropped his voice, cringing with the pain of a vomitus-tinged hangover.

"It's better to be certain than to be eaten is my motto, dude," N said as he put the device away.

"The Marcy woman human person did not say the man's name was Hank," N2 said.

"She didn't?" N asked uncertainly.

"No. But you just mentioned Hank like he was—"

"She said a janitor at the Los Alamos Labs with a background in Applied Mathematics..." N interrupted, connections finally being made in his alcohol soaked brain, "So, of course it's Hank! The QMJ must have worked! It made him smarter," he said happily.

"Good for Hank. He deserves a break," N2 said and looked at himself more carefully in the mirror. Noticing how absolutely strange he looked, he then looked at N for a comparison. They both didn't look "right" at all.

"Don't you see the significance?" N asked excitedly, "If he's getting smarter... it could affect the rest of mankind. Our interference has repercussions for the future of humanity and all other beings... including us," N continued.

"I think it's a bit too late to worry about our jobs at this stage, N. That UFO left the space station ages ago," N2 replied and snorted with laughter.

"This is bigger than our miserable cubicle jobs, N2. This human, Hank, is the key. He is our leverage, our bargaining chip. Whoever rules Hank can name their price. Don't you see? We won't work for Zycorp, Zycorp'll work for us," N said happily and then groaned, his excitement making his hangover headache pound all the harder.

"Wow, I haven't heard you get this excited since we won the first round of the office Intergalactic Amateur Championship Mind Games Competition. What do you think we should do?" N2 asked as he splashed some water on his face.

"We need to find the earthling," N said slowly, now feeling nauseous and looking positively viridescent.

"Far out! Let's find the Hankster. Plus, we'll get to see Marcy again," N2 said happily.

"But first... sustenance. We have not fed our bodies since we arrived, and they are beginning to show signs of upset. Besides, the dense gravity here is affecting us; we need to get more protein-based strength to combat it," N said.

N2 shrieked and looked into the mirror. His skin was saggy and furrowed; he was shocked to see that his face now had deep wrinkles, which lent it a certain Chinese Shar Pei quality. He grabbed at his skin and then took a good look at his original. N2 looked and saw that N's skin was equally green. Sure enough, in their human disguises, they were both noticeably thinner, and their skin was significantly more wrinkled.

"Yes, sustenance. I guess these forms need to eat regularly," N2 agreed, "I don't think human skin is supposed to look green and wrinkly."

Walking straight out of the motel, N and N2 looked weaker by the moment. They approached the silvery exterior and neon-trimmed UFO-shaped, Alien-themed fast food restaurant.

"I just feel so at home here," N2 said to N, admiring the alien décor as they entered the building and went to place an order at the counter.

"What can I get for y'all today?" the bright and breezy clerk asked, her name read, "Sandy."

"Human food, please," N answered.

"See anything you like on the breakfast menu?" Sandy answered, pretending to smile at the customer's supposed joke. The annoyed look on her face revealed that she obviously didn't think he was funny.

"Everything," answered N2.

"Everything?" Sandy responded, beginning to regret the interaction. "Anything in particular you'd like to order today?" she asked, still being polite.

"No, you don't understand. We want everything you've got," N said, his body beginning to sway with hunger.

"You want everything on the breakfast menu, is that what you want to order?" Sandy asked.

"Yes," N and N2 responded at the same time as N took out a wad of cash from his flat bag.

Seated inside the "spaceship" of the fast food joint, they soon were chowing down on the full menu of breakfast items spread before them.

"Oh, my. This breakfast is, I believe, my favorite human meal," N said, stuffing his face.

"I know, right? Micky D's is da bomb. The sodium and the fat... completely delicious," N2 agreed. N grunted. N2 thought for a moment.

"Though, technically, it's our only human meal so far. We didn't eat anything since landing," N2 said.

"Shush," N chided, looking around in case they were overheard, "If anyone asks, we didn't land here... we came on wheels."

"Yeah, that sounds more normal," N2 agreed, stuffing his face.

"We should get more fuel," N said happily, his face, lips, hands, and fingers greasy with fat. N2 nodded.

"More of these..." N2 said and held up an Egg McMuffin and hash browns, one in each hand, "These taste nothing like space food. I love it!"

N returned to the counter and ordered more food. Afterward, he returned and sat down with N2, grabbing more fast food.

"You guys doing okay?" a clerk asked as he bused an adjoining table. Due to the considerable amount of food the guys had ordered and their distinctly odd behavior, the clerks behind the counter watched with interest.

"Yes, we are very pleased with your human food," N answered, "I think we are awaiting more fuel, though."

"Yeah, it's important to eat a good breakfast, most important meal of the day, or so they say," the clerk answered, not quite sure how to respond, "Where are you guys from, anyway?"

"We are not from around here, and we landed, I mean we came here on wheels," N2 carefully answered.

Sandy arrived carrying two trays, heavily laden with N's recent order.

"Thank you so much," N2 said, nearly teary with gratitude.

"This means so much to us. It's the best human food we've ever eaten," N said.

"It's the only human food we've ever eaten," N2 corrected.

"Uh-huh," said the clerk and turned to share a private joke with Sandy, who grinned at him as she circled her index finger by her temple to indicate that they were total whack jobs.

"Freaking mental," she whispered as she turned to go. The other clerk laughed.

N and N2 both ate as rapidly as they were able. N2's body grew increasingly swollen as he shoveled in the chow. N, having eaten only slightly less than his clone, was soon catching up.

Moments later, having demolished everything edible, the table covered with trash, N looked at N2.

Instead of speaking, as he had intended, he burped loudly.

"What was that?" N2 asked, more curious than offended.

"I don't know," N responded innocently, "I was going to say something and instead..." N stopped. He noticed that N2 was gazing down at N's lower body.

"What?" N asked.

"Look at your body, dude. You just got super fat," N2 said.

N looked down to see that he had indeed gained weight, surprisingly quickly.

"So are you, dude," N said, now realizing that his clone was just as fat, if not fatter. N pinched his flesh between a thumb and forefinger. He was seriously swollen,

"You think that's normal?" N2 asked, looking himself over. "I mean, normal for humans?"

"Of course. It's called obesity. Many human subjects get like this," N answered.

"We should leave now," he decided. They both peered around nervously, then, as no one appeared to be paying them any attention, they hoisted themselves up. Helping each other balance, they wobbled towards a side exit, trying to stay upright.

Taking clumsy steps, they used the restaurant furniture to help themselves balance as they exited the Roswell McDonald's. Every clerk behind the counter stopped what they were doing to stare after them, some with open mouths; others in horrified shock. They had witnessed two guys who resembled sticks enter. Then, an hour later, two guys who resembled bulbous whales departed.

"Did you see that?" Sandy asked a co-worker. "They came in skinny, and now they both look like the Michelin Man. Tell me I ain't seeing things."

"You ain't seeing things," he answered, still staring.

N and N2 waddled awkwardly along the sidewalk as quickly as they could, doing their best to avoid falling over and yet still make good progress.

"I'm so swollen... it's disgusting," N2 said, looking at his ankles and freaking out.

N farted, groaned and rubbed his belly, "Oh, my middle region," he said.

N2 paused on the side of the road and, turning his head, quickly spewed into the bushes. N made a deep inarticulate sound, a combined moan and whimpering cry, partly a response to N2's disgusting action and partly a reaction to his own pain and despair.

"It must be the chemical and physical cocktail combination of the Earth's gravity, the human body skin spray, and the fat and salt, and other stuff in human food," he reasoned.

"Remember how skinny we were this morning?" he asked as N2 stood up straight after finishing retching.

"That's right, dude. This can't be permanent," N2 said, wiping his mouth, "How can humans live in these crappy bodies? This human body sucks, dude."

"Come on. Let's go get the spaceship," N said.

"We'll use up fuel as we walk and get thin again."

"Yeah, I think we made enough memories in Roswell. Let's go find the Hank subject," N2 said.

N and N2 waddled down Main Street toward the highway and, ultimately, trying to remember the way they came in, they turned down dirt roads that ran through the scrub desert outside of the town.

Walking for several hours through the dusty, beige, and peach sandy desert, they did indeed burn off their fuel and return to their normal size. They also grew more tired, hot, and desperate by the moment.

"Haven't we... seen... this... cactus... before?" N2 asked between panted breaths.

N studied the huge saguaro cactus, which was the size of a tall tree. "Yes... I think we have," he answered. "Let's go in a different direction," he said.

Too tried to question or argue, N2 silently agreed. With N in the lead, they turned and trudged away in the exact opposite direction. When N2 was too tired to go on, N pushed, dragged, and pulled N2 along. A few hours later, they found their way back to the other end of town.

"Now we're back in town," N2 complained. "We came right back to where we started from!"

"Perhaps it's on the other side of town? I know I could find it again if we get to where it is parked," N responded.

"Listen to yourself, dude. Why did I ever let you fly? You're a terrible pilot and you always forget where you parked the spaceship," N2 said.

Thin, dirty, thirsty, and exhausted, they approached a used car dealership.

"We can get Earth wheels and drive on the land!" N exclaimed as they surveyed the various car options. All of the vehicles had bright price signs on them, the automobiles ranging in price from several hundred to several thousand dollars. N2 burped and held his stomach. He was still a little queasy.

"It's not like we could do anything about the atomic power rod stabilizers anyway... unless we got it towed to Los Alamos," N said defensively.

N2 laughed derisively. "And what are you going to say to the humans? 'Hello dumb earthlings, I'm a representative of Zycorp in dire need of a power source... can you spot me some plutonium?'"

"Your stupidity always amazes me," N said and scowled.

"What?" N2 asked.

"Plutonium is used for nuclear power, ET-wad, not atomic power," N said.

"Oh!" N2 said, feeling immediately dejected. Feeling guilty, N lightly punched his buddy.

"Dude, I'm just joking. Nuclear and atomic are generally used synonymously. Plutonium, uranium... either would do the job," N said.

N2 spotted a pink 1950s Cadillac with fins and immediately perked up with excitement. It looked remarkably like their Starcar in interstellar pink Cadillac jetcar mode.

"Now that is a nice ride," N2 said and whistled long and low. He looked the vehicle over. The car wasn't pristine, and the sticker read $32,500.

"That's a lot of Earth money for a vehicle that doesn't do basic interstellar flight," N said as N2 looked the car over.

"This thing will drive like a dream. It has a 365 V-8 engine, air conditioning, power steering," N2 said, reading off the details. He walked around to the rear and looked under the car. "It has a solid trunk and bottom," he added.

"Yeah, but what kind of weird thing will happen to us in that car?" N asked.

"I'm sorry, I didn't think about the boozle and the human food... Yeah, sure, in retrospect, I shoulda listened to you and realized that our bodies might react poorly to it, and the physical environment of planet Earth, in some way. But I didn't. I'm real sorry, N," N2 said, sounding like he really meant it.

"Sorry don't get it done, Dude," N said, and his delivery was a dead ringer impersonation of John Wayne.

"Okay, no more junk food, booze, whining, uh, no more... lack of focus... and, you know, all of that which, uh, pisses you off," N2 promised.

"That's more like it. I will purchase this vehicle now," N said, feeling respected and vindicated.

"Yeah, let's purchase this puppy," N2 said happily.

N took out some cash and entered a little freestanding car lot office.

A short time later, with N2 in the passenger seat, N drove the caddy off the sales lot. Entirely ignorant of the rules of the road, causing two cars to brake and swerve to avoid a head-on collision, he drove down the street.

As the Starrv decelerated from hyperspace, Mantid piloted the rental jumper with precision. "I have no idea where we should land," Beetle Blatt said as he studied the Earth on a 3-D holographic map.

"Have an idea, Zibbie," Mantid said, emulating and expressing a close approximation of happiness. "Getting very close," he said as the Earth's moon became visible.

"Want to stop to look at the blue planet from up top?" Beetle Blatt asked Mantid.

"What Zibbie mean?" Mantid asked.

"According to the manual, the rental Starrv has an observation deck," Blatt said. Clitter, clitter, clitter, Mantid laughed, his laughter sounding like cricket noises.

"Air in the Earth's atmosphere is mainly composed of nitrogen, oxygen, and argon. Cannot breathe those gases," he said plainly, stating the obvious.

"Oh, of course," Beetle Blatt said sheepishly. "I meant when we... landed." It was entirely unlike him to be stupid to the point of being careless, especially with his life, he thought to himself. But, then again, he'd never been on vacation before, so he gave himself some slack. Taking this wild and crazy journey to a hostile planet made him feel entirely out of control.

"How much longer is it?" Beetle Blatt inquired, fidgeting with impatience, yet doing his best to sound calm.

Clitter, clitter, clitter. Mantid chuckled again, his mandibles scritching against one another, making a clitter sound just like a cricket might make.

"Seriously," Beetle Blatt said, "are we there yet?"

Clitter, clitter, clitter, clitter, clitter, Mantid laughed and laughed.

"Zibbie make joke, so Mantid zonk out loud again," Mantid said and gave Blatt a friendly tickle with one long stick appendage. Beetle Blatt, however, was not at all joking. He shivered. The touch of Mantid's appendage disgusted him.

"We look for the Earth subject named Hank, yes?" Mantid then asked, keeping his eyes fixed on the computer screen.

"Correct," Blatt responded, still smarting from Mantid's insensitive laughter.

"I hack Earth's web system and perform search," Mantid said, clicking away on his computer module.

"Terrific," Blatt said, totally uninterested.

"Do not worry, Zibbie. I will find the Hank person."

"Great," Blatt said without enthusiasm.

The sun shone golden rays upon the vast, semi-desert terrain. Waves of heat created a shimme—a heat haze—which rose off the black asphalt of the parking lot outside the convenience store, Hank's regular stomping ground. Marcy pulled up and parked her SUV.

Taking stock of some dark clouds which were blowing in from the east, Marcy got out of her vehicle and entered the store.

After grabbing water and snacks, Marcy headed to the

market's counter. The Native American clerk put down his book. Marcy glanced down to see that the man was reading something titled "Brain: The Man Who Wrote the Book That Changed the World."

Feeling unsure of herself, Marcy looked the guy up and down and decided to take a chance on asking him about Hank. Maybe the guy wouldn't talk, she considered, but then again, maybe he was a friendly local and an open kind of person.

She had just come from the Los Alamos National Research Laboratory, where she was refused entry. They then politely told her that she must send the facility a written request for whatever it was she wanted, which in her parlance was the usual blow-off BS.

The math genius story was making its way into the national media, and her editor was now more excited about the janitor story than ever. She had to find Hank, he urged her. He told her that some world-renowned, respected mathematicians and scientists had reviewed the guy's work, and despite all the skepticism and claims that it was a hoax, they had found no errors.

"I'm looking for a fella... lives around here," she said to the clerk as he rang up her items. "Maybe you might know him?"

"Will that be cash or credit?" the clerk asked, ignoring her question as if she hadn't spoken at all.

Undeterred, Marcy laid down some cash on the counter.

"His name is Hank Walsh. He's a mathematician, works out at Los Alamos," Marcy continued. The clerk made change and seemed to think about whether he would divulge his secrets or not. Seeing that she had kind eyes, he decided that she wasn't intending harm to anyone.

"There is a local guy named Hank. I don't know what he works at, but he recently received a call. He's a preacher now," the man finally said.

"Huh. Nah, don't think he's religious, probably not the same guy..." Marcy said, then she paused a moment, and thought hard, "Wait. What does he preach about?"

"I don't know. The usual crazy shit, I guess," the clerk answered, wanting to be done with the interrogation.

"Does he say anything about ETs in his preaching, by any chance?" she asked.

Looking like he was embarrassed by the question, he stumbled over his words, then finally spoke. Marcy knew that she had her answer. "I guess," the clerk answered.

Marcy's eyes widened with excitement as she collected her purchases. "Thank you very, very much," she said as she left quickly.

MARCY WAITED PATIENTLY AS SHE SAT ON THE STEPS outside Hank's trailer. A mailman walked on his rounds and put some mail into the mailbox by Hank's trailer.

"Hey, there. I'm looking for Hank Walsh," Marcy said, before the mailman even saw her.

"Are you ill?" asked the mailman.

"Am I... what?" asked Marcy, thrown by the question.

"Do you have an illness?" the mailman asked, but then, seeing the puzzled reaction on Marcy's face, he turned to walk on. "None of my business," he confessed as he walked away.

"Yes, I do have an illness," Marcy shot back, quickly getting to her feet. "I'm very sickly indeed," she added, not quite sure of the direction she was taking.

"He has healed many," the mailman said. "Are you a believer?" he then asked. "It's only the believers that get the cure."

"Oh, I'm a believer, alright," Marcy answered. "I totally believe."

"He preaches after supper on Fridays and all day Saturday,"

the mailman said. "He's the real deal," he added as he nodded a farewell and continued on his rounds.

"Have a good day," Marcy said as she watched him go, not knowing what to think. The story she was already drafting in her mind was becoming increasingly convoluted. A janitor who was also a genius mathematician, whose proof of life beyond Earth was being validated by the scientific community, was now apparently a mystic preacher who healed the sick in the remote New Mexico desert. Either this person was a master magician and hypnotist, or something else, or, as the mailman suggested, he was the real deal.

Unsure of what her next move should be, Marcy returned to the cooling air conditioning of her car.

Marcy was conscious of feeling both relieved and sad at the same time. She felt relieved because she would have time to find a place to stay for the night, get cleaned up, get some food, and maybe take a nap. She was sad because she would have to wait to track down and meet this man, who only grew more and more enigmatic the more she heard people talk about him.

IT WAS A BEAUTIFUL DAY, SUNNY WITH A BRIGHT, cloudless blue sky as the Starrv made its descent above the California skies.

Instantly morphing into a typical Earth recreational vehicle, the craft emitted a plume of vaporized water, which formed a dense white cloud around the vehicle, shielding it from view. It hovered and slowly descended, landing vertically in a remote and nearly empty region of the vast Disneyland Park parking lot.

"What Zibbie looking for?" Mantid asked as Beetle Blatt quickly looked through the rental jumper manual.

"The clerk said that the rental came standard with a cloaking device," Blatt answered, annoyed at not finding what he was looking for.

"What kind human you want to look like?" Mantid asked as a series of laser beams shot out from his console and began mapping Beetle Blatt's shape.

"Just a normal human," Ball answered. "Whatever kind of human that will blend in."

Mantid keyed in some commands, and Blatt's form began to be rearranged by the laser beams. When they finished their work, Blatt looked like a human version of himself: small, dark, skinny, and spindly-looking with a bit of an egg-head, except that now he had a nose and ears.

"Humans ugly, but you handsome," Mantid said and then turned the device on himself. Blatt checked himself out in a mirror and moved around, getting a feel for his new form, as laser beams rearranged Mantid's form.

"You look amazing," Beetle Blatt exclaimed as he stared at Mantid in his new human form. "Huge improvement," Blatt said, not meaning it as an insult. Also skinny and spindly, except for the upper torso, Mantid's human form was that of a very slender, yet voluptuous, female human.

"Do you have these?" Mantid asked Blatt, referring to his quite busty chest.

"No, mine is flat," Blatt answered. "Did you choose a human female on the device?"

"No," answered Mantid. "Device set to most appropriate form.

"Then, this body must be most appropriate for you," Blatt said admiringly. "I like it!" It was true. Though he couldn't really have said exactly why, Mantid's new form was much more attractive to Beetle Blatt.

"Let us find Hank subject," Mantid said happily, heading to the Starry door.

"Yes," Blatt agreed, resisting the urge to reach out and touch Mantid's busty chest. "Let us continue with purpose."

Entering the gates to Disneyland, Beetle Blatt and Mantid joined with other tourists to line up to buy tickets for the park. "Don't we need Earth money to get into this Earthling establishment?" Beetle Blatt asked.

"I am prepared... have Amex Black; welcome everywhere on earth," Mantid said proudly, holding up a recently manufactured credit card.

"I trust that such a thing will be sufficient... but why are we here?" Blatt asked.

"According to my search on Earth internet, subject Hank has sibling that is Disney Princess, and sibling is to be found inside this large earthling playground," Mantid stated softly. It looked at Beetle Blatt with adoring eyes.

Very impressed with Mantid's detective work, Beetle Blatt nodded appreciatively. "I am happy you came aboard the craft, Mantid. You are most definitely thinking outside the rectangular," he admitted with admiration.

After they bought their tickets, they entered the Disneyland Park and walked down Main Street, U.S.A. As Beetle Blatt and Mantid wandered, they found themselves being jostled along by teeming crowds of human pedestrians seeking pleasure. Overwhelmed by the spectacle, the energy, the noise, and, most of all, the people, both of them stared at everything: the lights, the banners, the rides, and the people —lots and lots of humans of all shapes, sizes, and colors.

"Humans are larger than they look on screen," Beetle Blatt remarked.

"We must go... to Fantasyland," Mantid said as he consulted

his hand-held computer. "Princess at Fantasyland, this way, Zibbie," he said, pointing.

Beetle Blatt turned to look and see where Mantid was pointing. In the distance, he saw a wave of people walking toward something, which to him seemed magnificent: Sleeping Beauty's Castle.

As Blatt and Mantid made their way through the amusement park, entering and then exiting the archway through Sleeping Beauty's Castle, only Beetle Blatt seemed impressed. He gazed in wonder at the riveting lights, sights, and sounds of the vast human playground.

Tired of Blatt's slow pace, Mantid grabbed his hand and pulled him toward Fantasyland. Beetle Blatt looked self-consciously down at their conjoined hands as Mantid fixed his gaze ahead.

"Come, Zibbie. She will be here somewhere. We must search diligently for the princess," Mantid said. Beetle Blatt found himself strangely aroused by the pressure of Mantid's human female hand upon his own.

"We will see well if we partake of some of the ride offerings," Blatt said, almost salivating at the thought of riding on the bright and sparkly King Arthur Carousel that was now before them.

"Yes, perhaps you are correct," Mantid said, not picking up on Blatt's ruse, "The most optimum is flying ride which will give us height advantage."

Beetle Blatt and Mantid are soon riding the Dumbo the Flying Elephant ride, gazing around the entire time. "So many humans," Mantid observed, scanning the crowds for any sign of, and not seeing, the princess in question.

"Yes," agreed Blatt, smiling and soaking up all the good memories.

Still in search of Hank's sister, they get on the It's a Small World ride. Mantid looks around the whole time, while Beetle Blatt can barely contain his mirth.

"Did you see anything?" Mantid asked as they exited the ride.

"What exactly are we looking for? I mean, what does the princess look like?" Beetle Blatt asks excitedly, barely trying to hide his obvious enjoyment.

"This is photograph of subject's sibling," Mantid said, his hand-held computer projecting her Facebook picture as a hologram. Dressed in Disneyland costume, her profile name caption read, "Rhymes with Cinderella."

"I think I saw the subject's sister, sitting in an oversized hot beverage container, a pink one with a handle," Beetle Blatt said thoughtfully, staring in the direction of the Mad Tea Party teacup ride. Mantid stared in the same direction.

"Let us hurry and find her," Mantid said, sweating in the warm California sunshine. Mantid, in his human female disguise, had begun to look a bit worse for wear.

The two of them hurried to get in line at the teacups, hoping to catch up with the sister of the Hank subject. After a relatively short wait, they found themselves twirling round and round on the colorful and brightly lit ride.

"This playground very exhausting," Mantid said.

"Yes, very exhausting," Blatt lied, hiding a smile, as they sat in a giant teacup. He was having more fun than he'd had in ages. As Blatt and Mantid spun wildly in the teacups, Beetle Blatt couldn't hold back his laughter and laughed uproariously the entire time. Mantid looked at him with unnerved suspicion.

"There!" Beetle Blatt pointed as they made a sudden turn due to the ride's rotation. He gestured wildly, attempting to keep the young lady in sight.

"Where?" Mantid looked around but was now turned around and disoriented.

"There," Blatt pointed again as they spun madly.

"Is this joke?" Mantid asked, totally at sea.

"No joke," Blatt said as the teacups slowed down to a stop. "Look. See?"

Looking in the direction of where Beetle Blatt was pointing, Mantid saw a poster with Hank's sister in full costume, smiling brightly. The headline read, "Find Cinderella at the Disney Princess Fantasy Faire."

Stepping from the teacups, wobbly and lightheaded, both Blatt and Mantid immediately fell to the ground.

Taken unawares by their dizzy state, they barely managed to help each other up and had to stand motionless for a few moments as their heads felt like they were spinning like crazy. Finally, they managed to walk away.

In the Disney Princess Fantasy Faire, Mantid and Beetle Blatt searched for Cinderella, but she was nowhere to be found.

"Have you seen Cinderella?" Mantid asked a young lady who was dressed as Snow White. Showing her the poster of Cinderella, which they had pulled from the wall, the young woman frowned and seemed to be thinking.

"Yeah, she should be here today, but she isn't," she said. Mantid and Blatt looked at each other, neither the wiser for her shared information.

"She should be here, but she is not?" Mantid repeated back to her, seeking further clarification.

"Yeah, she should be here, but she had pressing duties at the castle, which, um, unexpectedly prevented her from being here today," the young lady said, hoping to sound informed and educated and, at the same time, not give away personal information to random strangers.

"We must speak to her about the subject, Hank," Beetle Blatt said.

"The subject, what? Oh, you mean her brother? You guys are friends of Hank?" Snow White asked.

"Yes, yes—friend of subject Hank," replied Mantid.

"I was so sorry to hear about their father's passing," Snow White said sadly.

"Passing where?" Blatt asked, looking around.

"You guys didn't hear? Their father just passed," she said. "It was very sad for them both, I'm sure."

"Oh, yes. That sad indeed," responded Mantid, not entirely certain what she meant, but her face conveyed that this "passed" was not a good thing.

"You guys want to pose with me for a photo, instead?" she asked brightly, switching quickly into her Snow White persona.

Before they could ascertain exactly what she meant, she lined up with them and rearranged their standing positions as one of the resident photographers took their photo.

"Say cheese," the photographer said, but only Snow White complied.

Blatt and Mantid walked toward the exit as the sun was setting. Both of them were now wearing Disney hoodies, while Mantid had on a pair of Goofy ears. The pair was loaded down with souvenirs, including a framed photograph of themselves, unsmiling, posing with Snow White. They looked totally exhausted.

"I don't get it. Snow White said that Cinderella had a "family emergency" in Oklahoma City?" Beetle Blatt said.

"Perhaps it was top-secret super agent lover-woman code," said Mantid, "But then again, she seemed sincerely to be grieving... for her friend, I mean."

"Code? What is code? What are you talking about?" Beetle Blatt asked.

"Instructions, Zibbie. The mission... our next steps. We must go to the Oklahoma City, which, according to the Wiki entry here, is also appropriately known by the sobriquet, "The Cinderella City," Mantid replied, as he conferred with his hand-held computer device.

"I can't understand you, Mantid. I don't know what you're talking about," Beetle Blatt said.

"That is because in such a short time, my English is getting so good, but no worries, my beloved. You soon learn, Zibbie," Mantid said happily.

The pair finally arrived at their disguised Starrv and, once inside, they wasted little time in pulling out of the lot and driving off.

INSIDE THE LOS ALAMOS NATIONAL LAB PROJECT ROOM, late at night, Drs. Delaware and Blake faced Hank, who was positively glowing with enlightenment and what could only be described as Divine energy.

"The incontrovertible truth of your mathematical theorem has attracted positive attention from the highest levels," Dr. Delaware said to Hank.

"Yes, I spoke with the Supreme Being this morning," replied Hank, entirely earnest and looking spiritually ecstatic.

Drs. Delaware and Blake exchanged a nervous glance.

"Uh, yes, very good. Well, we want you to attend the conference in New York and present the theorem at the UN on our behalf," replied Dr. Delaware.

"We've made arrangements to bring you on as a Richard P. Feynman Distinguished Fellow with shared authorship on all papers and full credit for your contributions," Dr. Blake added, hoping that this information would seal the deal. Hank had zero reaction, which made the pair of scientists quite nervous.

"And there would be more money. You'd jump from your current base salary of $18K to about $105K or so and join our R&D national security technologies team," Dr. Delaware added, hoping to get a positive reaction out of Hank.

"Pending a DOE Q security clearance, of course... and verification of your US citizenship," Dr. Blake clarified nervously.

"So, will you do it? Will you go to New York?" Dr. Delaware inquired.

Hank gazed into the distance, as if gazing deeply into the future.

"It is clear that it is the highest good for all concerned reality. So, I must. And, of course, it is my destiny," Hank replied with all sincerity.

Drs. Blake and Delaware jumped up and shook Hank's hand.

"Good! Good!" Dr. Delaware said.

"Good man!" Dr. Blake added.

***

Marcy again waited on the steps of Hank's trailer; this time, she had brought reading material and some snacks. She nibbled some fruit and reclined.

Her attention drifted as she watched local folk slowly gathering and hanging out just a stone's throw away on an adjacent grassy knoll.

Perhaps they're assembling to hear him preach, Marcy thought, which means that he's expected to show up pretty soon. She found herself growing excited.

Once more, Marcy rehearsed in her mind what she would say to him. She just had to arrange an interview and considered it best to approach him before he spoke, rather than after, which was most likely when everyone else would want to speak with him.;

Just then, Hank, beatific and radiant, drove up in his beat-up pickup. Marcy didn't waste time and hurried to reach him before anyone else could.

"Dr. Weber?" she said breathlessly as he exited his pickup. Hank turned, and Marcy was stopped dead in her tracks upon making eye contact with him.

It was as if, in an instant, they were at one, and Marcy felt that she had fallen in love. Almost dumbstruck by her emotions and the ecstatic and highly energizing connection, Marcy felt excited yet deeply peaceful at the same time.

"Call me Hank, please. May I call you Marcy?" the saintly man asked as he gently shut his pickup truck door.

Marcy couldn't help but blush: her cheeks became hot and pink with emotion.

"Yes," she said and giggled. "Uh, did I tell you my name?"

"Your Soul told me," Hank replied softly and smiled.

Again, Marcy blushed, her skin deepening to a darker shade of pink.

"Oh," she said, not quite knowing how to respond. Hank walked toward his trailer, and Marcy, almost in a daze from amazement over how wonderful she was feeling, followed. Hank paused on the step.

"How can I help you?" he asked gently.

"Oh... Uh, I want to interview you about your theorem and your... work," Marcy said, feeling totally flustered.

"I must shower and change clothes right now. Then I must speak with the people. I hope you don't mind waiting," Hank said with great love.

Hank reached out his hand to open the trailer door, and without touching it, the knob turned, and the door swung open, even as Hank continued to gaze into Marcy's eyes with great love. She was stunned by her experience with the man.

"I don't... mind," she replied. Then, as the door closed, her legs gave way from under her, and she sank on the steps. She sat, contemplated, and waited.

<hr>

ENRAPTURED, MARCY COULDN'T TAKE HER EYES OFF OF Hank as he faced an ecstatic crowd. Looking vibrant and dressed entirely in white, he paused as a flock of beautiful, shimmering butterflies floated towards the group. Marcy watched as they approached and then smiled peacefully as she noticed molecules of sunlight that shone like gold on the green of the beautiful glade.

She had never known a peace like this, she thought to herself as Hank spoke.

As she listened to his words, she realized that she didn't truly know what he was saying, yet what he seemed to be saying made absolute sense. Only hearing and understanding a word here and there, she soon realized that she wasn't listening with her ears and her mind; she was listening with her heart.

"When I-you-we be that, the mind moves into alignment with the truth of our own being..." she heard Hank say, as a soft breeze cooled all in attendance.

"When two or more are gathered... our true self..." she further heard as the flock of butterflies fluttered above and then landed on all who were present. "...Our Divine nature and the knowing I-you-we are one follows." The crowd sighed.

Even though her brain wasn't making sense of the words it was hearing, Marcy, and indeed everyone in attendance, was rapt and feeling enveloped by a magnificent outpouring of pure love energy from the highest realms.

Marcy gazed in wonder at an approaching butterfly. As if time had slowed down, she watched as it gently opened and closed its wings and then softly lit on her outstretched finger. Many butterflies still fluttered in the air, and countless more were resting on individual members of the group.

The swirl of flying, iridescent, shimmering hues and colors elicited joy, awe, and, for some, ecstasy among all those gathered.

MALLOW DWEEB SAT AT HIS OFFICE DESK, PLAYING A VIDEO game on a high-tech console. Daftbrood, Mallow Dweeb's superior, a pin-headed being from the planet Zon, exploded into Dweeb's office with two Zyborg Space Troopers following smartly behind him. Terrified, Dweeb shut off his game and stood.

"Daftbrood, sir. What's gone wrong?" Mallow Dweeb blurted out as he looked down at the tiny head of his superior.

At the push of a button on his handheld device, Daftbrood projected a holographic image of an upward curve increasing in height.

"This! This is what is wrong!" shrieked Daftbrood, his high-pitched voice all the more terrifying because of his obvious rage.

Mallow Dweeb squinted at the image.

"Something's on an upward curve?" Mallow Dweeb inquired uncertainly.

"Not 'something,' you zitwit," Daftbrood yelled, "the consciousness of the farqing planet Earth!"

"The consciousness of the Earth, humanity, is... rising?" Mallow Dweeb gasped out.

"This projection, from your figures and research... indicates in the affirmative," Daftbrood said, his globular eyes narrowing in his tiny, squished-together face.

"The figures are wrong?" Mallow Dweeb said hopefully, "I can fix bad data," he said, not even allowing himself to think about any another possibility. It was improbable and entirely too appalling to contemplate that the data before them might actually be accurate.

"That would be a best case scenario," Daftbrood whinged and bared his extremely long, sharp teeth in a grimace that made Dweeb cringe and wobble.

"You will annex me if the figures are... incorrect?" Mallow Dweeb inquired, fearfully, yet fully cognizant of Zycorp regulations

Daftbrood flipped the device over and withdrew the hologram.

"Rising consciousness of the Earth has far-reaching consequences. You will be annexed if the problem, the data issue, remains. Fix it!" Daftbrood squeaked, his pinhead appearing to swell, his face increasingly scarlet.

Dweeb almost instinctively shielded his face, fearing that his boss's pinhead would actually pop.

"Yes, of course. I'll get... I will fix it," Mallow Dweeb said, practically groveling (which was ironic because he despised groveling and was known to throw anyone and everyone off the space rig before admitting that he was the one that had made a mistake. Yet here indeed was a mistake, which originated from his department, and there was no one to blame... except himself. He shuddered.

Daftbrood didn't bother to listen any further. He and the Zyborg Space Troopers stormed out, leaving Mallow Dweeb to deal with the fallout of the situation.

Daftbrood decided that he would deal with and fix the

problem immediately... and if it couldn't be fixed, he would... run away. He shuddered again.

On Main Street, in Oklahoma City, in the beautiful, rather flat state of Oklahoma, Beetle Blatt and Mantid sat parked in their vehicle.

From inside their RV, Blatt and Mantid watched a scant few automobiles and a small funeral procession pass by.

"Though I do not have feelings, Zibbie, except for the aforementioned love of your mind, I know that this occasion must be sad for the Cinderella princess," Mantid commented, almost sounding philosophical.

Beetle Blatt grunted. He really didn't know what to think or say.

Death, the nature of reality, consciousness, deep emotions, these were things he never thought about and had no opinion about.

When the last funeral procession vehicle passed by, Beetle Blatt pulled out behind it and followed it to the cemetery. When the first cars in the funeral procession reached the gates of a tiny cemetery, with a little stone chapel on its grounds, Blatt immediately parked on the street outside the gates.

Several cars were already parked on the side streets. The cemetery was small, and only the limo hearse entered the gates. It was parked beneath a solitary, green, shady tree. The driver, a man, a young woman, and two other people got out.

Blatt and Mantid watched the funeral from a distance. The young woman, a pretty, delicate blonde girl who could easily and did play Cinderella for a living, stood by the graveside. There were few attendees.

The RV was parked behind a VW Bug with California

plates, which had been parked there when they arrived. Blatt and Mantid got out and leaned against their vehicle, waiting idly in the early summer heat for the service to end.

When the funeral service finally ended, the few attendees departed. The blonde girl, who had been crying but now looked emotionally numb, walked past the limousine hearse she had arrived in and approached the parked Volkswagen Beetle.

Mantid stepped toward her. Startled, she looked up at the strange female.

"Human miss? Miss Cinderella?" Mantid softly inquired.

The blonde paused, confused and uncertain. "Yeah?" she asked.

"Please accept our condiments for the loss of the human life form," Mantid said.

"Thank you," the girl acknowledged. "But I think the word you meant to say is condolences," she said without malice, her red eyes swollen from earlier crying.

Despite his mix-up of words, Mantid's kindness had touched her heart; his unemotional, yet almost-seeming tender compassion was a source of comfort and had deeply affected her.

Beetle Blatt nudged Mantid, and the insect-like being, still disguised as a human female, spoke to the ethereal blonde girl again.

"The mathematician did not arrive?" Mantid inquired softly.

The girl looked between them, their RV, and the VW Bug, which was obviously her vehicle.

"No. I couldn't reach Hank, and, well, it happened so fast, and my father and he... well, you know how it is," the blonde said sadly.

As Mantid didn't understand what the human was saying, he was stuck desperately trying to find a rational response. He twitched awkwardly a bit in his human form, for no apparent reason that he could internally gauge.

"Well, you know it is," Beetle Blatt said, equally lost for a rational response and deciding to repeat the last words that the human spoke.

The aliens were truly at a loss for how to connect with this dreamy earth being, which they could not begin to understand. She was experiencing a tragic personal event, the effect on her being of which they could not begin to fathom.

The blonde was struck, however, by their strong and obviously caring outpouring of compassion, and she mistakenly perceived an unusual wisdom in Beetle Blatt's phrase. She stopped walking and looked straight into Beetle Blatt's eyes; then the girl grabbed his shoulders, which was actually terrifying to the alien.

"Yes. Yes. You know... it is what it is," she said. "It's horrible. It's life. It's death. It's the end and the beginning. It is what it is, and you know what it is," the young woman said and then hugged Beetle Blatt hard and began to sob.

Weeping loudly, her body shook with her inconsolable crying. Internally, Blatt was freaking the zarkwad out. Yet, he managed to control his urge to scream and run away and instead held the young lady and softly repeated: "It is what it is."

Mantid stood watching his companion with renewed love and appreciation.

What an amazing genius my good friend, Beetle Blatt, is, he thought to himself.

When the hug went on just a bit too long for his liking, Mantid's mood suddenly shifted to an unfamiliar feeling of mad, passionate insecurity and jealousy.

"At this time, don't you think we should convene with the Hank subject?" he asked as calmly as he possibly could, hiding that he was seething inside.

The beautiful, delicate blonde was now silent, her tears and emotion spent. She broke away from Beetle Blatt's embrace. Feeling serene, filled with a surprising peace, she soulfully watched an iridescent butterfly fly past. She rubbed her red, flushed face and wiped strands of her long blonde hair out of her eyes.

"Yes, I suppose we should," she then said, absentmindedly.

"You are too uncertain in your current emotional state to operate a vehicle," Beetle Blatt said. "Perhaps we should drive."

"Yes, perhaps you should," the young girl answered.

A MILLION STARS FILLED THE NIGHT SKY. HANK AND Marcy sat on the steps outside Hank's trailer. Marcy, silent, her expression sad, leaned against his shoulder.

"You could come with me," Hank said as he gazed into the distance, looking into a future that only he could see. "I'll be walking a fair part of the way and others will join me," he added. Marcy lifted her head.

"I like to walk," Marcy said, her face brightening.

"It's settled then," Hank said softly, his expression pure.

The telephone rang inside the trailer. "That's my sister. Be back in a bit," Hank said calmly and stood. Marcy looked up at him and watched as he left. Her expression said, "I'm totally devoted to you."

INSIDE THE RV, THE BLONDE TOOK A SEAT IN THE BACK.

"I need to call my brother," she said, "but my cell phone battery just died. You guys got a cell phone I could use?"

Mantid and Beetle Blatt looked at each other, each wondering what she might be referring to.

"We have the Star Spark Interstellar Communicator," Beetle Blatt answered, uncertainly, and looked at Mantid.

"I'll be real quick," the blonde said, not quite understanding what his concerns might be.

"Here it is," Mantid said, giving her a high-tech device that actually did rather resemble an Earth cellular phone.

"Press red button for Interstellar communication, green button for terrestrial," he added helpfully.

"What now?" she said, not recognizing any of the weird buttons. She stared down at the device, confused by the button symbols that resembled both Egyptian hieroglyphs and mathematical symbols.

"Press the green button and say the person's name three times," Beetle Blatt suggested.

"Oh, guys, this is no time for—" she said, but was interrupted.

"The device will find the recipient by their frequency," Mantid added quickly.

The young woman looked at the earnest expressions on their faces and then decided, What the heck.

"Hank Walsh, Hank Walsh, Hank Walsh," the blonde said, after hitting the green button. Looking at the two aliens, she waited, curious to know exactly what the punch line of their joke was going to be.

"Hello?" a masculine voice emanated from the communication device. She looked down at the mechanism in her hand.

"Is that you, Monique?" Freaked out beyond belief, Cinderella almost jumped out of her skin.

"Hank?" she asked into the device.

"Hello, baby sister," Hank said softly.

"Oh, Hank. I'm so glad to hear your voice. It's Daddy, Hank.

He passed," she said, and turning away for greater privacy, she listened to Hank speak.

"He is? You are?" the blonde said and was quiet again. "That's wonderful. Yes, I'll see you there. I love you, too, Hank," she said and paused. "Bye," she added softly, as she lowered the device from her ear.

"You won't believe it. He said Daddy is in a better place and that he loves me. Hank wants me to meet him in New York... in three days," the blonde said and wiped away a tear.

Beetle Blatt and Mantid exchanged a look: where or what is New York, they each wondered.

"This is like the coolest cell phone ever. What is this? This must be at least 6G or 7. I guess you geeky math guy scientists have some cutting-edge devices," the blonde said. Then she handed the machine back to Mantid.

Unsure of her question, Beetle Blatt decided that he would again answer her with her own last words of the question.

"At least," he said with a straight face as Mantid admired the amazing ingenuity of his buddy.

HANK OPENED THE TRAILER DOOR AS MARCY MADE ROOM for him to come out and sit beside her again. She smiled up at him.

"My sister's going to meet us in New York," Hank said.

Marcy nodded, and they sat in silence for a while. Looking at the stars and listening to the music of the night, the sound of insects, frogs, tiny reptiles, and mammals rustling in the cool evening air made them feel very close to each other.

After a moment, Marcy stood, her hand held gently in Hank's own, then spoke:

"I'll be back around—"

"Six A.M.," Hank finished her sentence for her, and she smiled.

"Six A.M.," she repeated, deeply peaceful and radiant.

N AND N2 DROVE SLOWLY THROUGH A LOS ALAMOS trailer park. They pulled up outside a mobile home surrounded by rusted old vehicles and other items in various stages of disrepair in the yard.

"What about this one, N?" N2 asked, "Does it look familiar... or not?"

"Not," N said, shaking his head.

"Hank's domicile seemed smaller. His tin box had no art installation in the yard," N commented, as he surveyed the rusted metal and debris, mistaking it for art. "Let us keep looking, dude," he said

They backed out the pink caddy and continued driving.

"That was no art installation," N2 said.

"What else could it be?" N asked.

"They were priceless antiques... some kind of display," N2 stated. N rolled his eyes, then laughed.

"You think you're the expert on everything human, don't you, Elvis?" he teased.

N2 grunted in irritation.

N surveyed the other trailers, most every mobile home had something old and rusty dumped in their yard.

"This is probably museum row. Look at all the priceless relics!" N said and turned his face away, so that N2 wouldn't see his wide grin.

"Over there. That's the trading post that Hank gets his beer cans and other sustenance items from," N2 said, bouncing with excitement. N parked the car outside the familiar convenience store. It was strange to be in the place they had observed on screen multiple times.

As they entered, they smiled with recognition. "Beer," N2 pointed out.

"Beef jerky," N said and pointed as they stood just inside the door. Observing them from behind the counter was the Native American store clerk.

"He looks larger in person," N whispered to N2.

"It's strange, but I feel like I know him," N2 whispered to N, as they smiled at the clerk who stood waiting to ring up any purchases they might wish to make.

"I know! Me too," N whispered to N2.

The Native American clerk simply stared at the guys and took them in stride. They were sure an odd-looking pair, he decided. Something was not quite right about those two. Well, we get all kinds here, he thought to himself.

***

SITTING IN THEIR FORMER CUBICLE, MALLOW DWEEB watched the scene with N and N2 unfold on the screen. Sensing something peculiar about the two beings on screen, Dweeb instructed the computer to do a biological analysis of the shoppers.

When the digital holographic results revealed a DNA match for N and N2, Dweeb's facial expression was one of utter astonishment.

"Idiots!" he snarled and keyed in some commands, bringing up another screen. He watched Beetle Blatt driving the RV with Mantid in the back and the blonde up front. She seemed fascinated by the intricate dashboard of their fancy vehicle.

"It's so nice of you guys to give me a ride," the blonde said. "So, are you guys married?"

"Married?" Beetle Blatt asked with obvious disgust.

"Just dating?" the blonde asked, sheepishly.

"You mean, as in... making sex?" Blatt almost screamed with revulsion. Mantid giggled nervously.

"Hey, none of my business, sorry I asked," the blonde said, irked by Beetle Blatt's shrieking and sudden negative mood swing.

"Let's have some music," she said quickly and pressed a button on the dash, assuming it was a radio power button. She didn't notice, but as a result, the roof became invisible and a compartment above opened. An object that appeared to be a nuclear warhead swiveled and pointed skyward.

"Don't touch the controls!" Beetle Blatt screamed. Monique stared in surprise as Beetle Blatt depressed the button to off. Still staring at Beetle Blatt, in shock at his apparent rudeness, she was oblivious as the warhead retracted above her, the compartment closing. And the roof became visible and opaque, once again.

"Forgive his crazy," Mantid hurriedly said as the blonde giggled nervously, unsure how to react.

"We do not appreciate human music. It disgusts the ears," Mantid explained.

"You don't like music? Where are you guys from? Outer space?" the blonde joked.

Blatt turned a different dial, and weird, atonal sounds emitted from the speakers. It was Schumann resonances (SR), a set of spectrum peaks in the extremely low-frequency (ELF) portion of the Earth's electromagnetic field spectrum, and Mantid immediately began to groove to it. He moved rhythmically.

"Of course we like music," said Beetle Blatt, contradicting his buddy.

"Just not all the time. Many humans do not like music all

the time," Beetle Blatt said. "This is a tune that is a pleasure to our... ears." Blatt frowned, thinking about how many beings lacked ears and didn't hear yet, instead, felt frequencies. Yet, the limitations of human language didn't make sense in the context of non-terrestrial anatomy, at least for many beings.

"Is that, like Mozart?" the blonde asked, with obvious dislike.

"It is Schumann... the, uh, resonances," Mantid replied.

"Never heard of it," the blonde said as she covered her ears. The music and the whole scene were just too weird for her.

"You will like it more and more with experience," Mantid assured her.

"Sure. Cool. Maybe it's too much trouble for you guys to drive me all the way to the Big Apple. Do you wanna drop me at the nearest bus station?" she asked, suddenly no longer certain about taking a cross-country road trip with these two.

N AND N2 PULLED UP OUTSIDE OF HANK'S TRAILER. Smiling with recognition, they both pointed at Hank's familiar abode.

"That's Hank's domicile!" N said.

"We found the Hank human! What next?" N2 asked.

"We will take the subject, Hank, and return to the space station to make a deal with Zycorp," N stated calmly.

"But the spaceship is broken," N2 pointed out helpfully.

"The Hank human will fix it," N retorted.

"Another problem is that we do not know where the spaceship is," N2 said.

"He will help us find it," N said flatly.

"So we really need the Hank human," N2 said, stating the obvious. N stared at his clone, unsure if he liked the human body his clone was cloaked in, as he couldn't easily read its expression.

"Correct," said N finally. "The Hank human will solve all our problems," he added and sighed, hoping that it would happen exactly that way.

"Good plan. Do we go now?" N2 said. N looked at the quiet trailer over and thought hard.

"Because his wheels are not here, it means that the Hank human has not come back from work and so therefore is not inside," he reasoned.

"So we do not go in?" N2 asked, shifting in his seat.

"No. We wait for him to return home," N said with a great deal of satisfaction.

"Peace and happiness are within our grasp?" N2 asked.

"Essentially, the restoration of our normal lives, and very likely a big promotion, is now within reach," N said, smiling, "So, we wait."

"Not quite sure of N's logic, N2 nevertheless agreed, and they both settled in their seats to watch and wait for Hank to, at some point, come home.

What the two aliens, masquerading as the humans named Elvis and Marilyn, did not know was that at that very moment, Hank and Marcy were long gone. Already on their way, they were driving east in Hank's pickup truck.

The beatific man and his female companion sang joyfully to a song on the radio, their packed bags stowed in the rear behind their seats, as they headed for New York.

ATTEMPTING TO FOCUS ON DRIVING, BEETLE BLATT TRIED to hide his disgust as the blonde incessantly talked and used the

Starrv passenger seat sun visor mirror to apply her make-up. Utterly bored, Mantid stared at the vehicle ceiling.

Inane pop music now played, obviously the blonde's choice, as her MP3 player was plugged into the dashboard audio input.

Mantid, in the back, was quite obviously equally repulsed, the music and the sound of her voice piercing his brain.

"So I was all, 'Don't touch the princess. Where does it say that it's okay to touch the princess?' And then he was all, 'But you're so pretty, baby. You've got such pretty blue eyes.' Then he kept petting my hair, like I was his dog. Have you guys ever heard such bull shit?" she asked.

"Not such bull shit, ever," Mantid agreed, looking like he was losing his mind.

Then, for no apparent reason, other than he was actually losing his mind, he guffawed loudly. Har, har, har... Mantid's human laugh was totally unlike his natural clicking-type laugh, and yet something about it was evocative of his actual natural laughter. Hearing Mantid laugh made Beetle Blatt laugh as well.

"Not such bull shit, ever," Beetle Blatt repeated as he and Mantid exchanged a meaningful look in the RV rear-view mirror. Then they both laughed some more.

Unsure if they were commiserating or making fun of her, the blonde rolled her eyes: these guys are just so utterly weird, she thought.

They drove for hours, Beetle Blatt fantasizing about the moment when they would reach their destination. He almost regretted not letting her take the bus. The pleasurable fantasy made him think that he now understood the expression:

"I could have died from happiness."

He reminded himself that they would soon be free of her. The thought made him smile. Then he had a new thought. They would soon be free of her unless the blonde's non-stop talking drove him and Mantid both out of their minds first. That terrible thought made him frown.

"It wasn't always my dream to be a princess. Well, in real life it was, I mean, how fun would that be? Right?" she said and laughed. To Mantid, her laughter was more donkey-like, a hee-haw, than the bell-like tones one would expect a feminine Earthling creature to make. She checked her makeup for the umpteenth time and fluffed her hair a bit, and then opened her oversized handbag.

Rummaging through the eclectic assortment of the contents of her bag, she pulled out a large metal spray can. Mantid looked at the can nervously. Was she on to them? Was she going to use some unknown human technology to disarm, change, or otherwise affect the two of them, he wondered. Blatt also observed her. She seemed entirely uninterested in the two of them, so it was possibly another of her grooming devices, he decided.

The blonde removed the metal spray can cap and sprayed her hair with a misty, noxious hair product. The chemicals were so repugnant to the disguised aliens that they immediately began to turn light purple, and bulbous, red pustules formed on their exposed skin. The more she sprayed, the more they coughed and choked on the toxic fumes. Mantid, being thin and small, was deeply affected.

In desperation, Beetle Blatt pulled out the RV's first-aid kit and quickly tossed it to Mantid. The being disguised as a human riffled through the items inside and finally found a device that might help. Its label claimed "protection from the noxious pollution of any planet." He held it up and showed it to Beetle Blatt.

Mantid quickly opened the device and shot one self-guiding caplet down his throat, which provided him immediate relief. He then shot another self-guiding caplet in Beetle Blatt's direction. The self-guiding caplet whirred around toward Blatt. As soon as he opened his mouth, it zoomed down his throat.

They instantly stopped coughing. The purple skin blotches on both their faces stopped forming, and existing ones slowly began to fade. Still staring into the visor mirror, the blonde was totally oblivious. She didn't at all notice that her riding companions had almost choked to death on her fumes. When she did turn to look at Blatt, she noticed his pustules, and as her eyes grew large, she gasped.

"Oh my gawd, what happened to your face?" she screeched.

"Adverse reaction from human food," Blatt said drily.

"Oh, yeah, spicy food does that to me too, and MSG makes me crazy," the blonde said and laughed loudly, then started in right where she had left off.

"Like I was saying, who doesn't want to marry a prince and live in a castle, maybe somewhere in the European Alps, pop out a few kids, topless summers on the Riviera. Know what I mean? We all want the fairy tale, right?" she mused aloud.

When they finally arrived at the bus station, despite it being at her request, the blonde now looked sad to be exiting the company of the aliens.

"I guess this is me," she said, barely moving.

Beetle Blatt stared ahead with resolve. No way was he going to allow this obnoxious human woman to remain in their midst one more second.

"Thanks for the ride, I guess," she said as she slowly opened the door.

"You are most welcome, Cinderella," Beetle Blatt said politely.

"Monique," the girl said. "You can call me Monique."

"Have a nice day, Monique," Mantid said, forcing a polite smile.

Monique finally left their vehicle and walked sadly towards

the depot. She turned to wave one last time, but the two disguised aliens pretended not to see her. Heaving huge sighs of relief, they watched her enter the building.

"What a sad excuse for an organism," Mantid stated.

"I totally understand why everyone hates humans," Beetle Blatt added.

"Talk, talk, talk..." Mantid said.

"About nothing!" Beetle Blatt said disparagingly.

"And what about those disgusting smells she put on her skin?" Mantid asked.

"Could you believe what she was putting on herself? All those chemical toxins? Entirely disgusting," Beetle Blatt said.

"If she hates herself so much, she should just stab herself in the soft part of her anatomy with a big, sharp, rusty food preparation implement. Am I right or am I right?" Mantid said.

Beetle Blatt laughed hysterically even as he noticed that Mantid's conversational skills had advanced considerably in the company of their recent human companion.

"You know, many times I had to restrain myself from hitting the ejector button? Twenty-seven times! Twenty-seven fobbing times!" Beetle Blatt stated.

"You are a saint, Zibbie," Mantid said and grinned slyly, his expression making him look remarkably like his normal alien self. "A saint."

N AND N2 SAT WAITING AND WATCHING FROM THEIR PINK Caddy, parked outside of Hank's trailer. In contrast to N, who was looking quite calm but was really bored out of his mind, N2 looked extremely anxious and fidgeted in his seat.

"How much longer?" he inquired, and it was clear by his tone that this was a question he'd already asked more than once.

"Subject normally returns home at dark," N stated, "We have observed him many times, remember?"

N2 reflected upon N's words and nodded his agreement.

"That is true. Or sometimes earlier," N2 agreed.

"You must stop arguing with me, N2. I am right. You will see. We wait for the Hank subject to show up," N said firmly. N2 shrugged and avoided N's eyes.

N2 had noticed that Marcy's SUV was parked nearby, yet he knew that if he mentioned it, then N would get angry. Then, most likely, he would explain why her parked SUV was of no importance.

N2 decided, therefore, that it was better to let N discover the fact himself. If the existence of the vehicle was a vital clue that the couple were missing, well, then it was N's own mistake, and he'd have to admit, for once, that he was wrong.

N2 had noticed the Earthling woman's vehicle right away, and he fretted about why Marcy's SUV would be parked beside Hank's trailer. She told them that she wanted to find Hank for an article she was writing for her magazine. Perhaps she was interviewing him in a private setting. Perhaps the meeting between the two of them had turned into more than an interview. Maybe they would mate and live a dream life together.

N2 wondered if and when he might meet his own "dream girl."

If they were forever marooned on earth, he realized that whoever his future dream girl might be, she would obviously have to be human. The only place that humans seemed to fall in love with alien-looking people was, coincidentally, the happiest place on earth, a place he longed to visit, Disney World. N2 decided that he would visit Disney World if it were the last thing he did on this planet.

Then he gazed with wonder at this small part of planet Earth: the plants and trees, the sky, and the distant mountains.

As a peace descended upon him, he sat back patiently and waited for N to figure it all out.

———

HANK AND MARCY PULLED OFF THE ROAD AND PARKED outside a roadside diner. Motorcycles jammed the parking lot. The couple made their way between them and entered the diner, which was quite busy. Most of the patrons were bikers, and Hank and Marcy looked oddly out of place as they sat in a red vinyl booth.

"What do you feel like eating?" Marcy asked.

"Something vegan or vegetarian feels right," Hank replied blissfully.

"Good luck," Marcy said, her voice devoid of sarcasm, as she noticed that the menu was mostly comprised of meat dishes.

A tired and cynical older waitress, her long grey hair braided into two buns, one on either side of her head, came to take their order.

"What can I get ya?" she asked mechanically.

"Do you have anything vegan or vegetarian?" Marcy asked.

The waitress almost sniggered.

"Got what's on the menu. If it ain't there, we don't got it, sugar," she answered. Her words were pleasant enough, yet her tone was not. Marcy noticed that something about the way that she said "sugar" made it sound like a swear word or some kind of slur. Marcy shrugged. People are needlessly nasty, she thought.

Marcy looked again at the menu and then smiled kindly at the waitress.

"What would you recommend?" Marcy asked.

"You look like you could use a steak, Twiggy," the waitress said and laughed. "We got steak and eggs, with toast and taters on the side."

"Oh, I don't think a steak..." Marcy said, and her voice trailed off as she looked over the menu and tried to find another alternative.

The waitress then turned to Hank. As soon as their eyes met, the waitress's expression instantly softened, and she smiled. Her demeanor changed so much and so quickly that she almost looked like a different person.

"What would you like to eat, sweetie?" she said sweetly to Hank.

"What I would really like to eat is not listed on the menu, I'm afraid," Hank said, looking up at her.

"Tell me what you want and I'll see what I can do," the waitress said softly.

Marcy looked up in shock, disarmed by the woman's change in attitude.

"Okay. How about a nice green salad with spinach, lettuce, and cucumber on a bed of sprouts, accompanied by some beans and coleslaw? No dressing," Hank said carefully as if he were describing something beloved.

"If it makes you happy, I'll go into the fields and pick 'em myself," the waitress replied as if she meant every word. Marcy stared at the woman, stunned.

As the waitress turned to walk away, Marcy called after her. "I'll have the same, please," she said, hoping that the woman had heard, since the waitress didn't turn or otherwise indicate recognition of Marcy's request.

MANTID DROVE WITH BEETLE BLATT IN THE PASSENGER seat. They closely followed Monique's bus east through Arkansas.

"That's the most insane transport I have ever seen," Beetle

Blatt said as he watched the plumes of dark exhaust spew from its tailpipe. "Just look at the noxious fumes spewing from the people mover."

"My brain is so stimulation starved, I've had to reboot it three times," Mantid said with an expression meant to indicate great sadness.

"Earthlings are so primitive, they still use internal combustion engines," Beetle Blatt announced as if he were revealing a shocking personal habit.

"What's combustion engine?" Mantid said.

"They mix air with ancient fossils and spark an explosion that powers metal rods, which turn the wheels," Beetle Blatt replied.

Mantid, bemused, thought that Beetle Blatt was joking.

"Not, seriously?" Mantid said. He was certain that Blatt would tell him he was attempting a joke, perhaps a form of human humor.

"Seriously," Beetle Blatt said.

Har, har, har. Mantid burst into laughter, and soon Beetle Blatt was laughing too. Then Mantid looked over at Beetle Blatt.

"Not such bull shit, ever," Mantid said, and Beetle Blatt got the joke. They both snorted and burst out laughing, almost unable to stop.

Inside the roadside diner, Hank enjoyed an enormous plate of green salad while Marcy struggled to cut and eat her way through a huge steak and finally gave up. Hank put some salad on a bread plate and gave it to Marcy.

Some biker dudes, really rough-looking with piercings, tattoos (possibly gang tats, in black and red, with lots of symbols, including crosses, roses, snakes, and blood drops), kept looking at Hank. When one of them made what was obviously a snide comment, the others laughed. Marcy was more than a little nervous about their interest.

"Your salad's getting attention," Marcy said quietly.

"It's probably the first plate of green food ever served here. Bound to attract some attention," Hank said kindly. He looked over at them and smiled kindly.

As if feeling insulted by his glance, or perhaps merely waiting for an excuse, three of the bikers stood up and stepped in the direction of Hank and Marcy's table. Marcy kept her eyes on her plate, terrified of what was about to take place.

"Hey, mister, what's that you're eatin'?" one of the dudes said.

"It's a green salad," Hank said, his voice filled with kindness.

"We saw it come out and figured that it must be for your horse," another of the biker dudes said and looked suggestively at Marcy. She blushed, turning bright red, and pushed her plate back. Marcy began to feel ill.

The biker dudes laughed meanly until Hank stood and looked them each straight in the eyes. Taken aback by his audacity, they stood closer in order to stare him down. As if his eyes were emitting a bright light that they could barely bear to look at, one glance into his gaze was enough to change them instantly.

"I don't own a horse," Hank said, his voice brimming with great love.

The biker dudes stood stunned and disorientated. They didn't respond, but neither did they go away. They were, apparently, speechless.

"Is everything okay here? Would you like to sit with us?" Hank asked.

The biker dudes seemed to thaw; they softened and smiled amicably. One of them quickly extended his hand.

"Name's Billy Joe. This here is Joey and Bobby Rose. Pleased to meetcha," the biggest, bawdiest, most tattooed and hairiest of the men said.

"Hank," Hank said and gently took the man's giant paw in his own. The men all shook Hank's hand with genuine admiration.

"It's a fine pleasure to meet you," said Joey, a swarthy, short biker, as he took Hank's hand in his.

"Hey, everybody!" Billy Joe shouted to the rest of the diners.

The entire restaurant fell quiet and looked on. Terror struck the faces of some non-biker patrons, especially those who appeared elderly, as if they sensed that something bad was about to happen.

"Ya'll come on over here and meet our new friend, Hank," Billy Joe said with a big, genuine smile. Marcy's mouth fell open, and she gaped, stunned by the turn of events.

With great relief, the non-biker other patrons went back to eating their meals, and soon the place was filled with the normal sounds of a packed afternoon diner.

All the bikers in the place got up from their seats and lined up to shake Hank's hand. Marcy stared in awe, as she had never seen anything quite like the effect that Hank seemed to have on people of all types. There seemed to be no one, rich, poor, or otherwise, who didn't appear to feel touched by him in some way.

SITTING INSIDE THEIR PINK CADDY, N AND N2 STARED fixedly at Hank's trailer.

"Perhaps the Hank human did not leave the tin box today,

after all. He could still be inside, perhaps watching TV or drinking some beer," N2 said, not meaning a word of it. He didn't want N to fall into a deep depression over his mistake.

"Hank human is not in his home," N said sadly.

"How can you be so sure?" N2 asked.

"His wheels are not to be seen," N said.

"So, the Hank human is located wherever the truck vehicle is located?" N2 asked.

"Always," N said.

"Perhaps he took his truck vehicle somewhere else?" N2 said.

"Since coming to earth and changing into this body, my logic has been blemished," N said, sadder than ever, "My brain may be deteriorating."

Unsure of how to respond or what to say to cheer his buddy up, they sat together quietly. N2 noticed how striking the light was, as it changed when the sun set in the sky and the twinkling light of the distant stars began to appear. He truly found planet Earth quite beautiful.

"It is peaceful here," N2 commented. "We are making good memories."

"Yes, yes, we are." N agreed as he too looked up at the sky and the dark silhouette of the mountains in the distance. "So peaceful and quiet," he acknowledged.

"And perhaps a complete waste of our time," N2 admitted.

"Yes. A total waste of time," N agreed and sighed.

"Those wheels belong to Marcy, remember?" N2 said as he pointed to Marcy's SUV, which was parked alongside the end of the road, closer to the mailbox. N stared in shock and then beat himself in the head and looked close to screaming.

"No, no, no, no, no," he yelled while punching himself in the face. "Stupid, stupid, stupid," he continued.

N2 grabbed N's fists in order to prevent him from harming himself.

"It's okay," N2 said. "It's all okay. It really is no biggie."

N2 pulled N into a bear hug as all the while N cried with rage, frustration, and self-awareness of how he, yet again, had harmed himself by insisting that he was correct... always, always correct. His face grew hot, apparently a physical reaction in his human body, as N realized that his obstinacy was mortifying.

Darkness had fallen outside, as inside, Hank and every single being in the diner—general customers, bikers, and staff—sang a heartfelt rendition of "We Are the World." Tears streamed down people's faces as their hearts opened with each word sung. Everyone present seemed to be uplifted to a place of transcendent love, peace, and harmony, a state they had never experienced before.

The more they sang together, the more everyone present felt deeply bonded to each other, as if they were all intimate travelers together on a journey through time.

Unbeknownst to the people singing, everyone present was changed, transformed in such a way that they would change others upon coming into contact with them. A vibration of uplifted consciousness, devotion, empathy, tranquility, and accord rippled outward from Hank, seeded in each Soul, and it seemed to be highly contagious.

Outside of the roadside diner, Hank and Marcy headed for the truck.

Bikers got on their bikes. Other people, including the waitresses and kitchen staff, got into their vehicles. Everyone moved together, in a group wave of movement, slowly as if with reverence and peace.

The stars seemed brighter, the night sky bluer; all reality seemed entirely rich and alive, with energy, with beauty, with the glory of something ecstatically Divine. Having secured Marcy into the passenger seat, Hank opened the driver-side door of his truck and waved goodbye to all.

"Good night, everyone," Hank called out as no one seemed in an actual hurry to leave.

"May the road rise up to meet you. May the wind be always at your back. May the sun shine warm upon your face; the rains fall soft upon your fields, and until we meet again, may God hold you in the palm of His hand," he said, reciting an old Irish blessing.

Tears in his eyes, the lead biker, Billy Joe, approached Hank. "You're not getting rid of us that easy, Hank. Where y'all headed?" he asked with great love.

"We're heading to New York to address the United Nations about forming a peaceful resolution to end all strife on earth and create a harmonious coexistence with all intelligent life forms in the galaxy," Hank said easily and naturally, as if he were certain that Billy Joe could and would understand every word. Judging by the earnest and compassionate expression on Billy Joe's face, he definitely did.

"Well, sign us up, bro. We're coming with ya and yer old lady," Billy Joe said and whooped aloud, meaning for all the bikers and their gals to join in, which they dutifully did. Marcy was startled by the instant camaraderie that developed between them.

Their voices were a wild cry of beauty, plaintive and deeply resonant, and the molecules in the air vibrated more and more rapidly.

Hank glowed with light and love, as did everyone present.

Hank smiled and touched Marcy's arm, checking in with

her. He knew that she was experiencing a unique heart opening herself. Almost unable to speak, she mouthed:

"Thank you so much," as tears of joy, past sadness and grief, and love streamed down her face. She was radiant, like everyone present, and beautiful.

Hank acknowledged her gratitude and turned back to Billy Joe.

"As you wish, my brother," Hank said to the biker, and smiled as Billy Joe threw his arms open and aloft, staring upward with his chin lifted in recognition of the Divine and those who wished to declare peace, love, and compassion among all beings.

In response, the bikers and others assembled raised their arms upward, looking to the sky, and made a group salute to peace, love, and all things holy.

Hank joined Marcy in the truck and cranked the vehicle. Soon, he pulled out onto the main road, followed by a huge, noisy gang of bikers. Riding in a tight-knit group, someone began singing, "We Are the World."

Pretty soon, others joined in, and others still expressed their collaborative contributions by adding their plaintive heart and Soul cries and wolf calls.

<hr>

THE SQUID-ALIEN MALLOW DWEEB WAS VISIBLY SHAKING with panic as he sat across from Daftbrood and some very scary-looking, high-level Zycorp officials. With the aid of a multi-dimensional media presentation, Dweeb explained the situation.

"So you see..." he said, pointing to an upward increasing red line on the graph, "...the evidence shows that one or more Zycorp employees interfered with human consciousness."

"Your employees, meaning subordinates, you mean," Daftbrood clarified.

"Yes," Mallow Dweeb admitted, swallowing hard. "Technically, ex-employees, as their current status is classified as criminal-to-be-iced-on-sight renegades."

"But you have told your employees never to interfere, correct?" Daftbrood continued, as he paced menacingly before Dweeb. "That if you interfere in the life of one human, you interfere in the lives of all?"

"Yes, of course. Standard Zycorp policy," responded Dweeb, "I've explained the ripple effect of consciousness to them many, many times and they do know Zycorp Reg. inside and out."

"Tell me, Dweeb," Daftbrood asked, leaning his massive face down to within inches of Mallow Dweeb's face, "How do we fix this?"

"It's quite simple, actually. If we take out the corrupted human, we can stop the ripple effect in its tracks. We destroy the contaminated human, retrieve and return with the QMJ so that no further contamination can take place," Dweeb answered, trying not to soil his pants.

"Very well, then," reasoned Daftbrood. "Fix it."

Looking extremely agitated and perplexed, Mallow Dweeb leaned back a little to give himself a little more personal space. He wiped his brow of green sweat.

"It will mean sending someone to the Earth planet," he concluded.

"That's right," Daftbrood nodded and, much to Mallow Dweeb's relief, stood upright again. Mallow Dweeb knew what Daftbrood was suggesting but he knew that he still had to ask.

"Me? You want me to go to planet Earth?" he nervously enquired.

"Or be annexed! Your choice," Daftbrood bellowed.

Despite Mallow Dweeb's intense internal panic, he knew

best not to argue or find fault with Daftbrood's logic. Cleaning up after yourself, especially if you'd made a mess, was the Zycorp way, after all. Quickly collecting his things, he headed to the door.

"Sure. No problem. Consider it done," Dweeb said as he was leaving.

As Mallow Dweeb exited, Daftbrood turned to his superior, Yikeshifter, a spiky, gelatinous being, for further instructions.

"Prepare for invasion," Yikeshifter demanded.

"Will we wipe out all of humanity, or will this be a partial cleansing?" Daftbrood asked happily and smiled, ready to be done with the lot of humanity.

"If their consciousness rises much more, every bleeding heart intergalactic liberal will cry to the council to save them. So we need to make some hard decisions, right now," Yikeshifter said as he looked to his alien business advisor, Bizgrate.

"We've pretty much milked humanity dry, really. It's hard to find pure specimens. Their actions have contributed to the planet's pollution to the extent that it has become almost uninhabitable. As a failed species, they don't have much time left, in any event. We could probably call it a loss," Bizgrate advised.

Yikeshifter looked to his furry bug-eyed alien legal advisor, Legalyeti.

"As we hold the patents for most of the lifeforms, it means that, for now, at least, we can do whatever we wish. We could even annihilate them and still legally retain the planet's air, water, and mineral rights, and the rights to any useful debris," Legalyeti said.

"So, we could cleanse the earth of their kind, entirely," Yikeshifter summed up, "Before the Arcturians or anyone else can stop us and tie the humans and their planet up in their bleeding heart peace marches, prayer vigils, or litigation."

As no one disagreed, Yikeshifter's face broke out in a broad smile. The others joined in, and soon they were all making blood-curdling alien war cries and engaging in other grotesque group-bonding acts of warrior-like excitement.

———

Zoom! Zoom! A sleek, shiny Starvette shot out of the docking bay and smoothly entered space. From inside the craft, Mallow Dweeb watched behind him as the space rig rapidly diminished in size.

Soon, it disappeared completely, in a flash of light, as his vehicle accelerated to warp speed.

Mallow Dweeb had no recent memories of being out of his offices, never mind being off the space rig, and he stared with fascination as outside his window a sea of white stars turned blue and elongated strangely as the Starvette streaked towards them. The stars turned gold in color as the Starvette moved through them and made the jump. He shuddered with horror at the excitement of it all.

As if the extraordinary change of environment and the abject vastness and loneliness of space affected his hippocampus and the more primitive areas of his brain, Mallow Dweeb began to cry and sob hysterically.

"I hate field work," he said out loud, "I hate, hate, hate fobbing field work!"

He had no clue that he was being sent on a fool's errand to a planet whose primary inhabitants were designated to be destroyed en masse.

———

News of the impending strike on Earthlings spread quickly throughout the galactic grapevine. In the grand meeting room of the Arcturian monitoring space station, a few hundred highly disturbed, higher-level, gentle, petite, and slender horse-like Arcturian beings gathered for an emergency meeting.

Acting chairman Lanzilott stood up before the assembled and waited for their full attention before sadly announcing his distressing news.

"Fellow Arcturians, we have news that the Zeta Reticuli Zycorp corporation plans to annihilate Earthlings. We must use every resource at our disposal to prevent this atrocious and egregious ethnic cleansing from taking place."

Rumblings of discord and dissent echoed throughout the vast room as many of the assembled whispered to their colleagues, and some smaller groups broke off into side discussions of their own. The Arcturian Commander-in-Chief, responsible for the military forces, stood up and pressed his talking light stick for permission to speak, which was immediately granted.

"Should we assemble and arm the space fleet?" he asked sadly, military action being a last resort for these diminutive and slender horse-like beings.

"Absolutely, we must," replied the chairman, without hesitation.

At the news of the Zeta Reticuli Zycorp corporation's plan to destroy the human race, high-level Lyrian beings gathered in their space station. They were orbiting planet Zxtet14, researching to understand how some mysterious, cosmic force was depleting the planet's oxygen levels.

"We must make our move and send a military fleet to Earth!" the chairman of the Lyrian heads of state and the top chiefs of staff declared, and in response, received shouts of excitement and war dances of approval from all gathered.

Higher-level Zeta Reticuli were the only race of beings that did not hold an emergency meeting. As a known warrior race and the originators of the plan to annihilate the objects of their financial interest on earth, they did not need to vote.

"Deploy all battle ships to Earth. First war, then spoils!" was the message that scrolled across every room, docking pad, and corridor of their space station.

<hr>

INSIDE THEIR COZY LITTLE PINK CADDY, N AND N2 WOKE up after falling asleep on their stake-out. It was morning. They both looked towards the trailer simultaneously. N was terribly disappointed to see that Hank had not returned. N2 rubbed his sore neck, and his stomach growled with pain due to a lack of food.

"My body needs fuel," N2 said, stretching his neck. N thought for some time.

"All right," N finally decided, "Let's go to the tin box and look for clues."

As they walked to the front door, N2 quickly noticed a note that was taped to the doorbell. "Would this be a clue?" he asked.

N grabbed the handwritten note but couldn't understand what was written on it. "It's a handwritten note in English cursive," he said.

"You know how to read English cursive?" N2 asked, impressed.

"No, of course not," N replied. Removing a tiny Zycorp Knife from his pocket, he selected "Translate" and scanned the document. The tiny gadget translated the note aloud in an androgynous computer voice:

"Gone to the UN building in New York to bring at-oneness to the world's superpowers. Love and blessings, Hank."

"This explains why the Hank subject's earth vehicle hasn't been here for these past 38 hours," N2 deduced.

"Where is New York?" asked N, looking desperately all around him.

"It can't be very far," N2 reasoned, in an attempt to reassure him. "That truck vehicle of Hank's didn't appear that it could last for more than two clicks."

SOMEWHERE OUT IN THE VASTNESS OF EAST TEXAS, HANK drove his truck, followed by a sea of bikers and a mixed cortege of other vehicles. Smoke spiraled from the hood as Hank's truck finally came to an abrupt stop. Hank waved off the smoke coming from the engine through the dashboard vents and turned off the ignition.

"This truck has given great service but wishes to go no further," he said calmly to Marcy. She grinned at his continuing equanimity.

"Is this the part where you say, 'Let's walk?'" she asked, smiling.

"Not yet," Hand said, smiling broadly and mischievously, "First... We ride!"

Hank and a few bikers helped to push the trunk safely onto the shoulder of the road. Marcy and Hank then climbed onto the back of one of the bikers' bikes. As they pulled out onto the deserted road, Hank looked joyful.

"Don't you just love the open road?" he shouted to Billy Joe.

"I live to ride, man. Live to ride!" Billy Joe replied as he peeled out, leaving rubber and, with a wave of his arm, led the huge biker posse heading east.

In deep and deserted space, light years from Earth's solar system, a large Arcturian spaceship armada headed towards the Orion-Cygnus arm of the Milky Way, en route to Earth.

In another part of deep and deserted space, a fleet of Zeta Reticuli spaceships headed towards the Orion-Cygnus arm of the Milky Way, en route to Earth.

In yet another deep and deserted region of space, a Lyrian spaceship armada headed towards the Orion-Cygnus arm of the Milky Way, en route to Earth.

Mallow Dweeb orbited past the moon as his tiny commuter Starvette approached earth's outer atmosphere. Inside the craft, Mallow Dweeb continued his crying and whining fit, as if he were a female minor Zyturd from the Xlich-tock galaxy (who were famed for their annoyingly immature histrionics and drama).

"I hate danger," he sobbed out loud, "I simply detest it!" To take his mind off things, he turned on the TV, which, at this far-out reach of the galaxy, had but one channel transmitting. On the screen was a multi-ethnic Alien reporter whose scales, large and garish snout, complete with tentacles galore, made Dweeb want to vomit. He'd never get work for a real TV station, Dweeb thought to himself.

"Tensions, concerning the fate of earthlings, heat up as competing interested parties vie for power, control, and dominance over their potential usefulness and possible annihilation," the Ashtag alien reported in a monotone voice.

"Mother of Reptilia," Dweeb shouted at his TV, "Yet another meaningless intergalactic war and I'm headed right into the middle of it."

Mallow Dweeb cried for several minutes, certain that he had been duped and punished, by being sent to planet earth.

"I don't want to be extinguished!" I'm too young to exit and not old enough to evade the draft, which is sure to follow, Dweeb considered to himself.

"I hate fieldwork!" he then shouted so loudly that his words seemed to reverberate throughout the darkness and emptiness of space.

A TV NEWS REPORTER, A PETITE, WELL-GROOMED brunette, Jill Chaves, positioned herself in front of the UN building in New York. Listening into her earpiece, she began her report the moment her producer's count-down came through.

"I'm standing outside the United Nations building where, in eighteen hours, an unprecedented meeting of the world's nations will meet to discuss the possible existence of, wait for it... Extraterrestrials. Do they really exist? Is it possible that we are not alone in the universe? Over to you, Lawrence."

In the broadcasting studio, Lawrence Feringold, a very handsome blonde gay male, sat behind a news desk and addressed the camera.

"Thank you, Jill. Martians, ETs, aliens... whatever you want to call them, up to now, they have only existed in movies. Well, thanks to a janitor working at a military research facility, the world's major leaders are starting to take the topic seriously," he said and smiled, revealing an impressive set of chops.

Beside Lawrence sat another reporter, Jen. Taking her cue, she took up the story.

"Why are the world's leaders listening to a humble janitor,

you may ask? This broom pusher is no ordinary custodian. Meet Hank Weber..."

The large screen behind her showed various mixed footage of Hank.

In one sequence, he shook hands with large crowds in the desert. He poured water from a clear glass pitcher into a glass. It seemed that he was turning water into wine, as it became red as soon as it hit the glass. In other shots, people carried sick and wounded people to him as he raised his hands before them and, in practicing the laying on of hands, the sick and wounded were healed, and the lame got up and walked. Hank smiled a beatific smile as if he loved both the world and everything living upon it.

"To many, Hank himself has become an emerging world leader, and it's his mathematical theorem, which allegedly proves the existence of other intelligent life in the universe, that has catapulted him to fame," Jen continued her report.

"And his fame is growing," said Lawrence, tag-teaming the report, "Some people go so far as to claim that they witnessed the man actually resurrect two people, who were allegedly fatally injured in an auto accident."

The screen behind showed cell phone footage with the words, "BYSTANDER FOOTAGE" flashing obliquely. On screen, Hank approaches a terrible road accident where two people lie motionless on the ground and appear dead. Laying his hands on the bodies, a bright light seemed to radiate from his hands and entire being. The light distorted the image, but as soon as Hank stood back, the two seemingly badly injured people got up, as if nothing had happened.

Confused, the two people expressed love and gratitude as crowds gathered alongside Hank and reacted to him with great awe and reverence.

"Whereas Hank Walsh will make history by giving the keynote address at the UN, and he's gotta be happy about that, not everybody is happy. His presence here in the city is causing headaches for local law enforcement," Jen added.

The screen showed recent footage of Hank walking with Marcy, being followed by his entourage of biker buddies, as well as huge and increasing crowds of reverent people who all seemed to be glowing with love. Behind the crowds came record numbers of law enforcement on foot, horseback, and bicycle.

"Hank has arrived, after walking to New York for several days now and, in the process, has attracted hundreds of thousands of followers who have all joined him on his trip. Mayor Cockburn has said that New York has never seen anything like this extraordinary event before," Lawrence said, ending the report.

On the outskirts of New York City, stuck in heavy traffic, N and N2 were getting nowhere fast in their spiffy pink caddy.

"Why does vehicular traffic pattern move on that side, but no vehicles move on this side?" N2 asked as they finally came to a complete stop. N didn't reply. Traffic was at a standstill for several minutes before N2 repeated his question.

"Let's get a look," N finally said. Getting out of the stopped vehicle, the two disguised aliens climbed up onto the hood. Looking as far forward as they could, all they managed to see was a huge backup of cars and, ahead of that, what looked like crowds of people walking, causing the maddening traffic jam.

Ahead, a multitude of people were walking with Hank and Marcy. Strangers approached Hank, shook his hand, and seemed instantly transformed into peaceful, harmonious humans. They acted and seemed like changed people, as if they were charged with some ineffable energy, a consciousness that rippled outward as the people all around them became more radiant and filled with love.

Standing on the hood of the hemmed-in and non-movable caddy, N and N2 considered their options. N finally got an idea. He looked at N2.

"For the rest of our journey, we must go on foot," N suggested.

The two of them dismounted from the hood of the car and began walking in the direction of the large, teeming mass of humanity.

MANTID SAT IN THE PASSENGER SEAT AND BABBLED ON about how strange the planet Earth was to him. Focused on his task, Beetle Blatt drove at a respectable distance behind the cross-country bus and nodded or grunted periodically in response.

"Just looking at all these horrible buildings, that don't even look like anything that nature would design, makes me question whether an individual mind is better than the hive mind, you know?" Mantid continued.

Looking to Beetle Blatt for a bigger response, disappointed Mantid, as Blatt merely stared ahead, his unblinking eyes fixed on the rear of the bus.

"It's almost as if the way they dress and everything the earthlings build is like a scream for attention, or possibly a desperate plea for help, don't you think?"

Again, Mantid looked to Beetle Blatt for a response that never came.

"Look at me, they all shout. Look at me, I'm an individual! A desperate entity," Mantid continued. "I did consider opting in with the hive-mind, you know?"

Much to Mantid's chagrin, Beetle Blatt continued to ignore his musings.

"Want to know why I decided not to opt in for the hive mind?" Mantid asked, almost pleading for a response. "I'll tell you why," Mantid said, deciding to answer himself. "Because those of my species that did opt in... they don't seem interesting or have very much to say, you know? I mean, in fairness, some of them weren't very interesting to begin with, but now not one of them can hold a decent conversation without repeating the party line, ad nauseum."

Again, Mantid looked to Blatt for some kind of acknowledgement that, again, was not forthcoming. Mantid felt extremely teary and couldn't identify why.

"Talk about boring!" Mantid continued, ten octaves of desperation entering his voice, "Of course, they don't think that they're being boring because if you're in the hive mind, you don't really think outside of the collective, right? But come on, eating the same food all the time, wearing the same uniform, the same routine every fobbing day... Beetle Blatt?" Mantid practically yelled, starving for his attention. Beetle Blatt didn't move, grunt, or otherwise acknowledge Mantid.

"Has your brain gone into sleep mode again?" Mantid asked, now realizing that Blatt hadn't blinked or moved his eyes in quite some time. "Slam!" Mantid shouted to himself, admonishing himself that he didn't realize it sooner.

Mantid climbed behind Beetle Blatt and positioned himself so that he could place his hands directly on Beetle Blatt's head.

"Be at peace, BB. I'm just searching around for your brain reset points, my dearest Zibbie," Mantid said, to all intents and purposes appearing to be a tiny, slender, female human caressing the other extraterrestrial. Mantid touched Beetle Blatt's head at three carefully selected acupuncture points.

"Here we go. C2, A2, and DL," he said as he tried to

remember his training. As soon as Mantid successfully found them, Beetle Blatt "Woke up."

"Dwork-fobber! Where am I?" Blatt asked, reorienting himself.

"It's okay!" assured Mantid. "You're on planet Earth. This is no dream or training exercise. I repeat, this is not a dream or a training exercise. You're driving on the planet's surface."

"It sure looks like a dream," Blatt remarked as he returned to full consciousness.

"Perhaps I should drive," Mantid suggested.

A light on the dashboard flashed, signaling an incoming message. "We're getting an IM on Earth?" Blatt asked, quite intrigued, and pressed the screen to respond. Mallow Dweeb instantly appeared on the screen. He looked very perturbed.

"Mallow Dweeb?" Mantid asked.

"Pull over," Mallow Dweeb said.

"What?" asked Blatt, confused about everything that had just happened.

"Pull over! We need to talk" Dweeb insisted.

"We can talk," Blatt answered, regaining his calm and realizing where he was.

"I mean face to face, you dwork-fobber!" Dweeb practically yelled.

"You're three thousand light years—" Blatt said but was interrupted by Dweeb.

"I'm right behind you, Blatt. Pull the zarkwad over!" Mallow Dweeb shouted.

Blatt and Mantid both turned around at the same time and practically froze in shock and confusion as they saw Dweeb right behind them driving the Starvette. "You are sure this is not a training exercise?" Blatt asked Mantid.

"I'm very sure," replied Mantid, sounding unsure, "Unless we're unknowingly taking part in a mind-wipe, collective hypnotic relocation simulation exercise, in which case, you should also do as you are told and pull over." Blatt nodded.

Mallow Dweeb wasted no time in getting out of his vehicle and awkwardly fighting with the unaccustomed dense gravity of Earth; he comically strutted up to meet Beetle Blatt and Mantid, who had also exited their vehicles.

"How did you—" Beetle Blatt began to ask.

"Questions are irrelevant," barked Mallow Dweeb. "Do you have the QMJ?"

"Yes," replied Blatt. "But we need it to—"

"You need to shut the zarkward up," Dweeb interrupted again. "We may be out of the office, but I'm still in charge, and we have precious little time to do damage control here... and then get off planet. Just in case my plan doesn't work."

"Yes, sir," Blatt demurred.

"We're going to the UN Building," Mallow Dweeb ordered, "Zycorp has people on the inside that can place us for maximum effect. We will destroy the contaminated human with the QMJ, then do a mind wipe on every witness present. You will follow orders. Clear?"

"Yes, sir," Blatt agreed.

"Yes, sir," Mantid agreed even though he was entirely ignored and totally excluded from the interaction.

N AND N2 WALKED THE CONGESTED STREETS OF NEW York, making their way through the swarming throngs, and looked at the UN Building on the skyline.

"It's simple," explained N, "We go to the UN Building, avoiding Mallow Dweeb. Then we find the Hank human and then take him to our space vehicle."

"And take him back to Zycorp as our bargaining chip," N2 realized. "It is a most perfect plan, dude."

Looking tense, yet excited, top executives gathered in the Zycorp conference room on their R&D space rig. The Venusian war veteran, Hemmelrouser II, raised his hand, saluted, then spoke to those present.

"How can we annihilate humanity without being sanctioned by the Intergalactic Space Federation Council? Not only would such action result in intergalactic sanctions imposed upon us, but we may ourselves have war declared upon us."

The diplomatic Yikeshifter took it upon himself to suggest an answer.

"As you all here have code F_1 security clearance, you should know that we have Zycorp employees disguised as humans planted at every level of human society. Acting as a shadow government, they control all banking, political, and military-industrial organizations worldwide. On our orders, we can arrange for Earth's superpowers to declare war against each other. We could have a full-scale world war in effect by the first phase of the opposing moon on planet Tetris."

"Humans love going to war, everyone knows it," Daftbrood added vehemently and, increasingly excited, a drop of saliva fell uncontrollably from his mouth.

"Precisely," continued Yikeshifter, then continued:

"As you all know, the Federation treaty, of which we are a signatory, prevents interference in the affairs of an alien planet. Unless, that is - and only if - that foreign civilization invites us to do so. Once chaos reigns, we will be invited in to restore order by the heads of the secret government. Once we have the invitation, the Intergalactic Space Federation Council will be unable to stop us. Mission accomplished."

"Ingenious," Daftbrood agreed excitedly, spittle flowing freely from his mouth.

***

IN THE CROWDED AND FRENETICALLY HECTIC CONFINES OF the UN Building foyer, international delegates passed through security and quickly proceeded to sign in with the busy yet efficient registration personnel.

After exchanging a secret signal, a security guard—with a distinctly extraterrestrial air—ushered the now-disguised Mallow Dweeb, Blatt, and Mantid straight past the security apparatus, granting them full entry to the building.

Further back in the line, N and N2 were stopped at security by a very beefy-looking outside private security guard, several of whom had been hired just for this event. N and N2 exchanged terrified glances.

"What's your purpose here?" the security guard asked.

"Our purpose on earth or our life's purpose?" asked N, confused by the question.

"Is that a religious question?" N2 wondered aloud.

"Your purpose at the United Nations," the guard clarified, suspiciously, "are you two delegates?" He looked down at the clipboard that he was holding.

"Yes," answered N2 immediately, "we are very delicate. Both of us. Very, very sensitive. I feel like crying right now."

And he found himself weeping from the stress of this insane experience, and all that had happened in the last few days.

To his complete and utter shock, he realized that he was, if not exactly afraid of death, entirely opposed to having that experience.

N ignored N2's outburst.

"What are your names and what country are you representing?" the security guard asked as he scanned his clipboard with a list of names and countries.

"What country?" asked N.

"Where are you from?" the security guard asked slowly and deliberately, realizing perhaps, for the first time, that English was not their first language.

"That's a very personal—" N began to respond.

"These guys are from Finland," a voice said, and Marcy materialized, as if out of thin air, in the midst of the thick crowd of bodies. Looking radiant, to the point of almost sparkling, N and N2 could barely contain their joy upon seeing her.

"Marcy," the aliens in human disguise shrieked.

"Finland isn't on the list," the guard commented. Completely surly, his eyes scanned the countries beginning with the letter F. "Guess they weren't invited."

Marcy turned to face the guard. She got his full attention and looked deeply into his eyes. The effect she had upon him caused him to wobble slightly on his feet. His eyes glowed, and he appeared looser, relaxed, and immediately friendlier.

"You don't want to be the one responsible for causing, or contributing to, an international incident, by refusing to allow the Finnish delegation to observe the proceedings, do you, officer?" she asked warmly, yet pointedly.

As if unable or unwilling to break his stare away from Marcy's beautiful and tender eyes, tears welled up in the eyes of the security guard.

"No, ma'am. I love Finnish people. I love all people. I love you," he said earnestly and smiled. The love that suffused his being made him very handsome.

"And I love you," Marcy replied happily, without a hint of sarcasm or untruth.

"Come, boys," she said, turning to N and N2, "Let's sign you in." Leading them past the guard, she ushered them toward the registration table.

Inside the large auditorium, global delegates sat at their respective desks. N and N2 sat at an empty desk, just as two Asian-looking delegates were about to sit down. Assuming that they were in the wrong place, the genuine delegates moved down the line in search of other vacant seats. N and N2 giggled nervously.

N looked around at the huge assembly of the planet's most important diplomats and politicians and was clearly in awe. Tearfully, he turned to N2.

"I want you to know that no matter what happens, being with you has given me such positive memories that I will cherish for the rest of my life. I love you, N2," he said.

N2 stared at his clone with shock and increasing love. Neither of the two alien beings realized that the consciousness of Marcy, Hank, and the other increasingly enlightened beings is affecting their awareness.

Already overwhelmed by the event, and now by the surprisingly appreciative words of N, N2 also teared up.

"I love you too, clone brother," he said, his voice quivering with intense emotion. They hugged each other tightly and wept softly.

Mallow Dweeb, Beetle Blatt, and Mantid sat at an unmarked desk near the front. Dweeb quickly checked his backpack, to make sure that the QMJ was still inside, its dials and switches at the ready, then pushed it beneath the seat.

In a guest side room off the main corridor, Hank and Marcy sat, looking lovingly into each other's eyes.

Hank's sister Monique was there. She sent text after text to friends from her cell phone. Much to her chagrin, none of her friends seemed to believe her texts, which began with the question, "Guess where I am right now?"

Drs. Blake and Delaware, also seemingly transformed into two loving individuals by their proximity and exposure to Hank, sat together in silence.

They looked affectionately into each other's eyes and felt a profound human kinship for the first time in their lives. It was thrilling and astonishing.

"No, I'm not screwing with you. I'm in the United Nations building with my brother Hank and his fiancée," the princess spoke into her phone. Reacting like the other person just hung up, she gave an "I don't believe this" roll of the eyes to no one in particular. None of the other room participants paid her the slightest attention.

"How come nobody believes me?" she addressed the room.

Hank remained silent but looked deeply into his sister's eyes with great love. Drs. Blake and Delaware, and Marcy also gazed silently at her with loving kindness. The room felt increasingly peaceful as the vibration went up.

"What?" she asked, as if everyone around her was acting too weird.

"Perhaps a better question is, why is it important to you... that they believe you?" Hank said softly. The former character actress stared in wonder.

Then, as if he had just mentioned precisely the words that she was expecting to hear right at that moment, she instinctively dropped her cell phone into a pitcher of water.

"You're so right," she declared. "I don't need anybody's approval except my own!" Her eyes filled with light as if she had just had a major epiphany.

"I do so love myself," she then said, joyfully.

The other room participants laughed happily, and she laughed with them.

Assembled in the Intergalactic Space Federation Council auditorium, alien delegates from across the galaxy sat at their respective desks, which displayed their respective flags and insignia. A giant screen before them streamed the UN auditorium live, courtesy of GSPANX, the extraterrestrial version of CSPAN.

The Intergalactic Space Federation Council moderator, Grandphaster, addressed the federation members:

"Today, you witness the most consequential gathering in the history of planet Earth. Should they agree to recognize the existence of off-planet intelligent life, then contact with us, and the federation, is but a step away."

Intense excitement prevailed as the delegates murmured to one another, and various factions, pro and con, sat and watched the proceedings on planet Earth with intense interest. They watched with respectful silence as the UN moderator stepped onto the dais to introduce the guest speaker, Hank.

"Up to make his address to the dignified assembled is Dr. Hank Walsh. As a distinguished astrophysicist, Dr. Walsh has been invited today to share a fascinating theorem with us, the content of which, no doubt, you are already aware of, as his theorem has been making headlines around the world over the past few weeks. Please welcome Dr. Hank Walsh to the podium."

Acknowledging the excited, yet polite applause of the assembled, Hank stepped out and smiled broadly at everyone as he made his way to the dais.

"Hello, my name is Hank Walsh. I'm a mathematician. The theorem in question is on page six of the session booklet before you," he said clearly and softly.

Hank paused to allow interested delegates to open up their booklets.

"I'm not going to speak just now; rather, I'd prefer if you'll simply look it over. What I'd like to do is come down there and walk among you and say howdy."

A mixed reaction, of surprise, curiosity, and interest, in this mysterious man's words, ran through the delegates in both auditoriums, earth and intergalactic. It was an unusual and uncustomary turn of events. Some delegates reacted with joyful expectation. Many expressed their displeasure by refusing to open their booklets and crossing their arms and legs as an open demonstration of defiance.

Undeterred, Hank began walking among the delegates and greeted them with a handshake and a smile. Those he came into proximity with were transformed immediately, without quite knowing what was happening to them. Self-actualization, truth, love, and peace became their core values, and it showed.

Knowing an opportunity was presenting itself, Mallow Dweeb reached into the backpack to ready the QMJ. Realizing that he had no idea how to operate the device, he turned to Beetle Blatt. "How do you work this thing?" he whispered.

"You must triangulate on his image," Blatt responded. "Let me show you."

Beetle Blatt took out the wand in order to point it at Hank. Hank, however, was taking his time, introducing himself to a row of delegates across the other aisle.

Climbing the stairs and still smiling, Hank shook every willing hand and bestowed his loving smiles on those unwilling to shake. As he did so, each delegate instantly reacted as they were enveloped in a massive wave of divine love and peace. Some hugged him and others hugged each other; some, judging by their expressions, felt love for the very first time.

As Hank approached N and N2, he immediately recognized them.

"You're those Finnish boys," he said delicately, recognizing their true identity.

"We're not really from Finland," N2 admitted softly, as if Hank's energy was affecting him in ways he wasn't at all expecting.

"Of course you aren't," responded Hank with a knowing wink.

"Actually, we're from a distant part of the galaxy," N2 confessed. "We plan to take you back there with us. Will you come?"

"I'd love to," replied Hank. "How about I finish here first?"

"Really?" asked N, who now shot up in his seat with absolute delight.

"Really," said Hank, entirely happy to do so, having seen it as a possible future.

As Hank moved on, N and N2 congratulated each other like crazy. Jumping up and down, they then hugged and high-fived each other. Then N and N2 joined in the group hug, which was spontaneously breaking out among the delegates as Hank passed, his energy transforming everyone within his radius of being.

Blatt stood up in his seat in order to get a better view of Hank. Trying to get a clear shot of him was difficult, however, as not only was he moving, but so were other people. Delegates kept getting in the way.

"What's the problem?" Mallow Dweeb asked, shoving the backpack out of sight, hoping that Beetle Blatt would finish the deed before attracting undue attention.

"He's too far away. I can't lock on," Blatt reported, twisting and turning.

Hank moved along, his sheer presence causing a huge

outward rippling effect that transformed every person he met. Delegations from former enemy states were now laughing, hugging, and expressing love and respect.

Hank moved to the center aisle and began his descent back to the podium. Beetle Blatt got terribly excited as he got a clear view of Hank. "Locked on!" he soon declared, holding out the laser array. "Turn up the dial."

Mallow Dweeb began slowly to turn the dial. "How far. All the way?" he asked.

"All the way!" agreed Blatt.

"Are you sure this is enough to be fatal?" Mallow Dweeb asked as he turned the dial as far as it would go.

"Oh, yeah," answered Blatt. "This is enough to explode his brains right across the galaxy. Prepare to be slimed."

As if feeling some disturbance in the force, Hank suddenly stopped in his tracks.

He immediately looked towards Mallow Dweeb and Beetle Blatt, who were unprepared to be discovered so soon. They stared back, wide-eyed and unable to move, like two deer caught in the headlights.

Hank fell to his knees as if overcome by tremendous pain. He grabbed his head in his hands as if he were being tortured from within. The entire auditorium stopped what they were doing and looked at him in silence, all eyes on him as both auditoriums now watched with greater interest.

Many of the delegates felt their eyes well with tears and compassion, and even greater love, due to the deep connection and at-one-ness they felt with Hank.

Dweeb and Beetle Blatt, having reviewed QMJ test footage, smiled smugly and prepared themselves for the horrific slime explosion. At the rear of the stage, Blake and Delaware stood, wondering if they should go to Hank's aid.

Equally perplexed as to what was happening, the alien delegates watched with fascination, turning to mutter to each other:

"What's happening on Earth?" "Who is that being?" "Why is he in pain?"

Hank remained on his knees, appearing to be in unbearable pain. All at once, Blake, Delaware, Marcy, N, and N2, who had been frozen with concern, rushed to his aid. Upon reaching him, they stopped abruptly when, very suddenly, Hank sprang up. He raised his arms upward, in the universal posture of winning.

He looked toward the heavens. His lips moved as if he were speaking.

"He's going through some major transformation," Marcy announced to the others, trying to remain calm and breath, "Stand back and give him space."

"What's happening?" Mallow Dweeb asked and looked down to see Beetle Blatt squat and scramble beneath his delegate desk.

"You need to get down. He's about to explode," Blatt answered sharply.

Without warning, Hank's body jerked up, his arms still outstretched as an explosion of energy, a vibration of light and love, rippled from his heart outward through his being and radiated through the room and all of the people present.

Just like the blast wave of a nuclear explosion, delegates were thrown backwards, and papers and other light debris flew into the air. People cried out. The molecules of the air, charged with high-frequency light, changed everyone there.

The invisible ripples of energy—fast-moving, vibrating molecules—exploded outward through the building and into the surrounding busy New York streets, affecting everyone and everything in their path. The city was instantly lighter. People wept and hugged each other in the streets. Peace and love went viral.

The energy wave rippled further out from New York and circled the globe, affecting the entire human race in its path. Everything became clearer, lighter, and seemed more beautiful. Even the sun seemed to shine more brightly.

The energy waves rippled out into space. They passed through hundreds of alien spaceships, many warships from numerous planets, filled with extraterrestrial races eager to destroy humanity, which hovered just beyond Earth's atmosphere.

The alien delegates in the intergalactic auditorium watched the events unfolding on Earth with awe and wonder. They muttered to each other, wondering what exactly had just happened and what the consequences would be.

The Intergalactic Space Federation Council moderator, Grandphaster, was just as confused as everyone else. "What just happened?" he asked Xerb, the Intergalactic Space Federation Council President, and his top advisors nearby.

"It would appear that Earth's consciousness just went through a miraculous evolutionary explosion, an unparalleled upliftment," Xerb answered, entirely dumbfounded, as he checked his handheld computer. The device displayed incoming messages and provided measurements and data.

Grandphaster nodded his head sagely. He realized the immense significance of what was happening on planet Earth. Xerb seemed flummoxed. The consciousness of earthlings could feasibly rival or surpass that of alien beings throughout reality.

"Well, I'll be gosh zarkwad!" he exclaimed, stunned by the implications of this unprecedented circumstance. They were too late. There would be no exterminating earthlings now. He stood there for a moment, eyes wide, trembling, wondering what would happen now.

In the UN, Hank remained standing, arms stretched upward, grounding the energy emanating from him. He relaxed his arms, stretched, yawned, and looked around at all the glowing faces in the auditorium, smiling beatifically.

The auditorium was sparkling and radiant with light. Everyone in the room had entered an enlightened state of consciousness and being. They all but floated on waves of goodwill, feeling an intense sense of global oneness and peace.

As if even the air in the room itself were different, everyone breathed more deeply. Their bodies were non-resistant, and they took full, deep, life-enhancing breaths, calming and integrating their energy, emotions, and thoughts.

Outside in the streets, in the cities and the towns and the fields, everywhere that there were natural and man-made objects—everything molecular, which in reality was everything—was brighter and more luminous. People everywhere stopped what they were doing and, in joyful accord, smiled, loved, danced, and hugged each other in an act of shared, blissful enjoyment of human community.

In the Middle East, Israeli, Palestinian, and other Arab leaders smiled and hugged each other as they raised their respective flags and national regalia together, joining in an impromptu dance of peace.

Pastors, priests, rabbis, reverends, and other religious leaders all over the globe embraced one another and began walking arm in arm, rapidly becoming loving sisters and brothers in harmony.

Armies of every nation disarmed themselves and abandoned their weapons, leaving them where they lay. Soldiers disrobed and simply walked away naked, leaving their tanks and assorted armored vehicles.

The extraterrestrial space ship armadas and warcraft dematerialized their weaponry, making adjustments to their death ray laser beams, and used their lasers to beam a happy, melodic, joyous music of universal love throughout the galaxy.

Yikeshifter tried his best to stay angry, finding himself feeling quite strangely, as he addressed the Zycorp employees on a bank of screens on his console.

"The order was wage war, not wage peace," he said weakly, fighting back tears that came from an unknown origin. The employees, on their screens, reacted with gestures of love, peace, and acceptance toward their employer. Some blew kisses, others made the peace sign, and all of them smiled with love and acceptance toward their difficult boss. Against his will, their expressions of love and goodwill, and the Divine energies emanating from earth, were enough to shift the tide of anger within him, to change and enlighten him.

Tears flowed freely from his eyes as he made the alien sign for peace.

"I love you guys," he said, meaning every word, and burst into tears.

In the auditorium, the UN delegates basked in the love and presence of Hank, and it appeared that they didn't wish to leave. Even Mallow Dweeb, Beetle Blatt and Mantid were not excluded from the transformation. They hugged each other and greeted N and N2 with immense love as they approached.

N was weeping when he put his arm around N2's shoulders.

"This is amazing and... incredible," he said, looking all around him. "I'm so grateful. There isn't a thing I could want or need more than this... what could anyone ask for?" He looked around with great joy at the love between all beings.

"Well, I can think of one thing," N2 said, wiping away his tears.

IT WAS A BEAUTIFUL, SUNNY DAY ON A BLACK SAND BEACH in Hawaii.

Hank and Marcy faced each other and exchanged vows in front of a minister from the planet Venus. It was a tiny ceremony filled with great love.

The guests included Mallow Dweeb, Beetle Blatt, Mantid, N and N2, each of whom didn't even try to hide the tears and emotions elicited by the touching and beautiful ceremony.

"I now pronounce you man and wife," said the minister. "You may kiss your bride."

Hank gently kissed Marcy with great love. A beautiful breeze blew. Sunlight shimmered on the water. Blooming tropical flowers scented the air. It was a beautiful, still moment, and it seemed that all creation sanctified their love.

Mantid sighed loudly and unsuccessfully tried to grab Beetle Blatt's only free hand, which was holding his communication device. Blatt, terribly embarrassed, jerked his hand away and looked down to see that he was getting a message.

He was being summoned back to Zycorp to face Yikeshifter for an employment status reassessment by the corporation. He sighed, but even the possibility of devastating news couldn't destroy his peace and love buzz.

BACK AT THE ZYCORP CORPORATION, MALLOW DWEEB AND Yikeshifter faced Beetle Blatt and Mantid. All of them exuded peaceful, loving vibes to each other.

"Wild as it sounds, I've decided to go on a retreat!" Yikeshifter began.

"I need to take some personal time to get to know myself... and I need someone to run the ship in my absence. Someone I can trust to..." he got lost in feelings of deep peace and lost his train of thought. He smiled sheepishly at the others.

"Maintain the one-love policy," Mallow Dweeb helped out.

"Maintain the one-love policy," Mantid repeated, as everyone in the room broke into a smile and then laughed.

"I see we're of like mind, heart, and Soul. Beautiful. I trust you two, and honestly, I really love the way that you think outside the rectangular, Blatt. So, that's it," Yikeshifter said, gently caressing them with an appendage, then exited.

Mallow Dweeb embraced the two of them and followed Yikeshifter out.

Blatt turned to Mantid, and they both laughed and congratulated each other.

"The promotion! You got the promotion!" Mantid practically shouted.

"So did you," Beetle Blatt said.

"And he said Zibbie think outside of the rectangular," Mantid said playfully.

"It's a dream come true," responded Beetle Blatt happily. Then he cried.

At the Los Alamos National Lab for advanced research, Drs. Blake and Delaware gave a tour of their laboratory facilities to a visiting group of strange and bizarre-looking interested extraterrestrials from throughout the multiverses.

"I appreciate that this may all seem very primitive to you, but this is the height of our advanced knowledge in this country, and most probably on the planet at this moment," explained Dr. Delaware kindly.

"Not at all entirely primitive," the spokesperson for the

group assured them. "We're very impressed with your... with the... the coffee in the canteen is excellent, we have no coffee," he continued, trying to find something to compliment truthfully.

"Thank you," replied an earnest Dr. Blake.

Neither Dr. Blake nor Dr. Delaware noticed that several members of the group were avoiding eye contact with each other, fearing they would erupt into uncontrollable laughter.

N AND N2'S FIRST STOP AFTER HANK AND MARCY'S wedding ceremony was Disneyland Park. Both of them shyly held hands with Monique, looking like normal tourists, standing outside Space Mountain in Tomorrowland.

N2 held up his high-tech device. Monique and N looked down at it.

"It was really nice of Mallow Dweeb to shoot all that footage of us," N2 said as they watched their Disneyland memories on the small screen.

"It was. Weird how we all love each other now," N said very happily, "And look at all these positive memories!"

"I told you it was the happiest place on earth," N2 said as they watched themselves. They started laughing so hard that they cried, the pair of them getting emotional while watching footage of N, N2, and the blonde, screaming and waving their hands in the air as they rode Space Mountain. Various quick snippets fast-forwarded as their trip to Disneyland played. They laughed and laughed over the footage of the three of them riding the tea cups, and N2 and the blonde were laughing, but N looked like he could throw up at any moment. As the video came to an end, N shut off the monitor.

The three of them were laughing so hard they cried. Then

they hugged there, in the happiest place on earth, and said their goodbyes, wiping away tears of love.

Back in their alien form, but wearing giant Mickey Mouse ears, N and N2 traveled through space in the Starcar, which was set to resemble an Earth hotrod circa the 80s.

"So, what's the plan, man?" N2 asked.

"Plans?" N asked playfully. "Plans? We don't need no stinking plans," he joked.

"Alrighty, dude," N2 exclaimed with glee. "You've finally developed a sense of humor, you're rocking the funny bone earth style. I like it!"

N absentmindedly rubbed the QMJ, which was sitting in his lap.

"You know," N said casually, "I did hear a rumor that there are some ultra-terrestrials in a parallel dimension connected to the Zargon quadrant that have an inter-dimensional plot to exploit... well, whatever planets and civilizations that they can."

"Geez, ultra terrestrials..." responded N2 doubtfully, "I suppose we could check it out, but, uh, those guys are you know... scary. I know we have the QMJ and some other Zycorp tricks, and all that, but maybe we shouldn't mess with ultra-terrestrials just yet. We're kind of new at this consciousness-raising gig. I mean, those guys are seriously bad-ass. Just the thought of facing them makes me kinda nervous." N2 looked at N and shrugged, a little embarrassed.

"Well, pilgrim," responded N in his best John Wayne imitation, "All battles are fought by scared men who'd rather be someplace else! Whaddya say we go kiss some ultra-terrestrial ass?" N2 looked somewhat terrified until N broke into a laugh, bringing some relief to his anxiety.

"I'm just joshing with you," said N, "Not. Seriously, an ultra-terrestrial who doesn't want to make up may need to do some inner work. But hey, it's their Soul. Right? Am I right, or am I right?"

"I guess so," N2 responded, reflecting, "We could just check it out."

They both laughed, and N2 hit a button, starting some music.

"What is this dwork-fobbing music?" N asked in a joking way.

"Dude, don't you know Elephunk's, "Where is the Love?" It's awesome!"

"You're awesome," N replied. N2 grinned.

"No, your face is awesome," N2 said, as he was then thrown backward by the explosive acceleration of the Starcar as N floored it.

"I was just kidding," N added, and he and N2 both began singing along with the music. They turned the music up. As the tiny vehicle shot through the vast emptiness of space, N and N2 crooned along with Elephunk.

N2 punched the button for quantum speed, and a sea of white stars appeared to elongate and turn blue as the Starcar streaked towards them, the stars appearing gold once the Starcar had moved through them and made the quantum jump.

DERMOT DAVIS

Irish writer Dermot Davis divides his time between Ireland and the United States. An award-winning author, playwright, and screenwriter, his creative work spans diverse genres and explores human themes and characters transformed by life experiences. His published work includes a satirical novel, *Brain: The Man Who Wrote the Book That Changed the World*, which was a GREADER'S FAVORITE INTERNATIONAL BOOK AWARD Gold Medalist Winner, a SOMERSET AWARDS FIRST PLACE WINNER, a USA BEST BOOK AWARDS 1st Place Winner, and an INTERNATIONAL BOOK AWARDS Finalist. As a playwright, Dermot is a recipient of the OZ Whitehead Award (co-sponsored by Irish Pen and the Society of Irish Playwrights). In 2025, he won both best Irish play and best play overall in the 5th annual Carlow International One-Act Playwriting competition. His plays have been produced at Theatre Banshee, Burbank, the Celtic Arts Center, Hollywood, and Playwright's Platform, Boston, and he has directed his produced work on occasion. As a founding member of Laughing Gravy Theatre, he toured the East Coast of the US. Laughing Gravy was subsequently invited as a resident theatre group at the prestigious Piccolo Spoleto Festival, Charleston, SC. Dermot is an Irish Writers Centre Members' nominee to the IWC Board. Follow Dermot online:

https://dermotdavis.com/

H RAVEN ROSE

H Raven Rose bleeds star-dust tinted ink and writes story worlds from beyond the stars. Her MFA and PhD are in creative writing, and she is an award-winning screenwriter/director, author, poet, playwright, and creativity researcher; her poem painted in film—*Sacred Birthday, Sacred Wales - Pen-Blwydd yn Gysegredig, Cymru Sanctaidd*—won the 2021 Wales International Film Festival Illustrated Poem Jury's Award Special Prize. In 2018, her Super 8 short film, Sleep Disturbance, was shot in Bristol and screened at The Cube Microplex in the UK. Her play, Dark Eros, adapted into a suspenseful novella of the same title, was staged as readings in Los Angeles, with Jessica Biel starring in one production in the lead role as Leila. An excerpt of the play version of *Sleep Disturbance* was staged as readings at the Taliesin Create Space.

Recent publications include creative nonfiction, 'Waking up Wild' and ' Snow', published in *Tofu Ink Arts Press*, the ecopoem '23 Species from 19 States lost to extinction' published in the Winter 2022 edition of *In Parentheses*, and 'Mars or Bust: How Science Fiction Films will Promote Mars Colonization Reality' published in the newly released *The Book of Mars: An Anthology of Fact and Fiction* edited by Dr Stuart Clark (presented initially at The Mars Society 21st Annual International Convention in 2018 in Pasadena, CA). Follow H online:

https://hravenroseauthor.com/

Love Encounter? Then you might like *Bugocalypse: La Cucaracha V 1*, written by H Raven Rose alone. It's about a young Los Angeles actress who survives an alien invasion at the DNA level and then must escape from Los Angeles.

★★★★★ **Excellent. A fresh, funny take on the end of the world as we know it.**, March 25, 2015

By **Sherwin**

Verified Purchase (What's this?)

This review is from: **Bugocalypse (La Cucaracha Book 1) (Kindle Edition)**

Just finished Bugocalypse. Nearly passed it up; I've had my fill of dystopias. Realized it isn't a mysterious virus, zombies or vampires/werewolves, so I got it. IT IS TERRIFIC! The plot is fresh and fascinating, the hero(ine) is believable, admirable, and funny, and the dialogue is realistic. And the menace! I didn't think anyone could revive the creepy crawlies after what the movies did to them in the1950's (I'm 80 years old, man; I watched those things), but H. Raven Rose has reinvented the genre, and done it just right. Get it, read it, get the sequels, and enjoy!

Bugocalypse tells the story of wannabe actress Lacey and

the unusual events that occur the week of Halloween. The story is very much a classic alien invasion bug war of a bygone era.

Please enjoy the following excerpt from BUGOCALYPSE!

PROLOGUE

BEFORE EVERYTHING WENT to H E double toothpicks, I so had not been making it as an actress.

Sure, I'm skinny and have long blonde hair. Girls with those attributes are a dime a dozen, or at least no more than non-union rates, in La La Land.

I go to auditions when I can motivate myself. I have an agent, of sorts, though I think the skeeze ball may just want to bang me.

I take classes when I can afford them. I study acting and improvisation, elocution, dance, and even fencing.

I have my platinum blonde hair re-colored; I touch up before the darker roots get so bad that I'm shamed into it. I get regular manicures and pedicures because my friend and I trade them. I get spa treatments rarely.

I am yoga-obsessed. I do yoga, often instead of having hobbies, to maintain a perfect skinny size "O" body and butt.

Less is always more in La La land, where I live.

None of my efforts have helped my career take off. So, between the odd, rare acting gig, I tend bar and always have just enough money to get by.

I just manage to pay my bills, including my SAG-AFTRA union dues, but that is all. Maybe it is because I am from the Valley. Maybe it is because I didn't grow up in an industry or entertainment-connected family.

My dad, Avi, was in pest control. Don't laugh. I'm serious. Then he retired and moved to Florida. Although he invited me, I wouldn't leave La La Land with him—later, I will regret my obstinacy. It's sad, but I never knew my mom well. She died of breast cancer when I was an itty-bitty girl.

All I have left of her is stuff. I have photos and a super-fab copy of a screen test she did for a B movie (she got the role, one of several). I also have her funky, fabulous rhinestone costume jewelry and clothes from the '60s and '70s. Plus, I have her new-age crystals, spiritual books, and rad pink Cadillac.

My mom would have had a great career as an actress. The camera loved my mother. She lit up the screen. My dad never got over her. He has been alone ever since her death. He always says:

"You can't replace the love of your life."

My dad is sweet that way. I miss her, too.

Her final resting place is in Hollywood Forever, the cemetery. When my dad was here, we went to Cinespia together. We went to the movie screenings, visiting my mom beforehand.

My dad told the best stories about my mom and her career. He loved recounting every detail of every audition and each role that she had gotten. My father thought she would have been an enormous B-movie star if she had lived.

She was fearless. My dad always skirted the details of her bodacious success, me being his daughter and all.

The gist was that she could heave her ample bosom and toss her long blonde hair, screaming and running from beasts, with the best of the celluloid sirens. She was beautiful, sexy, and strong. She was top-notch at surviving in the end. She still lives in celluloid, in her onscreen roles, after fighting off a terrifying giant ant or another horrible monster, insect or otherwise.

Sometimes, I visit Rudolph Valentino at Hollywood Forever, but only after I visit my mother. With my dad gone, I sometimes go to HF at other times. Then, if a movie is showing, I head over to the Fairbanks lawn with my picnic hamper full of wine, cheese, fruit, and chocolate. I lie on the grass and dream about how I will somehow get screen time someday.

Sometimes, I think that, unlike my mother, maybe I am failing because I lack something. Perhaps I wasn't born with or never found the fire to pursue my creative goals and dreams relentlessly. Until recently, I seemed to lack drive.

It seemed that I was always late to or missed auditions, but even if I made it to the cattle call, I often learned that I was:

"You're too blonde," "too young," "too old," "too thin," "too tall," "too busty," or "not busty enough."

I live with Marisol, my best, best friend in the whole world. We've known each other since the fourth grade. While I spectacularly fail at life, at the ripe old age of 22, Soli is totes bad-ass.

Soli is a teacher. She's almost finished her Master's in Education coursework and student teaching. She has uncanny, bad-ass ambition. She did dual enrollment while still in high school.

Her parents are still together, hard-working, and devoted. They always treat me like a daughter. Marisol loves me. Always supportive and non-judgmental, she is the best girlfriend a girl could have. She always tells me:

"Lacey, you have a gift, something that you were born to do, and it comes from God. Life will reveal it to you."

And, although I hope that it's true and that everyone has a God-given gift, and that I will discover mine, I fear that it may not be true. I may be in the wrong place at the wrong time because nothing ever seems to work out for me.

Little do I know it, but Marisol is right.

I do have a gift—something I will excel at and was born to do—and I will find it, to my surprise. By the time I make the discovery, I won't be the same person at all.

Almost everything I have known and believed in, all ordinary reality, is about to fragment.

My God-given life purpose is about to become all-consuming. Allow me to re-introduce myself:

"I'm Lacey, Stellar Pest-Control of Los Angeles. I hear you have a bug problem."

CHAPTER 1

FOR MOST LOS ANGELENOS, when the fit hit the shan, it was the end of the world. It was Judgment Day, as they knew it, and the worst thing that had ever happened to them. For me, it was the best *and* worst thing that ever happened to me. The horrid part was that everything went to H E double toothpicks really rapidly. I mean, LA totally went to the devil, but the wonderful part was discovering my life's purpose.

By providence, when the mind-blowing cosmic events began, I wasn't really even all that disturbed, as I'd recently begun reading New Age books that had belonged to my mother. They were half doom-and-gloom-conspiracy-theory and half it's all love and Light, and a couple included detailed, if contradictory, info about the coming apocalypse.

So, when the stars fell from the night sky and the other weird stuff started going down, watching reports of shooting stars and meteors on the news or reviewing footage caught on amateur video and posted on Facebook, YouTube, or elsewhere didn't really frighten me or fill me with awe at first.

It was one thing to hear about or watch reports of shooting stars and meteors streaming across the night sky just before villages, towns, and cities were struck down with the Black Death. It was quite another thing to see a flaming ball of orange and yellow-white fire, larger than a building, fly through the blue-black sky.

It happened the day of the earthquake.

I'd had a not-so-great audition that afternoon, even though I had spent hours preparing physically, mentally, and emotionally. My hair was freshly colored and highlighted, washed and flat-ironed, and looked as much like golden wheat as I could get it.

I had a line, really just a sentence, about how great this one type of tampon is—it's "so comfortable, I forget I'm wearing it!" As if that would be a selling point?! What girl or woman wants to forget she's on her period and needs to check her tampon? Whatever...

I just wanted the gig. I needed an influx of cash; it takes beaucoup d'argent to pursue the creative life, plus my car requires mega quantities of gasoline. If the commercial played a while, I'd get residuals, and I'd heard that the director was getting into features... that meant if he liked me, maybe he'd use me in something bigger. So, I put a lot into nailing the role.

I did a few hours of yoga and meditated on being one with the character in the commercial.

I'd never tried that before; I figured it couldn't hurt.

Before I got ready for my audition, I cleaned up the apartment and then took out the trash because I preferred to clean when I was already sweaty.

I went downstairs with a bag of trash in each hand. I hoped neither bag would break since Marisol insisted we use cheap trash bags. I slowly approached the dumpster outside of and behind the apartment building. I sneezed from the funky smell.

I was about to heft the two bags and toss them into the green rusty metal bin when, to my disgust, I noticed a cockroach, at eye level, staring at me. Why was this critter out in farqing broad daylight? Bold, it was a ginormous cockroach, too.

I hefted the full garbage bags, and the entire bin rattled as the bags thumped and fell in. To my satisfaction, I noticed that the sound and movement had gotten rid of the weirdly huge roach. I went back inside the building to get ready for my audition. I took my time.

I mused about a recent incident where Marisol and I were at her parents' home, and a bug got in the house. We were watching a movie, and Roberto got up to kill the bug while I watched. Then Marisol freaked.

"Take it outside. Take it outside," Marisol screeched.

"Marisol and her 'bugs are living creatures, too,' sentiments," said her father. Then, he said some things in Spanish, and the boys laughed.

Marisol pouted while her mom tried to soothe her.

Roberto rolled his eyes but didn't say anything. Instead, he grabbed an empty plastic cup and napkin off a nearby table and scooped up the insect. Then he did, in fact, take it outside.

At home, I was the designated debugger, that chick creeping downstairs at 1:00 AM with a cup or some random piece of Tupperware with a piece of paper or cardboard over a spider-moth-ant-beetle-whatever to release into the wild.

And I really don't mind, I do love bees, butterflies, ladybirds, bumble bees and such. But, I admit, that stuff gets old, and by stuff, I mean standing barefoot at some ungodly hour, helping another insect escape. Still, I love a great many insects and wish to save them, when and if I can.

In this instance, I was happy to watch Roberto and his muscles in action.

Marisol was happy that the bug lived. I didn't like to kill insects unnecessarily, yet my best friend was entirely against killing them.

After getting ready for my audition, I got in my car and drove to the location. Maybe it was because of the cockroach, but to raise my spirits and get my energy up, I floored my vehicle and sang 'La Cucaracha' as I drove to the production offices.

I couldn't really remember the lyrics to the song, so I kept screaming the chorus at the top of my lungs.

'La Cucaracha, la cucaracha,' I sang, as my pink Cadillac crested a hill, with a dip just after, and sailed through the air. Bump. Bump. I loved the funny feeling that I got in the pit of my stomach when I accelerated and took a hill with a drop just over it super fast.

I checked my appearance when I parked and got out of the car. I was freshly coiffed and showered, lightly made-up with a fresh French manicure, and looked exactly like the especially sweet and clean blue-eyed blonde girl-next-door cheerleader type.

That type of chick would obviously use the best tampons, so I figured that's the look they were going for... but then I didn't get the role. They gave it to a short, plumpish girl with dark hair and big boobs wearing a black leather mini-skirt and dark glasses.

They said I was too groomed, tall, and blonde for the role, so I didn't even get to read for it.

When I saw the other girls on the cattle call, I wondered why my agent had even sent me out. I'm all classic chic blonde doll, but all the other girls were edgy, dark, modern, hipster, grunge, cool chicks. I was totally wrong for the role and the audition.

I felt terribly sad. I needed to make money, and I was increasingly worried that this audition failure was yet another sign that I would never make it in Hollywood.

My only consolation was that I had plans for later.

I tried to focus on the positive as I hiked back to the Pink Lady, which I still thought of as my mom's car, named after the all-girl club from the movie *Grease*. Whenever I approach my gorgeous pink vehicle, I hear the sing-song of the Pink Ladies in my head:

"Ba-Ba-Bum-Bum. Ba-Ba-Bum-Bum."

Thank goodness Marisol and I have a Halloween party to attend tonight; otherwise, I'd spend the evening obsessing about yet another career failure. Instead, I thought about the bash.

I looked great, and my hair was perfect. I'd already done my yoga for the day, but the best part was that I had hours and hours to plan and make the perfect Halloween costume.

Unlike most girls, we don't use All Hallows' Eve as an excuse to wear skimpy slutty lingerie and high heels.

It's not that we don't believe in cute or sexy costumes; adorable and hot are not enough for us. We like to show our sass, not our unmentionables.

Ever since the fourth grade, Marisol and I always make or assemble our costumes. We never buy them. It's one of our things.

We've been characters from literature, film and television, Egyptian goddesses, super heroines, everyday objects (such as a teapot or a bag of jelly beans), animals, insects, plants, food, planets and other celestial bodies, extra-terrestrials, magical creatures (a mermaid and a unicorn), professionals (a police officer, nurse, and so on), or even abstract ideas.

So, we had a tradition to uphold, among our friends, of being annual eye candy that was often food for thought. Naturally, my roomie determined what she would be and created her costume weeks ago.

She was going as Madame Curie. I'm a little miffed that I didn't think of that myself, being as Marie Curie is my all-time favorite real-life heroine. She, along with her husband Pierre, was obsessed with research and became the first female Nobel Prize winner.

Renowned for their discoveries in radioactivity, they both received Nobel Prizes. They had a small laboratory, a rehabilitated shed, and she, ultimately, got sick and died from years of radiation exposure. Now, that dedication to one's art and craft was something that I needed to emulate.

I'd been considering and discarding various costume ideas for weeks. Happily, thinking about Soli's guise and Madame Curie's discovery of a chemical element, polonium (which she named after Poland, her home country), led me to a brilliant thought.

I would go as the element gold. I'd dress in shimmery gold clothing or tights and a leotard and then use gold body paint and glitter on my skin.

I was watching the heat haze, the heat shimmer. The late afternoon sun blurred and created a shimmering effect above the hot parking lot asphalt.

The sunlight beat down. Gazing at the pavement, I got increasingly excited about my Halloween guise concept and the idea that I would soon be shimmering myself as the sparkling, fabulous element gold.

Then it hit. I only had time for one thought: earthquake. Then the whole world shook, and I was slammed onto the ground as the parking lot pavement roiled and rolled, unable to stay on my feet. I hit the ground hard and stayed down there for several seconds, dazed. Everything stopped.

Earthquakes are common in California—the state sits upon the San Andreas Fault, the tectonic boundary between the Pacific and North American Plates—so Californians experience thousands of earthquakes each year. Some of the tremors are so tiny that they're virtually imperceptible.

But a big one, which this obviously was, is felt.

I was about to sit up when the shaking began again, this time even stronger. I realized belatedly that the first one was a foreshock.

My thoughts occurred in slow motion as intense shaking occurred for over half a minute. I heard a boom in the distance and knew it had to be a gas main. I lay there on the ground, shaking and afraid, and rode the parking lot up and down. Then, finally, everything stopped.

I lay still, feeling numb and unable to move, and listened. Emergency sirens wailed in the distance. Buildings and vehicles shifted, twisting metal screeched, and window glass shattered.

The whole of creation cried out, from popping noises to small explosions, dogs barking, and hard and sharp things shattering and breaking.

Finally, things seemed stable, and the cacophony of noises subsided to a nearly inaudible din, or maybe I'd grown numb to it all. I, very tentatively, sat up.

Both of my arms were fairly scraped up from the elbow to the palm from trying to grasp onto the parking lot. I felt hot, dizzy, and overwhelmed, but not so besieged that I didn't get to my feet and make my way to the car. I wondered about the epicenter of the quake.

Then concern for my best girlfriend, Marisol, and thoughts of my father flickered through my being. I realized that I wanted to call her and make sure that she was all right. I also needed to call my dad in Florida as soon as possible and let him know I was okay.

I was almost at the car, using a pink cardigan sweater to wipe trickling blood away from my left elbow, when the first aftershock hit. It wasn't as strong as the foreshock or actual quake, but the movement and the stress of the situation made me feel very ill.

My mind skittered about a million miles a minute, and my heart beat a staccato rhythm as I sweated and rubbed tears from my eyes. I considered whether or not to get into the car or find somewhere else to go.

People rushed out of the production office location, some

pulling others along, and headed to their cars, obviously upset, as they tried to make or were already on cell phone calls.

Screw it, I thought and jumped into my beautiful Pink Lady, my bubble gum pink Cadillac. I figured I should go right home or go and get Soli. I wasn't sure if I should take surface streets or the highway, and decided I'd figure out the best route on the way.

It turned out that there was no rush. I made the mistake of getting onto the freeway and, after a couple of miles of driving at a snail's pace, there I sat.

I flipped on the radio and listened to various radio show hosts describe the damage and take calls from "survivors." I felt sad when I realized that people had lost their homes or businesses and that some people had actually died in the quake.

I sat and listened, tapping the steering wheel, and felt anxious and sick, fighting off despair.

A moment of overwhelming gratitude swept over me. I knew that my father would be thrilled that I was fine, except for a few scrapes.

Traffic was apparently backed up for miles due to damage to streets and roads, so, no longer bleeding, I dug through my purse until I found my cell phone.

~end sample~

Will Lacey manage to evade capture by giant, man-sized cockroaches? Can she escape from LA?

You'll find out the rest of Lacey's story in *Bugocalypse: LA Cucaracha V1*.

Love Encounter (co-written by H Raven Rose and Dermot Davis)? Then you might like BRAIN: *The Man Who Wrote the Book That Changed the World*. Written by Dermot Davis alone, the story is about an author who faces the classic dilemma of the writer.

Do you write what's in your heart, or do you write what sells? In this modern age of publishing, there is a huge chasm between the best-selling authors who are rich beyond their dreams and... well, everybody else.

Reviewers say fantastic things about *Brain*.

...an entertaining farce about modern society, a deft, fast-paced tale that will leave self-aware readers giggling.

— PUBLISHERS WEEKLY

⭐⭐⭐⭐⭐ **You Have a Brain - laugh with it!,**
June 21, 2013
By **John Reviews**
Verified Purchase (What's this?)
This review is from: **Brain: The Man Who Wrote the Book That Changed the World: A Satire (Kindle Edition)**
Brain is a must read for all authors trying to make sense of the world of publishing.
It reminded me of Bonfire of the Vanities and Tom Sharpe's work.
Essentially a comedy and satire, Brain is a modern fable about the power of imagination and marketing with unforeseen consequences.
It also includes some great set pieces and observations about life which resonate with this reader.
I loved the story and I believe it would make a great comedy film in the right hands. Monty Python
would be a great touchstone for the tone and humor.
Roll on the follow-up.
Oh and I'd love to see You Have a Brain - Use it! published!

Award-winning *Brain* tells the story of Daniel. He's an author struggling to make a living. His agent won't accept his latest masterpiece, which he poured his soul into: apparently, it's not commercial enough. In a final act of desperation, Daniel decides to write—not what's in his heart but—what he thinks will sell. What follows is bound to make you laugh!

Please enjoy the following excerpt from BRAIN!

BRAIN: THE MAN WHO WROTE THE BOOK THAT CHANGED THE WORLD

It was graduation day at the University of Tollston in Illinois. Before the assembled students and their families, Dean Reynolds stood at the podium to announce the recipient of the prestigious Marcus and Imelda Rogerspoon award for the student showing the brightest promise for a future literary career.

Although the majority of the persons in attendance didn't give a whit about the prestigious award, or who that year's recipient might be, the handful of literary types present knew that it was short-listed to just two people: the intense intellectual, Daniel Waterstone and the artsy, anti-establishment, outspoken radical, "Crazy" Mary McIntyre.

The Dean spoke into the microphone, the incorrect placement of speakers producing a faint echoing effect. "Founder of the campus publication, *Superior Review,* and the student deemed to be most likely to succeed in the art of story-telling, the award goes to... Daniel Waterstone."

Daniel jumped to his feet with glee and was only half successful in suppressing his impulse to punch the air with a clenched fist. He energetically shook the hands of several disinterested students, who just happened to be sitting in his row, and made his way to the raised platform. Perhaps, in his head, he equated being the recipient of this obscure award with winning an Oscar, so, to the accompaniment of very modest applause, he summarily shook the hand of each of the male faculty and kissed the cheeks of each of the indifferent females he met on his way to the podium.

He then bear-hugged the impatient dean who did not see the hug coming and who subsequently failed, in an awkward way, to complete the hug from his end. Beaming with pride and self-confidence, Daniel received the award in his left hand whilst vigorously pumping the Dean's hand with his right. Expecting Daniel to return to his seat, the Dean replaced his reading glasses and checked his notes to move on to whatever was next on the agenda.

Daniel, however, was not about to let his five seconds of minor fame conclude so quickly and so he proceeded to pull out, from an inside pocket, what appeared to be a prepared speech. Adjusting the microphone to his desired height, Daniel addressed what was now a puzzled and somewhat bemused audience.

"Dean, members of the staff, ladies and gentlemen, it is with tremendous pride and heartfelt honor that I accept this highly-esteemed and influential award," he began and then looked around to make sure he had everyone's attention.

"We are living in dangerous times," he then said, pausing, for dramatic effect. "Having progressed through the age of reason and enlightenment, civilization is now poised to enter the age of insanity. I tell you, in no uncertain terms that what we are currently witnessing, at least here, in the West, is the decline of culture itself."

Whereas the academically inclined did perk up somewhat to these stark revelations, the majority of the persons in attendance were mentally preoccupied and paid his words of doom no heed. "We live in a time, reminiscent of the declining Roman Empire, perhaps, where style is rewarded over content and where worthy conversation concerning the evolution of our culture is replaced with inconsequential nonsense such as gossip about the lifestyles of the rich and famous. Our literature has been in decline for decades. Loopy fads and fantasy genres, of questionable merit, now clog our once-great literary arteries."

As many in the audience took this opportunity to pay a much needed visit to the lavatories (or to check their email, update their FaceBook and Twitter accounts), Daniel continued his treatise on cultural decline. Mentioning a short list of literary greats, including Faulkner, Steinbeck, Hemingway, et al, he challenged those in attendance to mention even just three contemporary authors who were presently carrying the mantle for—and laudable descendents of—these great literary forebears and legendary authors and who were currently contributing to creating an even greater literary age.

Various authors like Dan Brown, Stephen King and

Nicholas Sparks were volunteered by audience members and some jokers shouted out names like Baron Munchausen, Dr. Seuss and Harry Potter. Whether the last three names were said in jest was questionable, as no one was heard laughing in response.

Undeterred, Daniel talked excitedly and passionately about the need for writers and intellectuals to rediscover their passion for the timeless classics and "true" literature. He ranted about the necessity of the re-ignition of "the great quest," (the quest to write the great American novel, that is) and the need, nay, the *urgency* for a renaissance in American literature for which he would lead the way.

Raising his right hand, in a pose reminiscent of a presidential inauguration, Daniel continued: "People before me; fellow citizens of this great nation, to you I make a promise. I vow to be a defender of the hallowed halls of timeless classics, those that make a nation, a culture and a civilization great. With all the innate literary genius and creative wherewithal at my disposal... this is my promise to you. You have put your faith in the right person... I, Daniel Waterstone. Remember that name."

As he paused to take a grand intake of breath, the audience applauded wildly. One got the impression, however, that the rambunctious applause was not so much a validation of his speech and his stated noble quest but more a wild hope that he had concluded and, if not, a ruse to drown out whatever more he might want to say. Many students gave him a standing ovation with mock serious expressions, shouting, "Bravo, Bravo."

Despite her outward show of apathy, a disappointed "Crazy" Mary stood at the rear of the assembled and waited to catch Daniel's eye as he returned to his seat. When he did finally see her and gave her some semblance of acknowledgement, she stuck out her tongue, turned her back, pulled up her weird-looking, homemade, non-traditional gown... and mooned him.

IT HAD BEEN TEN YEARS SINCE DANIEL'S GRADUATION AND it's fair to say that the intervening years had not been very kind to him, personally or professionally. Despite some early signs of success, where Daniel acquired a literary agent and had two novels published by a small, yet well regarded, independent publisher, his books did not sell well. His most recent book advance was rapidly approaching complete exhaustion.

Encouraged by his agent to move to a larger metropolis, a shift which she sold to him as a necessary career move (to take meetings and, generally, to be taken seriously by the literary establishment), Daniel moved to Beverly Hills. Soon after that he prudently chose to relocate to West Hollywood and then slowly but surely he continued to down-size and move to less affluent neighborhoods as his funds continued to evaporate.

Upon his final move to a poor and quite noisy neighborhood in the San Fernando Valley, he tempered his self-disappointment with the justification that he was a true artist and like the then unknown and struggling literary expatriates of Paris (Sherwood Anderson, John Dos Passos, F. Scott Fitzgerald, Ernest Hemingway, et al), at the turn of the twentieth century, he too only required a bed, a desk and a typewriter.

His light brown wavy hair made curlier by the heat (and his failure to shower immediately upon waking), Daniel stood over his printer as it printed the remaining few pages of his latest novel, *The Impossible Dream: Part Two*. Bought at the local thrift store, his once-reliable printer was now on its last legs and white streaks were beginning to run down the freshly printed pages. Daniel wiped his sweaty brow and, with excited satisfaction, watched his document print.

Excited about his imminent luncheon appointment with his agent, Suzanne, he was confident that she would not judge him for the poor quality of the manuscript but instead would, once she had read the initial few pages, revel in the prose. In fact, Daniel was one hundred percent sure that the quality of his brilliant writing would obfuscate any short-comings with the print and toner issues in the document. As his new novel was a sequel, he expected it to be a highly desirable property. It answered many questions which were left tantalizingly unanswered in *The Impossible Dream: Part One.*

He didn't want to second guess the publisher's marketing rationale for not having *Part One* out in print yet but he assumed that it was because they were waiting for him to finish *Part Two* so that they could better strategize promotional and marketing opportunities for both books. The publishing and marketing of books was a foreign country to Daniel; one that he didn't know nor truly care to understand but he did appreciate that it was sure to have its intricacies and indeed, for himself and other authors, its necessity.

Like his printer, and most other mechanical and electrical items which he owned, Daniel's fifteen year old car was also on its last legs. As he sat behind the wheel, with ignition key in hand, he made a silent wish that it would start up and without incident transport him to his meeting with Suzanne, on time. Having untold trouble with the vehicle in the past few weeks, he finally had taken it to a mechanic. He had hoped to get a free estimate of its laundry list of issues. Then, he could prioritize repairs and determine what he could afford to have remedied. To his shock, the low ball estimate of the mechanic required a great deal more money than the actual car was worth.

As well as a change of residence (and the repayment of a

slew of personal loans, bank and other debts), Daniel needed a new car, or even a new, used one. Back in Illinois, Daniel drove so little that he didn't even remember the model name of his hand-me-down Ford that his father gifted him with. Now living in Los Angeles, where a car was so necessary to one's successful navigation of the sprawling city, Daniel had gotten to know his Toyota Celica more intimately than he had wanted to or was even comfortable with.

Thankfully, with the imminent publication of his new novels, he would at last begin to see some financial daylight. He was sure that when the new novels finally hit bookstore shelves, they would be considered revelations in print and reader interest would re-ignite sales of his other two back-list books, *All Alone in an Insane World* and *Heartache*. Financially, things were dire. Yet he was certain that he just had to hang on for a few more weeks.

Daniel turned the vehicle ignition key. The starter motor engaged but the engine didn't turn over. He tried again. And again. On the seventh nail-biting attempt, the car eventually roared into a loud and smoky state of reluctant engagement. The more he drove the vehicle, in its current condition of disrepair, the more he understood the car's dysfunctional state. He knew that if he turned the starter motor repeatedly, for short bursts only, that the car would eventually start up. Once started, he knew that as soon as he took his foot off the gas that the engine would slowly fade and die. Therefore, it was imperative that he keep his foot on the gas.

His challenge, once he got the car moving, was not to let the engine die when he had to slow down or come to a stop. Luckily, the car was a stick shift (which, he was sure, was the reason he got it so cheaply in the first place) and he could depress the clutch while still keeping his foot on the gas pedal, thus preventing the engine from dying. At the very first stop light that Daniel encountered (despite his feet being securely planted on both the clutch and gas pedal), the engine sputtered and died.

Unfortunately, just like life, no amount of planning and understanding is foolproof and with the declining state of the vehicle's overall health, it was getting harder for Daniel to anticipate the car's behavior. His ignition theory was being put to the test and to his chagrin, each and every time he turned the key, his understanding of what worked and didn't work, was found wanting. Despite the number of quick turns of the ignition key, the car would just not start.

In a controlled state of panic, Daniel didn't know what else to do and turned the key so many times without result that the patience of the drivers in the cars stuck behind him began to wear thin and much honking of horns was heard in the otherwise quiet intersection.

Daniel pushed his car to the side of the road and opened the hood more as an act of desperation than as a show of competence. He knew that if he took a good hard look at the wires and coils and tubes and sundry parts of the interior and didn't see something, something which was obviously disconnected or broken or a part that was leaking liquid or protruding smoke, then he had no idea what he was looking at or how to go about fixing.

Sure enough, save for a minor leak in a radiator hose, which he already knew about (and carried a five gallon container of water in the trunk for constant radiator replenishment); he failed to see anything overtly amiss. This was not the first time he had stared cluelessly at the inner sanctum of his increasingly familiar, personal Rubik's cube of an engine. Taking a cloth in one hand he proceeded to tighten and secure everything that looked like it should be tight and secure: wires, tubes and connections of all shapes and sizes.

Having performed the task to his satisfaction, he once again got behind the wheel and turned the key... again and again. After several attempts, the car started. He had no idea why.

Waiting for him at a Beverly Hills adjacent restaurant, Suzanne sipped some imported sparkling water and, on her smart phone, caught up with her emails. Working as a literary agent in a town like Los Angeles, for all these years, Suzanne knew that so much counted on appearances. Meeting clients in restaurants frequented by studio executives, and industry people, in general, was a way of showing that she was busy making deals and that she was in the game. She knew that by being seen she was reinforcing her brand recognition and through her constant presence, advertizing her services. Seeing and being seen meant that she might get a call sooner than a competitor who relied on the telephone directory alone, for new business.

When Daniel finally made it to the underground parking garage, he was shocked to remember that there was no option for motorists to Self Park: everyone had to pull up to the valet stand. As he did so, a Hispanic valet, Carlos, opened his door with a friendly greeting. Daniel, however, did not move from his seat.

"If the engine stops, it won't get started again," Daniel explained, "You need to switch with me."

"Yes," said Carlos, not understanding. He held the door open wider and stood in puzzlement as Daniel remained seated.

"I can't take my foot off of the accelerator," Daniel said more animatedly, realizing that English might not be the valet's first language. "I need you to switch with me to keep the motor running. Understand?"

"Oh. Yes," answered Carlos as he fixed his eyes on Daniel's right foot which remained pressed on the gas pedal, "I put my foot on gas or car die."

"That's right," said Daniel. "I'm sorry but I didn't have time to go to the mechanic."

"Understand," said Carlos, as he gamely extended his foot to replace Daniel's on the gas pedal. In order to do so, he was now practically sitting on Daniel's lap as Daniel tried to slide out from under the valet and scoot over to the passenger side of the car.

"Is your foot on the accelerator?" asked Daniel, masking his embarrassment.

"Yes. Yes, you go," answered Carlos with good sportsmanship cheerfulness.

Leaving Carlos sitting in the driver seat, Daniel grabbed his manuscript and awkwardly opened and then slipped out of the front passenger door. Then he ran around to the other side of the car and, reaching behind the driver's seat, pulled out a large rock which he had kept for this express purpose. He held the rock up to Carlos.

"Okay. When you park it, put this on the gas pedal. If the engine dies, then I'll have to get a..." Daniel didn't finish the sentence because he didn't have any money to call a tow truck and he didn't want to implant the idea into the valet's head that a tow truck was an option.

"Please don't let the engine die. I won't be long."

"Yes, yes, understand."

Daniel watched tensely as Carlos drove the car away. From Carlos' friendly response to the embarrassing episode, Daniel got the impression that Carlos did indeed understand.

"Suzanne, I'm so sorry," Daniel apologized as he approached Suzanne. Slightly out of breath, he sat and immediately placed his manuscript in her hands. She awkwardly juggled it and then made room for it, placing it on the table.

"Your car broke down," Suzanne said calmly.

"Yes. How did you know?"

"Mechanic's hands," Suzanne said, referring to his somewhat blackened, grease-stained hands. Daniel stared at his hands in embarrassment.

A friendly, yet no nonsense, efficient waiter appeared and smiled as he addressed Daniel. "Can I start you off with a drink? A glass of wine, perhaps?"

Daniel managed to hide his panic and pretended to casually browse the menu. As he looked at the menu options, he was mentally computing what he could order with the nineteen dollars and fifty-two cents cash which he carried in his pocket. As it turned out, what he could pay for, tax and tip included, was not very much. Yet, if he ordered a green salad and a glass of tap water only it would be all too obvious what his pathetic financial situation was.

After a moment's contemplation of etiquette, he decided that it didn't matter. Since the restaurant luncheon was at Suzanne's invitation, he was sure that the accepted, non-written protocol was that the onus to pay was on the inviter and not the invitee. Suzanne was likely to pick up the tab. Then again, he felt that he had to consider the gender factor. If the waiter served the man with the check, which they still tend to do in this day and age of supposed sex equality, then things could get very embarrassing indeed. The waiter hovered, still smiling but looking a tad more impatient. "Do you need a minute?" he asked.

"Yes, please," responded Daniel in a gentle, yet commanding tone. As the waiter shuffled off, Daniel kept his eyes on the menu and mentally wondered how best to ask Suzanne if she was actually paying for this meal.

"Have the steak," Suzanne helpfully suggested. "They're known here for their steaks."

"You're having steak, Suzanne?"

"Can't decide between the tenderloin and the filet mignon. I had the tenderloin here last time and it was exquisite."

"Nice," said Daniel, as he looked at the exorbitant menu prices for both.

"If we both order one of each, we can split them," Suzanne suggested.

"We could do that," Daniel replied unconvincingly. "Don't know if I'm in the mood for steak, though."

The waiter returned and again beamed a smile at Daniel. "Decided on anything to drink?"

"A glass of water would be great. To start with," Daniel said before realizing that there were already two poured glasses of water on the table, complete with ice and a slice of lemon in each.

"Certainly," said the waiter, "domestic or imported?"

"Domestic is fine," said Daniel, wondering what in the heck he had just ordered. At that moment, before his internal panic became external and obvious, Daniel realized that he just had to come out and ask her. So, in as neutral a tone as he could muster, he blurted his query. "How are we doing this, Suzanne? Is this going on your business card as a business expense, is this a business lunch... are you paying?" Daniel asked, all too quickly, his words jumbled together.

Suzanne looked at Daniel for a few beats before answering but it was unclear to Daniel what she may have been thinking.

"Oh, no, honey," Suzanne said with just a slight hint of human feeling, "I assumed we were going to go Dutch."

Daniel wasn't sure if his agent saw his Adam's apple take an impromptu and uncontrolled leap into the base of his throat but he knew he had to stall with a thoughtful facial expression as it might be a moment before he possessed the ability to speak again.

"Is that a problem?" Suzanne asked.

What Daniel knew was (as did every rapidly, out of control, vibrating cell of his entire body), that this was terrible news on many fronts; it was not merely bad news as far as the present meal was concerned. This was not the, 'the publishers love your novel and can't wait for the next installment' celebratory meal that he had joyfully anticipated.

In his gut, he now knew that this get-together was going to go someplace so ghastly, someplace so terribly, terribly, catastrophically appalling, that he wasn't sure he could take it and hold himself together as a fully functioning human being; which was probably why his agent chose someplace public; someplace where he couldn't shout and scream and throw things and smash whatever was before him into tiny little pieces.

"I can't sell your novel," Suzanne finally said. "I'm sorry."

As Daniel's world imploded upon itself, the waiter returned with another fixed and friendly smile, "How are we doing here? Have you two decided?"

Daniel didn't hear the questions being addressed to him or, if he did, he didn't show it. He looked frozen in place: his body, his face, his unblinking stare... frozen.

"Give us a few more minutes," said Suzanne to the waiter, who once more, and less joyfully this time, shuttled off. Suzanne stared at her client.

"Are you okay, Daniel?"

Daniel did not look at all okay. In fact, if he were a computer, what would be showing would be the blue screen of death, along with the error message, 'a fatal error has occurred and this application cannot continue,' familiar to all PC users, especially those still using operating systems XP and older.

Suzanne watched Daniel with concern and uncertainty as to what to do next. If he truly were a computer, she could simply press control-alt-delete and have him reboot, perhaps restoring him to an acceptable level of functioning. He was not a computer, however, and in any event, as she was not thinking of him as a machine, the thought did not occur to her. Suzanne did, however, wonder if sprinkling him with some drops of water would do the trick. Perhaps a good splash would get him back to the here and now. Before she could consider whether it was best to use imported or domestic, sparkling or tap water, Daniel's eyes blinked.

"Daniel?"

Daniel's facial expression looked as if his brain were indeed rebooting: his eyes flickered and his eyelids fluttered.

"Are you okay?" Suzanne asked.

"You can't sell *The Impossible Dream: Part One?*" Daniel asked, incredulously and hoping that perhaps he had misunderstood her in the first place.

"I'm sorry, Daniel. The market's very soft right now. Maybe down the road."

"It's my best work?" Daniel said with such incomprehension that his statement sounded more like a question.

"It's wonderful, Daniel. It's... a classic."

"Then... what? It needs work? They gave you notes to improve it? What?"

"No, Daniel. They didn't give any notes. They really don't... they feel that they can't take it out, right now."

"They didn't like it?"

"No, they loved it. Everyone thinks it's terrific, your best work yet. It's a minor masterpiece, no question."

"Then why won't they publish it?"

"Because they don't think it will sell, Daniel. They just

don't see a market for it. It's not the kind of work that people want to buy, right now."

~end sample~

Find the rest of Daniel's story in *Brain*.

Love *Encounter*? Then you might like *Mr. Psychic*. Co-written by Dermot Davis and H Raven Rose, this book is a light-hearted comedy about a man who must lose nearly everything in order to find himself and meet his soulmate.

 Linda S. Amstutz

★★★★★ **Mr. Psychic stole my heart**
Reviewed in the United States on November 13, 2013
Verified Purchase

George's best-laid plans come crashing down when he loses his accounting job and is unable to find work. So what's a straight-laced accountant to do? He dons a disguise and takes a job as a telephone psychic! George doesn't know it at first, but he's found his calling and his phone personality, Mr. Psychic, soon becomes wildly popular. As Mr. Psychic transforms the lives of others, he discovers he has transformed himself as well -- into a kinder, more loving, happier human being. Along the way, he starts a new romance and finds new friendships. And we, the lucky readers, get to go along for the ride!

Mr. Psychic is a wonderful read! Dermot Davis and H. Raven Rose transform the main character, George, from a priggish elitist who thinks he has his life perfectly planned into Mr. Psychic, a soulful, open and loving human being. It's a fun journey and you'll love the characters.

Mr. Psychic tells the story of George, a divorced accountant with a grown son, who has spent decades alone, with only retirement to look forward to.

After carefully scrimping and saving for his future life of expectant ease, he gets the shock of his life when he is let go from his employment. With his entire retirement in serious jeopardy, George is thrown into a panicked tailspin.

Facing a job market heavily skewed towards youth, he finds it almost impossible to locate a comparable job in his field.

After many entirely useless excursions into the employment market (can you say humiliating job interviews?), George accepts the only job offered to him: he becomes a telephone psychic.

Please enjoy the following excerpt from MR. Psychic!

MR. PSYCHIC

Aite no nai kenka wa denkinu.
(One cannot quarrel without an opponent.)

- JAPANESE PROVERB

GEORGE Beresford II COULD NOT BELIEVE his son's arrogance in telling him to get back out there and "find someone."

"There's more to live for in life than your precious roses, Dad," George III had said the previous weekend—as if the boy knew a rose from a rhododendron.

"Don't wait too long, George the second," his daughter-in-law had helpfully added in a joking tone. She was an attractive young woman with a pleasant demeanor, and it was hard to feel angry at her.

Her playful manner separated George, her husband, from

George, her father-in-law, and always made George II smile. He couldn't help smiling now.

Her blue eyes twinkling, she smiled back and, flipping her long blonde hair, continued, "All the good ones get taken in their forties and fifties, after they've gotten divorced or been widowed. You don't want to end up speed-dating leftovers... women with issues who are incapable of love."

It wasn't the first time that this pair had bombarded their elder with unsolicited romantic advice.

George had ignored them both for months. A man of the world in his sixties, he had his career, investments, a beautiful home, and hobbies to enrich and sustain his soul. He didn't believe that he needed a woman in his life, much less a wife. Nobody had a dire need for romance, love, or communion.

He had everything and then some, and he knew that the idea of needing another half was a mad myth that ruined many a perfectly good life.

Yes, that's what he had, he decided, a perfectly good life comprised of satisfaction and select, cultivated pleasures.

GEORGE PRUNED HIS ROSES HAPPILY, ENJOYING THE LATE afternoon sun and the pattern of light and shadow created by the golden sunlight and green plants on the wall behind the shrubbery.

He leaned close to a rose bush with lush green leaves and gorgeous reddish-pink, velvety blossoms, so fragrant and sweet-smelling. The scent made him dizzy for a moment. He closed his eyes and breathed in the delicious fragrance. The heavenly scent was the perfume of his perfectly good life.

He opened his eyes to gaze upon his prize-winning roses lovingly. What? He stared. He did a double-take. Then he looked closer. Phytophthora. A genus within the group of fungus-like organisms known as oomycetes had dared to settle upon his roses. The evidence was slight, yet he was sure that it was there.

He alternately examined the root and crown of his rose bush. He stared at the soil. Traitor. The treacherous Phytophthora species can infect a wide range of trees, shrubs, and bedding plants, and they sometimes lie in wait, persisting in the soil, for many years before settling upon a victim.

As he mentally debated whether the phytophthora had progressed enough to be diagnosable, knowing full well that chemical management of the disease was both impractical and uneconomical, he noticed Ed creeping about.

Ed was his forty-something-year-old neighbor. Or maybe Ed was in his fifties; it was hard to tell. Whatever his age, he was one of those men who perpetually looked pubescent and never seemed to age.

The man had retained his acne, gangly, awkward, overly fatty, immature-looking body, oily hair, smudged glasses, and surly teenage attitude throughout his life.

For some ghastly, unknown reason, perhaps boredom or jealousy (it's not just a myth that the married man with kids envies the life of a single man), Ed was constantly spying on George.

Watching from the corner of his eyes, he saw Ed pretend to check on an ugly and neglected bush growing on the side of his lawn; George grimaced internally while keeping his visage neutral.

"What a jerk," he muttered softly to himself.

There was a ginormous "Neighborhood Watch" decal on Ed's house window and a station wagon parked in Ed's drive-way. George was surprised that one or more of Ed's snotty-nosed children wasn't clutching his pants leg or otherwise hanging off of his body, as was their wont.

He had a half dozen or so offspring of varying ages and levels of cleanliness, in addition to a wife who somehow managed to put up with Ed's annoying personality.

The man's inanity seemed irreparable to George, but he also knew that in life, you don't get to choose everything you desire for yourself, least of all your next-door neighbors. Other people, along with the family you are born into, fall into the "luck of the draw" category.

Ed ambled in George's general direction, as if he were strolling without purpose. There was nothing subtle about Ed, nothing ephemeral. Ed was, in fact, one of those on-the-nose humans, an oaf who was exactly what he appeared to be: difficult, obnoxious, and combative... the opposite of well-meaning.

"Morning, Ed. Special plans?" George asked, knowing full well that Ed usually had a singular purpose in mind.

Ed reached the far side of George II's front lawn and continued to walk toward his neighbor. Ed grinned and laughed loudly; his smile and laughter were mean and false. George stared at the front tooth gap in Ed's not-so-white toothy grin.

"Oh, you know... same old, same old. Spend some quality time with the wife and kiddies," Ed answered casually as George nonchalantly opened his garage with the remote.

"Guess you miss having little ones around," Ed said half-heartedly as he stared obsessively into the garage. As usual, once George II's garage was open, Ed was awestruck and nigh speechless. The man had a morally perverse, covetous appreciation of George II's belongings, specifically his cars.

Slobbering with desire, Ed stared, as he always did, at the beautiful antique roadster. It was parked right next to George II's Prius. George entered the garage and put away his pruning shears. He emptied the rose cuttings into the plant waste recycling bin.

Giving Ed a surreptitious glance, George took out his antique car cleaning kit and pulled out a blue surgical towel. Then, with Ed's eyes watching his every move, like a hungry snake might watch a mouse, George carefully wiped down his roadster with the cloth.

Ed didn't dare step inside George II's garage, or even on the intimate parts of his private property. The fallacy of their friendship didn't extend that far. Truth be told, they weren't friends at all. They had a simple relationship: George owned a few things; he had a lovely home with well-tended gardens and lived a carefree single life that Ed lusted after.

"What about you, George? Got plans?" Ed called to George II, from just out of his sight.

George smiled to himself and then carefully replied:

"Taking Miss Betty out for a ride in the beautiful sunshine." George heard a grunt and then footsteps and knew that Ed was returning to his own home. Smiling, George polished Miss Betty, his beautiful roadster, all the more slowly, the better to enjoy himself.

As Ed returned to the boisterous chaos of his family life, he looked at George II's manicured lawn and beautifully maintained home.

He was unaware that the gash of his toothy grin had slowly developed into a full-blown sneer. His mind was tight and bitter, weighted down and tired of the constant assault of raucous subconscious memories of the personal injustices that he had experienced throughout his life.

Unable to purge painful and unconstructive memories of his accumulated past, his thoughts were overwrought and began to verge on ruthless and hate-filled.

Thump. Thump. Thump. Crossing the edge of the yard and

perhaps in an unconscious desire to rid his being of such unwanted negativity, Ed took wide, stomping steps.

With each reverberation, each angry footfall that boomed, the corners of Ed's mouth turned further down. He glowered and shook his head, disturbed by George II's apparent gentlemanly contentment and by the sounds of pandemonium made by four clamoring kids as he grew closer and closer to the inside of his dilapidated house of discontent.

Restless, filled with unhappiness and displeasure, which he had no way to cure, Ed paused in the yard to look into his residence. He looked through the plate glass window of his front room.

Inside, his four children ran amok. A couple of the rug rats shrieked and screamed with guttural laughter as the older siblings wrestled the younger ones with serious intent. The littler ones screamed with pain, tears streaming down their red, blubbering faces. Someone had punched or pinched, or otherwise assaulted, the two younger children.

Lindsay, Ed's very pregnant wife, appeared by the kitchen door and shouted at the kids, demanding fair play. Mocked by her children for her efforts, she unsuccessfully chased the older two kids, who only laughed and shouted in response to their mother's demands.

Ed, who really didn't wish to go back inside his own house, glanced back at George II. The wide open front door of George II's home revealed his quiet, tidy dwelling, a comparative bastion of peace and bliss.

George had finished polishing his fine-looking vehicle, which didn't need shining—it was pristine. He always kept it garaged and free of dust and dirt outside of brief weekend use.

George closed the door to his home, then got into the antique roadster and cranked up his beauty with one turn of the ignition key. As always, the sound of the purring engine elicited a satisfied smile as he backed her up, out of the garage, down his drive, and into the street.

To his great satisfaction, he noticed that Ed had stopped to watch him as he zoomed smartly out of the suburban neighborhood. A moment later, as George accelerated, the side of the street began to blur.

Shades of green and earth tones smeared in a hazy kaleidoscope as the car sped away. Checking in his rear-view mirror, George smiled as he watched a sad and envious-looking Ed slowly appear smaller and smaller and, finally, disappear from view.

GEORGE DROVE HIS MISS BETTY LEISURELY THROUGH THE beauteous, verdant suburban countryside. His windshield glass was immaculate and so clear he could see right through it. It seemed almost invisible.

The driver's side window rolled down; his left arm rested on the driver's side door. George drove with a single hand on the steering wheel, as casually as a seasoned cowboy might control the reins of his champion horse. Warmed by the golden midday sunshine, he luxuriated in the heat.

Sunshine streamed from the sky, and the simple act of driving in silence filled him with a deep peace. Thoughts of his son, George III, his only child, named after his father, as he was, were long gone.

George sighed with deep peace and surveyed the blue sky, with hardly a cloud, emerald grass, and newly leafing trees. In late May, growing things were shades of green and beautiful. It felt like early summer as he drove: balmy, bright, and as if the day stretched endlessly before him.

George's weekends were sacrosanct. Truth be told, every detail of his life could be considered something of a ritual.

Over the years, caring for his home, cars, and other belongings had become somewhat ritualized. In addition to his household chores, grocery shopping, running daily errands, and indeed most details of his life, he followed a strict regimen designed to create a quiet, easy life based on routine safety.

Today, just like every Saturday, after caring for his roses and wiping down Miss Betty, he chose to do his weekly shopping.

Very happily, he shopped at three distinct stores: an ethnic market for certain staples, such as vegetables, meat, and rice (which were much less expensive there, even though the quality was the same); a dollar store for odd lots of brand-name items (which, for some reason, were sold at a significant discount); and an upscale health food store that sold whole foods, chic gourmet items, and other tasty foodstuffs.

Upon reaching the increasingly trendy upscale health food market, he happily parked his vehicle and went inside. He spent an hour carefully shopping for items he would need for tonight's dinner party with his friends.

Entertaining made him feel especially prosperous.

HE PERUSED THE AISLES OF THE NATURAL FOODS MARKET, singularly focused upon his task. He diligently avoided the gazes or other attempts by single women to catch his eye, such as the plump-looking brunette he was sure was following at a discreet distance. She most likely hoped to "bump" into him.

For a single male, the mere act of grocery shopping could be a hazardous affair, he had often noted to himself.

Having had years of experience in this endeavor (avoiding

grasping females), George could instantly turn on an air of distraction and utter disinterest.

It wasn't that he would never be interested in a woman ever again. It was just that it wasn't a priority at this particular time of his life. A relationship was likely to be a distraction from the goals that were his primary concern.

It was all a matter of timing, he reasoned. A man needs to have his finances in order before considering adding a woman who needs looking after into the mix. Affairs of the heart would have to wait until he had his retirement package squared away; there would be no exceptions. So, he disciplined himself.

His marriage had been an utter fiasco, psychologically, financially, and in every other way. When George III was small, George II had determined to get his life sorted entirely before he even considered a serious relationship again. His mind hadn't changed since.

He pondered the merits of adding capers to the mixed greens salad in the gourmet section. Capers, artichoke hearts, and maybe some hearts of palm might go nicely on the evening meal menu.

He mused about the virtues of capers at length. This was partly because the brunette lingered overly close, and he knew he could wait her out. He was determined that way. George pondered the jars of capers before him. Real capers are the flower buds of a caper bush, Capparis spinosa (its large seedpod is called a caper berry), which was also called Flinders rose.

While young and green, the seedpods of nasturtiums look and taste a great deal like the buds of the caper plant. However, most cultured classes consider them "poor man's capers," so obviously, George was not considering those.

Naturally, the capers he was considering were the real deal, imported from the Mediterranean. They were picked, sun-dried, and then pickled in a vinegar brine. George glanced at the tiny yet beautiful jar in his hand. Would it be too much green? He wondered.

He planned to slice fresh tomatoes or red or orange bell peppers to add a splash of color to the top of the salad and then add pine nuts, lightly toasted with Celtic sea salt.

He would gently toss the salad in imported red wine balsamic vinaigrette with extra virgin olive oil. He would prepare and offer warmed, lightly breaded goat cheese medallions on the side of this salad.

Yes, he decided, looking at the tiny container of beautifully preserved capers. They would add extra texture and flavor to accentuate the salad's other attributes. He put two jars into his cart.

After a lengthy mental debate, George spent a fair amount of enjoyable time considering the wine choices. He chose a couple of moderately expensive cabernets and a single Californian Sauvignon Blanc for Marcus, the sole white wine drinker.

Of course, he had a completely stunning Le Cache European Country 5200 wine cellar, a free-standing furniture-style wine cellar with a chocolate cherry finish. It combined state-of-the-art wine storage technology with exceptional design artistry.

Made of premium cherry wood with crown and base molding, hand-carved wood trim, hardwood French doors, and digital temperature display and control, among other features, it was a highlight of George II's dining room. It was well-stocked with hand-picked wines, holding 544 racked bottles.

George did not like things to be empty. A place for everything, and everything in its place, was a motto he truly took to heart.

After paying cash for his groceries, he headed to the other two stores to finish shopping. A couple of hours later, the day still warm and illuminated by sunlight, he felt as satisfied as he had ever felt. The trunk of his car was stocked with luxurious, delicious, and sundry household items.

Sure, he had a perfidious phytophthora situation to deal with. Yet, thankfully, the rest of his life was blissfully perfect. Sure, he couldn't relax entirely until he was safely retired and living off the interest of his retirement fund, but he was on track to reach his financial goals in the next few years.

It would take more than phytophthora, that fungus of black death threatening his rose garden, to seriously mar his perfect life. With a sigh of contentment, he cranked his vehicle and seconds later was returning to his immaculate ordered home.

Everything about my life is on schedule, he thought happily to himself. Reaching his home, filled with an aura of satisfaction, he parked and unloaded his car.

***

HE PUT THE GROCERIES AND OTHER ITEMS AWAY INSIDE HIS traditional, elegantly decorated dwelling. He then washed and pounded several chicken breasts and prepared a marinade with a bit of fresh rosemary, lemon juice, lemon zest, white wine, and garlic.

Leaving the chicken in the refrigerator, resting gently in the marinade, he carefully rinsed the vegetables needed to create a mixed salad. Preparing the veggies for the side dish, he washed and drained them in the colander and then left them on thick paper towels to dry naturally.

He had a few hours before he needed to prepare further for his guests, so he decided to check his retirement fund and other accounts just like he did every day (sometimes more than once).

It only took a couple of minutes. He kept his dinosaur of a

computer in his home office, stripped of unnecessary programs so that it could run his financial investment software.

He continually tracked his personal banking, credit card, loan, 401(K), investment accounts, and personal balance sheet, not just to assure himself that he was on the right track but also because seeing his wealth accumulate gave him a great sense of inner peace and security of mind. The app on his phone was too small and induced too much anxiety for him to try and look at everything at once.

Most of his assets were investments, stocks and bonds, mutual funds, and other assets that formed part of his overall retirement plan. His liabilities were primarily the residual balance on his mortgage loan.

His parents were considered "well off," but they were young for their age, and even though he was their only child, he had never taken anything, much less money, from them. He had no intentions of starting now, not that he had the need.

George III and Georgie IV, his grandson, could inherit if his parents chose to choose heirs.

Settling into his home office desk chair, George looked at a computer-generated image of his current "real-time" retirement stock portfolio projections.

On screen, as thrilling as always, he was happy to see that the graph line on his portfolio was close to his $2M end goal. Obviously, $2M was barely enough to retire in the current fiscal environment in the United States.

However, it was a decent start and, when he reached that number, he planned to implement plan B, an aggressive series of investment strategies to seek to double his retirement fund.

He pulled out and glanced at his OMEGA 1932 Olympic pocket chronograph watch. A Rattrapante Chronograph in 18-carat yellow gold was powered by rediscovered unassembled movement kits that had miraculously been discovered in storage at OMEGA's headquarters in Biel.

The parts had been stored since 1932, when the watch brand first served as "Official Timekeeper" of that year's Olympic Games. In addition to being rare, the timepiece was a thing of great beauty.

The horological wonder of it all—an OMEGA product with mythological status—the 1932 pocket chronograph was impossibly seductive for him. When he learned of its existence, he had to have one. He had, at first, tried to resist his impulse to acquire one.

When he bought the watch, George was quite aware that, at upwards of $70K, it could not legitimately be perceived as an investment. Instead, when unable to resist his yearning, he justified it as a talisman to motivate him to create the future of independence he desired. It was a thing of beauty, and when he checked the time several times a day, he carefully held it.

Glancing at the timepiece, he felt wealthy and in control; the watch reminded him of who he would be if he industriously followed his financial plan. It gave him tremendous pleasure to check the time. Looking at it now, he got a quick fright as he realized he had barely enough time to shower and prepare for his guests.

GEORGE SHOWERED AND DRESSED IN HIS STANDARD weekend attire, which he wore with such unwavering regularity, it could almost be considered his weekend uniform.

Putting on a pair of dark, cuffed slacks and a white linen long-sleeved shirt, he added a touch of after-shave and slipped his watch into his left trouser pocket. He noted with great satisfaction that his hair hadn't grown much since his most recent monthly haircut, taken care of the last Saturday of the previous month.

Sure, his clothes and suits were several years old, perhaps even a decade or two. Still, they fit perfectly as he meticulously watched his diet because it was cost-effective and so as not to succumb to that dreaded middle-age spread. They were freshly pressed, medium starch from the dry cleaner, just as he preferred, and nothing was worn, stained, or otherwise in obvious disrepair.

He felt very strongly that the compulsion to spend unnecessarily was a symptom of the dissolution and dissatisfaction rampant in the Western world, a debauchery which he found repugnant.

George was sure that his lifestyle choices would seem idiosyncratic to some, extreme even. Yet one doesn't become a middle-class self-made millionaire without generally being a very frugal person. He bought quality items, whether clothing or otherwise, and cared for them meticulously.

He did all the home and lawn maintenance himself, using a couple of books about how to do that. He only replaced clothing when it didn't fit, was irreparably stained or damaged, or was too worn to maintain its shape and hue.

He wasn't as well-off as his parents, being a self-made man. Truthfully, he jettisoned his work clothes first before getting rid of his at-home attire. He did this primarily because, for some idiotic reason, upper-level management increasingly seemed to think that clothes made the man.

Over the years, he had seen many a young upstart punk, with little to offer intellectually, yet inexplicably given an advanced degree, dressed in impeccable high-end attire, and with those and an arrogant, overbearing, and self-important attitude to match, get hired or promoted above their senior peers.

He felt content that all his promotions over the last forty

years were based solely on merit. He was still at the same company, though the current president was now the son of the man who had initially hired him. Like his father before him, George was a man of rare employment longevity. And he hoped that he had passed on to his son his belief that endurance in service is akin to moral fortitude.

George was the current comptroller of the finance department for the Chief Financial Officer of Teleseismology Hub NS, a well-respected, small yet highly successful organization. Even though less than two years ago, George had previously been passed over for the CFO position—the job had been given to his younger direct report and former mentee—this time around, he expected to be promoted finally.

At first, getting used to reporting to a former direct report had been strange, yet he had managed. He was determined to do whatever it took to get promoted. He routinely spent hours and hours, above and beyond those worked by others in his department, doing whatever was required to provide timely, relevant financial data to support the company's planning and control activities.

If promoted, he would be responsible for directing the corporation's fiscal functions according to generally accepted accounting principles, which the Securities and Exchange Commission regulates, the Financial Accounting Standards Board, and other regulatory and advisory organizations.

He would finally be a Vice President and a bona fide senior management team member. The most senior and experienced—and, in fact, most loyal—member of the finance division, he had spent the last eighteen months endeavoring to show that he could handle any challenge.

Said challenges included being passed over for a promotion, working well with other managers despite that fact, and understanding and communicating technical financial data to others simply and straightforwardly. Thus, he was no longer worried about his competition.

George III, his ever-annoying son, loved to remind him, even though he had repeatedly asked him not to, that Teleseismology Hub NS was an anagram for "The Soulless Big Money."

George thought people who had time to play around with words were obviously irresponsible, possibly even lazy, and could lack drive. The SBM, as his son laughingly called the company, had made it possible for George to raise his boy. Alone.

Teleseismology was seismology that dealt with records obtained at long distances. The company had clients worldwide, from academics to government agencies. George dealt with the company's financial aspects and spent a growing amount of his time as an internal and external business consultant.

Long since liberated from the mechanical aspects of accounting and finance, he felt he was a trusted advisor and an increasingly capable intellect.

Despite being accused of micromanaging his duties and subordinates in the past, he felt that his research, analysis, reporting, and managerial skills were finally about to be recognized and duly rewarded.

Spotting outsourcing trends in other industries, he had recently submitted an unsolicited report to senior management detailing ways the company could immediately slash its bottom line and substantially increase its profits. Certainly, THNS had considered outsourcing years ago, yet other companies had lost business due to poor quality external hires. So, they had never leapt. George had found evidence that judicious outsourcing to language-tested, financial whizzes of the sort they could use would eliminate the hiring issues that reduced client or customer satisfaction and got such bad press.

Judging by some comments he had overheard through the

office gossip grapevine, he felt certain that the report had struck a chord and, in private, was being very well received.

In contrast to the insinuation of his son's ignorant, almost slanderous, words, George felt that his company was not soulless. Naturally, they dealt with big and grand money concerns as befits any successful capitalist organization.

Thoughts flickered through his mind, like dust motes. Brushing aside thoughts of work, George switched gears and mentally prepared the dinner party meal in his head, then did an informal system check on the evening ahead.

RETURNING TO THE KITCHEN, GEORGE'S THOUGHTS returned to the salad. Capers have a particular flavor; enjoyment of the garnishment could be considered an acquired taste. He loved introducing coworkers to this type of tiny life delight. You wouldn't get capers on the dinner party menu just anywhere.

He knew the capers' sharp, piquant, and salty taste would beautifully contrast with and complement the rest of the meal. After checking that the salad fixings were dry, he drained the sun-dried Mediterranean capers and set them aside.

The marinated chicken breasts were put into the oven, and he started brown rice in the steamer. His ex-wife had accused him of being obsessive, overly considering food and meal preparation, yet he found it so soothing, and life was so long and tedious. Really, what else was he to focus on?

He very precisely ripped beautiful green lettuce and sliced several fresh tomatoes, for the top of the salad, for a splash of color. After lightly toasted pine nuts with Celtic sea salt in a pan, he made red wine balsamic vinaigrette with extra virgin olive oil.

He put the salad together and then set it aside without dressing it. Then, he carefully poured the vinaigrette into a beautiful, tiny cut crystal decanter.

After steaming artichokes for the side and preparing an olive oil and fresh herb dip for them, he sliced up some pungent goat cheese and lightly breaded it in a rough-ground blue corn meal breading to serve as medallions on the side of the salad.

The white wine was chilled. He took two bottles from the wine storage and placed them in ice-filled clay wine holders. Then he took the bottles outside to the backyard patio. With great satisfaction, he noted the absolute splendor of his backyard. Looking around his garden felt peaceful, almost healing.

The setting sun cast an orange-gold glow over his award-winning roses, filling the backyard's air with a subtle, sweet fragrance in shades of red and pink. Greenery, vines, and precisely clipped grass and bushes created a deepening peace in his soul and being.

He placed the clay wine holders on a side table and returned to the house to get the red wines, candles for the tables, and place settings. He carefully created a beautiful arrangement of serving ware and settings for an intimate dinner for four.

With dusk rapidly approaching, he turned on the subtle outside lighting once back inside the house. Then he returned to the patio to light the candles and survey the table.

It was perfect. He hurried back into the house to make the final preparations.

Back in the kitchen, he warmed hearth-baked Bialy artisanal bread. The rich, hearty alternative grain bread, with black olives, thinly sliced sun-dried, caramelized, seasoned onions, and poppy seeds, would be delicious and taste almost cheesy in the middle.

Glancing at his OMEGA Rattrapante Chronograph, George sighed with satisfaction.

It was time.

———

WITH THE DINNER PARTY IN FULL SWING, GEORGE STOOD back briefly to survey and assess his kingdom. George II's coworkers, Marco, James, and Bethany, chatted and laughed as they enjoyed the elegant backyard dinner party.

Due to George's diligent construction and organization, and despite the presence of the chatting and laughing party people, the garden and patio continued to be a haven of peace and elegance.

Verdant plants and blossoming flowers, including his beloved roses, exuded a delicate scent which increased the harmony. Flickering lit cream candles, inside Amber glass and wrought iron candle holders, cast a soft glow over the scene.

He smiled to himself to see Marco's face already a little shiny and red. He had swigged down a couple of glasses of wine as soon as he arrived. James had arrived first, though.

There had been a moment when, in a confidential tone, James had mumbled that he had something important to talk to George about, and it was clear that he didn't want the others to participate in the conversation. But then Marco arrived, and the opportunity to talk privately was lost.

Marco loved his wine and was an effusive guest. His general conviviality and appreciation of George's hosting efforts made him a pleasure to be around. He savored the food, the drink, the conversation, and the moment, and not being a shy type of person, he was always vocal with compliments and toasts.

James and he had been in the same division—the finance division—at Teleseismology Hub NS. George had tried to mentor him, to a certain degree, being that he had a good decade in years and work experience over him. They had an unspoken camaraderie that made work more pleasant.

Not too surprisingly, the guy had catapulted up the career ladder. So, oddly, he was now in a unique career position, having created his little department of one. He no longer reported to George because his department was an adjunct to finance. It was not an issue, George and he had much mutual respect.

Marco lifted his glass in a toast as if on cue and brought George out of his reverie. George refilled every stemless wine glass with more wine. He realized that he hadn't answered Bethany and strained to remember what she had just asked.

"Capparis spinosa..." George finally said to Bethany, pouring her another glass of red wine, "Its large seedpod is called a caper berry... but the plant itself is known as Flinders rose."

"Ah," Bethany remarked in response.

"Honestly, George, can't you invest in a decent bottle of wine?" Marco joked as he drank deeply. James frowned at Marco, obviously mistaking his tone.

"Pretentious much, Marco? You know George only has the best..."

Marco shrugged and laughed. He was amused that James didn't get the joke.

"That's right, the best..." added Bethany. Trailing off, she carefully sipped her glass of red wine. She then leaned back and luxuriated in the scene and setting.

"...the best retirement fund at this table," James added. "So he has no intention of wasting his hard-earned Benjamin's on your beloved Syrah et Shiraz... French import or otherwise."

James laughed and gave George a conspiratorial wink. George knew that he knew that the one area where he didn't scrimp and save was on the wine and food.

"Well, I think it is lovely..." Bethany replied, lifting her wine glass carefully and uncharacteristically proceeding to guzzle her wine. " George's portfolio, I mean."

The guests and George laughed. More coworkers than bosom buddies, they were only half joking. George II's cell phone buzzed in his pocket.

He wasn't expecting a call, but—cautious man that he was—he would never irresponsibly leave his cell phone unattended or ignore his calls. Still buzzing, he pulled it out and checked the caller ID.

He sighed, stood, and motioned that he'd be right back to his friends, who were happily continuing their meals. Then he stepped away to take the call. George took several steps away, close enough to the patio speakers that played soft jazz music and near enough that he could still hear snippets of the conversation at the table.

"Hello?" he said into his phone. Hearing his son's normal voice, George sighed in relief, realizing there was no emergency. Even though the conversation behind him became more raucous, George could still hear every word on the phone.

Still unsure about the purpose of the call, George listened patiently as George III rambled on about having a family vacation.

"He can retire in five years or even less... and, I admit it, I'm a bit jealous," Bethany said and smiled. Her just audible words made George II smile just a bit.

"George is a saver. Big deal," Marcus said. George knew that Marcus would be waving his hands to punctuate his words. Bethany giggled and sipped her wine.

"Oh, admit it, Marcus, we're all a little jealous," James said good-naturedly.

Their voices faded away as George concentrated more fully on his conversation.

"Well, what do you think? You don't seem too excited about it," George III said.

Given his rising emotion, George quietly spoke as kindly as possible into his phone. His expression revealed uncharacteristic irritation.

"I told you, son, I have guests."

THE MASTER BEDROOM OF GEORGE III'S HOME WAS A mess. It wasn't dirty. It was just a jumble, the kind of disarray often seen in the house of a happy, harried family. Baskets of clean laundry, half-chewed dog bones, articles of clothing, a couple of tennis rackets, and baby toys were strewn about the room.

George III, patrician good looks, lay in bed, flipping channels on the muted television set while talking on the phone to his dad. A golden retriever lay on a dog bed on the floor.

Jenn wrangled their toddler Georgie IV into the bath in the adjacent bathroom.

"I want to nail down some dates for the family holiday... Don't you remember? You said you'd think about it, Dad," said George III.

George stood surveying his backyard patio.

"I said that because you wouldn't take 'No' for an answer, son," George finally said gravely.

"I'm sick of taking 'No' for an answer, Dad. Come on vacation with us. Don't you want to see your grandchild growing up?" George III said with apparent increasing exasperation.

Jenn, from the bathroom, looked at George III with apparent sympathy. He shrugged his shoulders, as if to say,

"Dad is still being obstinate and driving me dotty." She nodded at him and scrubbed their child.

"As I have told you repeatedly, son, wasting money on a holiday will prevent me from meeting my retirement contribution milestones and objectives in a timely fashion," George II said calmly. His face grew quite red due to some emotion that was not audible in his tone of voice.

He tried to understand why this was such a sore point with George III. He had virtually raised the boy alone after he was divorced when the child was three years of age.

They had both lost her, his wife and George III's mother, when the woman, a self-professed gypsy, had gone off to *find herself.*

Being a single father, raising a child on one income, and being forced to pay for child care when the boy wasn't in school, all by himself, required fortitude, self-sacrifice, and fiscal discipline.

He had raised his child to understand the value of a dollar and the necessity of planning one's life carefully.

He hoped these conversations weren't an indicator that the boy's mother's slacker genes were finally expressing themselves. Was there a genetic predisposition to laziness and profligacy? He almost shuddered.

"Dad, you've scrimped and saved for years. You don't enjoy life. You don't date. You hang out with a bunch of losers who eat your food and guzzle your cheap wine," George III growled.

Jenn, rinsing soap off of George IV, as he giggled and wriggled, and in an attempt to warn her husband to tread lightly, she shook her head, no.

Caught up in the call and the resoluteness of his position, George III didn't see her movements or get the message. Would he have heeded her guidance if he had?

GEORGE STARED AT HIS FRIENDS. HIS COWORKERS WERE rapidly and quite rabidly consuming the meal he had prepared. They were also hurriedly imbibing the wine, which wasn't 'cheap' at all.

Unbeknownst to his guests, George had decided to treat them to a combination of his rare, special, and select private vintage. Perhaps only James would know the value of it.

As George looked at the group while gathering his thoughts to respond to his son, James looked up at him and gave him a genuine smile of gratitude.

James lifted his wine glass in a private toast. George immediately felt warmth in his heart at the gesture.

He thought of a couple of times when James, when the company was in a tight spot, had given him the heads-up about a situation at work when he didn't need to.

More importantly, probably, because of the risk to the guy's job security, he shouldn't have.

They weren't bosom buddies... but the younger man was a friend.

Despite his son's claim, none of them were moochers.

True, they didn't carefully craft intimate little dinner parties or other gatherings in their homes and invite George to partake.

Instead, they generally insisted on picking up his tab at any outing, luncheon, or other meal-related event.

Come to think of it, he rarely, if ever, had to pay for a lunch or dinner when he was out with any one of the three. Plus, he knew that Bethany had more than platonic feelings for him. She really and truly cared for him, as a man and a person.

Unfortunately, a romantic relationship was out of the question because he did not reciprocate Bethany's feelings.

Although they were merely platonic friends—and that was all they would ever be—he and Bethany were still relatively close. They exchanged holiday gifts, as a matter of fact.

Coming out of his daydream and realizing that his son was mid-litany and showed no signs of stopping his diatribe, George decided it was time to nip this irksome conversation in the bud.

"Georgie, you're out of line," George said sternly, and in a sharper tone than he could remember having used in a long time.

"My retirement fund is what will keep me from being a burden upon you and Jenn in my old age."

George III did not respond.

George II listened to the silence that followed. He half wondered if his son had actually had the audacity. Did George III hang up on him? Finally, his only child spoke.

"I'm sick of hearing about your retirement fund, Dad. Your grandson is growing up, and you... If you don't change your ways... you're going to end up a lonely old man with nothing to keep you company but an old hunk of metal and those stupid roses," George III barked.

Click!

George III hung up on his father and then flung the television remote to the other end of the sofa. Jenn, carrying their now clean yet sleepy toddler, entered the room.

George III took their son from her arms. Jenn sat near her husband and gently rubbed his temples. Neither spoke.

THE CITY'S WHITE LIGHTS SPARKLED AGAINST THE BLUE-black, darkening night sky. Disheveled from a night on the town, wearing a rumpled dark tux with the bow tie undone, George strolled down the sidewalk adjacent to an empty city street.

He was oblivious to an indigent homeless man and almost passed right by. The man grabbed George by the ankle.

In shock, George stared down at the dirty, sickly looking man. The man spoke:

"I used to have all the cards. Bet you have all the cards in your wallet."

"You used to have all the cards," George mumbled, almost incoherently. In a dead sleep, he tossed and turned, clearly dreaming—he was having a nightmare.

"What? What cards?" George responded.

"Saks Fifth Avenue, Nordstrom, Neiman Marcus, all of 'em," the homeless man gasped in a gravelly voice. Then the man coughed until he hacked something up.

George stared at the dirty, unkempt man with increasing horror and then, pulling himself together, managed to wrench his leg free.

He hoped that, whatever disease or malady the man might have, the fellow wasn't contagious. The destitute man laughed bitterly and stared at George with scorn.

"I used to have your life," the homeless man said, rubbing his eyes with a grimy hand. Then he whispered the words. "I used to have your life."

"You used to have my life," George muttered in his sleep, tossing his head from side to side, grimacing, obviously upset.

George pulled out his wallet. Progressively more upset, George wanted to find a way to shut the guy up and get away as quickly as possible. He slipped cash from his wallet and held it out.

As the sick, impoverished man stared up at him, George felt a wave of pity. Then the man wiped his oily hair out of his eyes, and George gasped.

The dirty, bereft, sickly man before him, the man who had once had a life like his own, had George's face. George stared in shock, and the blackness of the dark street and the bright white city lights in the distance seemed to melt.

The scene slipped sideways, and the homeless man's face and eyes stretched like a reflection in a funhouse mirror.

The man reached toward him, and George jumped back in panic.

GEORGE JUMPED IN HIS SLEEP. HE TWITCHED AND WOKE with a start. He looked around wildly.

The sight of his beautifully kept bedroom, masculine and ordered, a place for everything and everything in its place, was immediately somewhat calming.

He sighed heavily and yawned.

"A dream," he whispered, "it was only a dream."

Groggily, he rubbed his temples and closed his eyes. It wasn't real, he told himself. Yet the dream, it... he had been dreaming, hadn't he?

It had been so real. It had felt real.

It couldn't have been real, he decided, still not absolutely sure that he was in his bedroom or what had happened. Had he been truly dreaming?

Of course, he was, he decided, because he would never allow himself to be that disheveled in reality. Ever.

The thought of walking down a public street, unkempt and sweating after a night on the town, was horrifying.

But even worse of a shock was that the grimy, down-and-out man had his face, as if, in some way, he was the down-and-out, impoverished man.

Could this be an omen, he wondered? What he had just experienced was obviously a nightmarish dream. Possibly, he had caught something from one of his dinner guests.

Stumbling from his bed, George stood and headed straight to the bathroom.

A SHORT WHILE LATER, GEORGE II, IMMACULATELY groomed, towel wrapped around his waist, slapped Old Spice on each cheek and looked himself over carefully. He was again his controlled, calm, usual persona.

It had been a bad dream, likely induced by his son's telephone call of the night before.

After deciding to wear an older three-piece custom bespoke suit, he stood over his kitchen sink and carefully ate his regular weekday breakfast: a banana and a bran muffin. He leaned to his right and circumspectly sipped his tea.

He placed his mug on the counter, finished his fruit, and baked breakfast food. After disposing of the muffin wrapper, he obsessively picked up each errant muffin crumb with his index finger from the kitchen sink basin. When the sink was crumb-free, he rinsed it quickly and dried it with a kitchen towel.

Outside his home, George II checked his mail, as he did every morning. His peculiar habit was to check his mail daily before leaving for work.

Not checking after work (when he could be reasonably sure there would not be mail in the box) made him feel nicely restrained and in control. He felt sure that most people would not have the self-discipline to delay the pleasure of getting their mail overnight.

Once he had gotten his mail from the previous day, George got into and cranked his Prius and drove away.

George exited his parked vehicle and glanced around the parking lot of his Fortune 500 Company, Teleseismology Hub NS. He was pleased to note that, as usual, he was one of the very first employees to arrive at work that morning.

SEATED IN HIS IMMACULATE PRIVATE ACCOUNTING department office, George finally relaxed. He looked over a stack of documents. Joe, a handsome young man in his thirties, dressed in the latest edgy, smart GQ business fashion, entered George's office without knocking.

George looked up in surprise. Although Joe was George II's current boss—the current CFO—it was unlike him to be disrespectful in that way. He always knocked first before entering.

"Can I see you in my office?" Joe asked brusquely, and it sounded more like a command than a request.

George managed to nod and answer in the affirmative. Before he could stand, however, Joe had turned and was gone.

George entered Joe's much nicer corner office; this was the same office that George expected would be his when Joe moved onto his new opportunity.

It was rumored that Joe, the younger guy who had previously surpassed George, would be moving on soon. George looked around in surprise.

The floor was covered with boxes full of files and papers.

All kinds of forms from HR were spread everywhere. Joe's office was generally always tidy.

Joe sat behind his desk. He nodded at his subordinate, George, who sat carefully and uneasily. Joe looked at George II. Yet, for the longest time, as if mentally deciding how best to say what he had to, he managed not to say a word.

George grew increasingly nervous. His mind raced, filled with thoughts, fears, and questions.

What was going on? Was there an issue with his work or with the department? Was it possible that Joe no longer supported George for the CFO position?

"You know what BPO is, right?" Joe finally asked, after much sighing.

George breathed a sigh of relief. It was some kind of impromptu investigative meeting that Joe had called. Maybe the files were part of new research. George gathered his thoughts and replied calmly.

"Business Process Outsourcing. As you know, I just compiled and shared a corporate-culture-changing cost-benefit analysis and in-depth report on BPO... It's quite profitable," George said, and finally, he could relax entirely.

Perhaps he needed to consult on or explain some of the finer points of his findings. The report wasn't for finance at all; it was an overview of the benefits of outsourcing some Teleseismology Hub NS departments, primarily those involved in production or marketing. Joe nodded at him.

"Yes. Very, very profitable... So much so that they want to extend the program... to accounting," Joe replied drily. George stared. It was almost impossible for him to comprehend the turn of the conversation. Had he heard correctly?

"You're outsourcing accounting?" George asked dumbly.

"Don't take it personally... the entire department's going,

plus that one-person on-site internal audit department guy, what's-his-name..." Joe added.

He stared at George for a long moment.

George was now gobsmacked and, therefore, speechless. He stared at Joe, his eyes wide. His throat felt tight.

After a long moment, Joe spoke the thoughts that explained the growing smirk on his face."It's pretty ironic, don't you think?"

George was still too shocked to answer or even consider what Joe might be referring to.

"I had forgotten that you wrote that report! Well done. You managed to demolish your entire department with one document." Joe laughed. Yet how he did so made the younger man sound sad, not amused.

"You're letting us go?" George asked querulously.

WHAT WILL HAPPEN TO GEORGE?

Get *Mr. Psychic: The Bean Counter Who Lost It All, Only to Fall in Love and Live Happily Ever After* to read the rest of George's story and discover how an uptight accountant recovers from the shock of his life and overcomes the struggle to find a job.

In the rest of this light-hearted comedy, you will discover how, in the act of being forced down a path that he did not choose, George finds not just himself, and figures out his finances and gains a better future, yet meets and falls in love with the woman—his soul mate—who has been missing from his life all along.

www.ingramcontent.com/pod-product-compliance
Lightning Source LLC
Chambersburg PA
CBHW061648190726
48289CB00006B/1792